"A mix of *The Lord of the Rings* and
Buffy the Vampire Slayer."
—*New York Times* bestselling author Kevin J. Anderson

**Praise for Barb Hendee's
Vampire Memories Novels**

Blood Memories

"A satisfying story line coupled with engaging characters,
fast action, and a hint of things to come make this a
winner."   —Monsters and Critics

"Fast-paced and intriguing."
                    —*News and Sentinel* (Parkersburg, WV)

"A fascinating tale with wonderful characters and delicious
villains who solicit the readers into loathing them."
                                              —SFRevu

"A terrific vampire stand-alone thriller that fans will enjoy."
                                    —*Midwest Book Review*

"Intriguing. . . . Ms. Hendee's fans will be gratified to know
she writes just as well on her own as she does in tandem."
                                    —Huntress Book Reviews

"Don't miss *Blood Memories*, the first in what promises to be a
fantastic new series."   —Romance Reviews Today

"An engrossing tale of vampire death and evolution."
                                    —Patricia's Vampire Notes

**Praise for
The Noble Dead Saga**

Child of a Dead God

"Readers who love vampire novels will appreciate the full
works of Barb and J. C. Hendee as they consistently provide
some of the genre's best."   —*Midwest Book Review*

continued . . .

W9-CCO-215

"A great adult look at the world of *dhampirs*, and the always-constant battle, in any world, between good and evil."

—MyShelf.com

"Complex and bloody. . . . Interspecies distrust, grand ambitions, and the lure of dangerous secrets protected by the undead drive the action in this neat mix of horror with more traditional fantasy elements."　　　　—*Publishers Weekly*

Rebel Fay

"A tale of ancient enmities, long-standing treacheries, and a hidden evil . . . peopled . . . with fascinatingly complex characters."　　　　—*Library Journal*

"Entertaining . . . a hybrid crossing Tolkienesque fantasy with vampire-infused horror . . . intriguing."

—*Publishers Weekly*

"A real page-turner."　　　　—*Booklist*

Traitor to the Blood

"A rousing and sometimes creepy fantasy adventure . . . this is one of those books for which the term 'dark fantasy' was definitely intended."　　　　—*Chronicle*

"There is a lot of intrigue in *Traitor to the Blood*, which is one of the reasons it is so hard to put down. . . . Readers will eagerly await the next book in this terrific series."

—The Best Reviews

"Winning. . . . Fans of the series are sure to be pleased, while the novel stands well enough on its own to attract new readers."　　　　—*Publishers Weekly*

"A unique tale of vampires and half-vampire undead hunters set against a dark fantasy world ruled by tyrants. The personal conflicts of the heroes mirror the larger struggles in their world and provide a solid foundation for this tale of love and loyalty in a world of betrayal."　　　　—*Library Journal*

Sister of the Dead

"A spellbinding work that is creative and addicting."
—*Midwest Book Review*

"A treat."   —*SFRevu*

"An amazing adventure that will keep you engrossed until the final chapter."   —*SF Site*

"The Hendees continue their intelligent dark fantasy series by cleverly interweaving the sagas and personal demons of their heroes with rousing physical battles against the forces of evil."   —*Romantic Times* (4 stars)

Thief of Lives

"Readers will turn the pages of this satisfying medieval thriller with gusto."   —*Booklist*

"Fans of Anita Blake will enjoy this novel. The characters are cleverly drawn so that the several supernatural species that play key roles in the plot seem natural and real."
—*Midwest Book Review*

"*Thief of Lives* takes the whole vampire-slayer mythos and moves into an entirely new setting."   —*SF Site*

"The Hendees unveil new details economically and with excellent timing, while maintaining a taut sexual tension."
—*SFX Magazine*

Dhampir

"*Dhampir* maintains a high level of excitement through interesting characters, both heroes and villains, colliding in well-written action scenes."   —*The Denver Post*

"An engaging adventure that is both humorous and exciting."
—*New York Times* bestselling author Kevin J. Anderson

"Take Anita Blake, vampire hunter, and drop her into a standard fantasy world, and you might end up with something like this exciting first novel."   —*Chronicle*

HUNTING MEMORIES

A VAMPIRE MEMORIES NOVEL

BARB HENDEE

A ROC BOOK

ROC
Published by New American Library, a division of
Penguin Group (USA) Inc., 375 Hudson Street,
New York, New York 10014, USA
Penguin Group (Canada), 90 Eglinton Avenue East, Suite 700, Toronto,
Ontario M4P 2Y3, Canada (a division of Pearson Penguin Canada Inc.)
Penguin Books Ltd., 80 Strand, London WC2R 0RL, England
Penguin Ireland, 25 St. Stephen's Green, Dublin 2,
Ireland (a division of Penguin Books Ltd.)
Penguin Group (Australia), 250 Camberwell Road, Camberwell, Victoria 3124,
Australia (a division of Pearson Australia Group Pty. Ltd.)
Penguin Books India Pvt. Ltd., 11 Community Centre, Panchsheel Park,
New Delhi - 110 017, India
Penguin Group (NZ), 67 Apollo Drive, Rosedale, North Shore 0632,
New Zealand (a division of Pearson New Zealand Ltd.)
Penguin Books (South Africa) (Pty.) Ltd., 24 Sturdee Avenue,
Rosebank, Johannesburg 2196, South Africa

Penguin Books Ltd., Registered Offices:
80 Strand, London WC2R 0RL, England

Published by Roc, an imprint of New American Library, a division of Penguin
Group (USA) Inc. Previously published in Roc trade paperback edition.

First Roc Mass Market Printing, October 2010
10 9 8 7 6 5 4 3 2 1

For my editor, Susan, and my daughter, Jaclyn, who both put an amazing amount of thought, time, and work into helping me with this novel.

prologue

Rose de Spenser sat at an antique desk with her pen poised above a sheet of pristine stationery. Night lights from Chinatown glinted through her bedroom window as she stared outside.

She knew what she had to do, but fear and uncertainty kept her pen in midair.

"Don't do it." A voice came from behind her. "You'll give us away."

"I have to," she whispered. "We cannot go on like this." Then she turned partway in her chair, facing inside the room.

Her nephew stood in the doorway. His form was transparent as always, so she could see out into the living room behind him. Though long dead, he looked eternally seventeen years old, his brown hair hanging to his shoulders. He wore the same blue-and-yellow Scottish plaid draped across his shoulder and held by a belt over the black breeches he had died in. The knife sheath at his hip was empty. After all these years with her in America, he'd never lost his accent.

"The world has shifted, Seamus," she said, "and if we do not act now, we'll lose our chance."

He looked at the wall and did not respond. But he must have known she was right.

What choice did they have? To continue rotting away in this apartment for another hundred years? To leave all the others, the lost ones in hiding, to rot away for another hundred years?

No.

Her attempt to convince him somehow strengthened her own resolution, and she turned back to the desk, this time lowering her pen to the sheet of paper. She wrote:

> *You are not alone. There are others like you. Respond to the Elizabeth Bathory Underground. P.O. Box 27750, San Francisco, CA 94973.*

She folded the sheet and placed it inside an ivory envelope, addressing it carefully:

ELEISHA CLEVON
1412 QUEEN ANNE DRIVE
SEATTLE, WA 98102

She stood up and walked to the door. Seamus didn't move, but she had never once walked through him.

"Where are you going?" he asked.

"Downstairs. To mail it."

She could see the pain on his face, the worry for her, but she just stood there quietly, waiting. After a long moment, he stepped aside.

chapter 1

"If you want to see the new *Rambo* movie, you'll have to take Wade . . . or go by yourself," Eleisha told Philip. "There's no way I'm sitting through that." She looked down the dark street into Pike Place Market. "Now focus. You need to practice so you can do this by yourself."

Philip was so tall that she realized she was standing under his chin, so she stepped away to see his face. He frowned, but she couldn't tell if his bad mood was due to her refusal to see *Rambo* or her insistence that he focus on the task at hand. Philip was hard to read, and they'd promised not to use telepathy on each other without permission.

"Your gift is better than mine for hunting like this," he said in his thick French accent, not bothering to look down at her.

"No, it isn't."

A month ago, Eleisha had discovered that she could feed without killing. . . .Well, more important, a few weeks before that, she had learned that most vampires were latent telepaths who simply required another telepath to help their abilities surface. Not long after developing her own psychic powers, she had fed upon a mortal, left him alive, and then altered his memories so that he never remembered meeting her.

To her, this was a revelation. She had always hated killing to exist, and now she didn't need to.

She'd expected Philip to be equally pleased . . . and relieved.

But to Philip, this new method of hunting felt more like a bridle—something to hold him back. He was a killer by nature, and Eleisha knew this. But he wasn't stupid, and he understood the freedom of feeding without having to worry about hiding or dumping bodies.

He also cared what she thought of him. He wanted her approval. She didn't like using this against him, but she would if she had to.

"Your gift is good for any kind of hunting," she said.

And it was.

Of the few other vampires she'd met, Philip's gift made hunting look the most effortless.

Within a few nights of becoming undead, a specific element of their previous personality developed into an overwhelming aura—which could be turned on and off at will. Eleisha's gift was the illusion of helplessness. She was perceived as a helpless teenage waif who needed assistance. The fact that she was small with wheat gold hair contributed to the strength of her gift. Her victims longed either to take care of her or to take advantage of her—and she used to feed only upon the latter.

Philip's gift was sexual attraction.

She glanced up at him again, and this time he looked down, tilting his pale, perfect face. He was slender and muscular at the same time, wearing Levi's and a long-sleeved Hugo Boss T-shirt. Thick red-brown hair hung halfway down his back.

Eleisha wasn't affected by his handsome appearance, but she understood its purpose.

And when he used it in combination with his gift, victims practically fell into his lap.

"Come on," she said, walking away, knowing he would follow.

Western Avenue grew less crowded as she moved away from the market, toward the parking garage.

By now, Philip knew the drill, and although he'd already complained a few times about the monotony, he agreed with the sensible nature of Eleisha's preference to get somebody inside of a parked car—as long as the car was in the shadows.

They paced the lowest level together, not speaking, just keeping an eye out until they'd reached the darkest sector, and Philip stopped.

A young woman wearing a Market Spice apron walked alone toward a Ford Taurus positioned behind a column. She looked tired, probably just getting off work.

Philip didn't hesitate. He'd been undead since 1819, and he knew how to pick someone.

"Pardon," he said, approaching her.

The woman turned at the sound of his voice in partial annoyance and partial alarm. She hit the unlock beeper on her keychain instantly. What was she doing down here by herself anyway? Stupid.

But then she froze at the sight of Philip, and he let his gift flow outward, surrounding and permeating her.

Eleisha fought to block it. She wasn't immune to his gift, and he wasn't immune to hers, so they had to be careful when hunting together. But she could still see Philip as this woman did: beautiful, strong, and passionate, like a hero from some cheesy book cover on the romance shelf at Barnes & Noble.

Yet even as Eleisha had this last thought, she could feel the pull of his gift, and she regretted every nasty comment she'd ever made about his taste in films and music.

He was perfect.

She shook her head hard, trying to clear it.

Focus, she told herself.

The woman stood there, watching as Philip walked up to her. She had brown-black hair in a ponytail. She wore a stylish leather messenger bag over one shoulder and large gold hoops in her ears.

"My sister and I have car trouble," he said, letting his French accent mesh the words together. "Can you help?"

"Do you need my phone?" she asked, taking shallow breaths, her eyes locked on his face.

"No, we are late for a family dinner on Capitol Hill. Can you take us?"

Letting strangers into her car was probably not something this woman did every day, but if he'd asked for her Visa card, she would have given it to him.

Eleisha decided not to talk—as he'd introduced her as his sister, and she couldn't fake a French accent.

"Um . . . okay," the woman said. "How far up on the hill?"

"I'll show you." He smiled and held out his hand. "Philip."

"Trudy," she responded, taking his hand, her voice shaking.

Eleisha climbed into the backseat quickly, as this was the only difficult part of her new routine. They couldn't let their intended victim start the car. So far, while training Philip, Eleisha had handled this part.

Earlier tonight, she told him he'd be on his own. He needed to learn how to do this.

But as Trudy put on her seat belt and fiddled with the keys, Philip just sat there, examining the stereo.

Without invading his private thoughts, Eleisha flashed out telepathically.

Put her to sleep!

He flinched and then frowned. Maybe he wanted to go for a ride up to Capitol Hill? He reached out to touch Trudy's face with the tips of his fingers just before she put her keys in the ignition.

"Wait," he said softly.

Her hand paused in midair.

Eleisha watched Philip's face as his eyes narrowed

slightly in concentration. He was getting better at controlling his newfound abilities. Right now, he was inside Trudy's mind, lulling her to sleep.

Within seconds, her head fell back against the seat. Her eyes were closed.

He'd done it.

"Good," Eleisha said. "Remember to feed from her wrist."

"I know!"

His whole body looked tense, as if it took all his effort not to rip out Trudy's throat. His lips twisted back over his teeth, and his eyes were hard. Eleisha had seen him struggle in their earlier practice sessions but never like this.

"Philip?" she asked, getting ready to launch over the seat.

He moved closer to Trudy, took her right wrist in his hand, and bit down, being careful not to tear too much skin—just as Eleisha had taught him.

She relaxed slightly. He seemed to have gained control of himself, and the worst was over. All he had to do now was keep Trudy asleep, take enough blood . . . enough life force to sustain himself, and then replace her memories of meeting him with one that convinced her she'd fallen and gashed her own wrist and then climbed into the car before passing out.

Accomplishing this last part was easy, or at least Eleisha thought so. They would be out of the car in a few moments.

But then Philip's feeding sounds grew louder, and he suddenly used both hands to grip Trudy's arm inside his mouth as he tore down deeper, draining and drinking her blood fast enough to kill her. His features were taut, and his eyes were glowing.

He'd lost himself.

Eleisha knew better than to touch him when he got like this. On instinct, she flashed out telepathically.

Stop it!

To her relief, he jerked his head back, pulling his teeth from Trudy's arm.

But this broke his mental hold on her, and she opened her eyes, seeing his blood-smeared face, seeing her torn arm, and she began to scream. Anyone within a hundred yards would hear her.

He snarled and covered her mouth with his hand.

"No!" Eleisha said, and this time, she reached over the seat, grabbing his shoulder, trying to pull him back. "Get off!"

Instantly, she reached out with her thoughts, taking control of Trudy's mind, rushing her back in time to the moment she walked into the parking garage.

The inside of the car fell silent, and even while she focused on Trudy's memories, Eleisha could feel Philip's tight shoulder easing beneath her fingers.

The memory of a simple fall would no longer work.

Eleisha created the image of a mugger as she rebuilt the last ten minutes in Trudy's mind. Trudy walked toward her waiting Taurus. A man jumped out from behind the column, waving a knife and shouting for her bag. He slashed at her, and when she raised her arm, he cut her several times. She dropped the bag. He grabbed it and ran. Terrified, she made it inside the car and then passed out.

Eleisha opened her eyes and reached to Philip.

"Give me your knife."

He was staring at her in confusion, as if he wasn't sure what was happening, but he reached down into his boot and pulled out the hunting knife he always carried. Eleisha took it and leaned all the way over the seat, making a few shallow cuts in Trudy's arm, hoping to cover the mess Philip had made. Then she handed the blade back to him.

"Get her bag from the floor," she said. "Hurry."

She was out of the car before he was, but he followed quickly, slamming the door and carrying Trudy's bag. Eleisha headed for the stairs.

He followed.

Either no one had heard Trudy screaming or no one cared, but Eleisha didn't even start to relax until they were back up Western Avenue again, moving farther away from the market.

Then Philip stepped in front of her, wiping the blood from his mouth onto his black sleeve. He didn't touch her, but he wouldn't let her pass.

"You're angry," he said.

Was she angry? She didn't think so. She wasn't sure what she felt. He shouldn't be having this much trouble. The fact that they didn't have to kill anymore shifted the entire balance of their existence. Why couldn't he see that?

She shook her head.

"Then what is wrong?" he asked. "You are different tonight, even before . . . before that in the car. So quiet and no fun at all." When agitated, he had more trouble with English.

But Philip always said she was no fun if she didn't do exactly what he wanted. She was used to that.

Tonight he could somehow sense more. And he was right. She'd had something on her mind for weeks now . . . something she had not told him or Wade.

"Let's just get a taxi and go back to the house," she said. "We can talk there."

"No." He didn't move. "Tell me you are not angry."

He could be such a child sometimes. He looked ten years older than her. He *was* thirty years older, and he'd recently passed the two-century mark. Yet he often made her feel like the grown-up.

Still, she understood him. Philip hated being alone more than anything, and he'd spent one hundred and eighty-three years of his undead existence alone. Now that he had companionship, he feared losing it.

She reached out to take the bag from him, tossing it into a Dumpster.

"I'm not angry," she said. "But you need to try harder."

He had to learn to control his blood lust while focusing his telepathy at the same time.

His expression melted into relief. "Is that all? Yes, yes, I will try harder." Then, as if forgetting the entire event in the parking garage had taken place, he turned and sidestepped so she could walk beside him.

"Did you rent a new movie for tonight?" he asked. "With guns and explosions?"

"No, I want to talk to you and Wade about something."

"About what?"

"Let's just go to the house."

*   *   *

Wade often felt at odds, rattling around the house by himself as if he had nothing better to do than wait for Eleisha and Philip to come back.

Unfortunately . . . he didn't have anything better to do.

Not quite three months ago, he'd enjoyed an orderly life, one he'd worked hard to create. He had a posh loft in Portland, Oregon, a career as a police psychologist, and the respect of his peers.

Now he had no job, no home of his own, and he was living in Seattle with two vampires.

What the hell happened to his life?

But he already knew the answer.

Eleisha.

Wade had always been a little out of the ordinary. For one, he'd been born telepathic, so he'd never expected a completely normal life . . . but this?

He wandered from the kitchen and into the living room, glancing at the television and the small pile of Philip's DVDs on the floor. Eleisha never watched TV of her own accord. Yet for someone who'd been around since the early 1800s, she was surprisingly well-adjusted to the modern world. Philip, however, was not, and sometimes, Wade regretted having taught him to use the DVD player. Philip had developed a fascination with action movies—especially anything by John Woo with Chow Yun-Fat—and he tended to play one after the other when he was bored.

And if he wasn't hunting, he was always bored.

A creak on the front porch sounded, and Wade

turned to look hopefully at the door. Were they home already?

No one came in. The house must just be settling.

With that thought, he suddenly realized that none of them ever referred to this place as "home." All three of them still referred to it as "the house."

But that was probably due to the fact that they'd been living here only a month, and before that, the place had belonged to another vampire named Maggie Latour . . . who was dead now, turned to dust.

So none of them had roots or memories in this house.

He dropped into a chair near the fireplace, trying not to feel sorry for himself. He knew Eleisha and Philip were both working to come to terms with the chain of events that had brought them here, too.

Wade let his mind roll back. When had it started?

Last March? When a vampire named Edward Claymore had committed suicide by jumping off his own front porch in broad daylight, bursting into flames?

Or when the police investigation had dropped Wade right into Eleisha's path, and he discovered someone just as telepathic as he was?

Or maybe it really began when he had quit his job in Portland to follow her here?

No, it began long before that, in Wales, in 1839 when a vampire named Julian Ashton had turned her undead and then cut her loose, sending her to America with no information and no real idea what she was, forcing her to figure things out on her own.

No . . . it started even before that, in France, in 1825,

when Eleisha's maker, Julian, had realized that unlike most vampires, he was incapable of developing psychic powers, and he fell into an obsession of fear and began killing his own kind. He'd spared any vampires who had not expressed telepathic abilities—and this included Eleisha and Philip.

But Wade had changed all that. He'd woken Eleisha's and Philip's latent abilities and, in doing so, turned them into targets.

And then Julian had come hunting them.

Somehow—and Wade still didn't know exactly how—on the night Julian found them, Eleisha had forced her thoughts inside Julian's mind and shown him something terrifying that caused him to freeze up . . . after which Philip kicked him out a twelfth-story window. Eleisha firmly believed that she had permanently driven him away, and they were all safe from him.

Philip didn't seem so sure.

But four weeks had passed since that night, and Julian had not come after them, and now the three of them seemed to be existing in a state of limbo, waiting for something, but none of them knew what. Eleisha had suggested that Wade find a new job here in Seattle. He agreed. She had suggested he might feel better if he found an apartment of his own. He partially agreed. She had suggested that they might clear out all of Maggie's things, buy new furniture, and make the house their own. He agreed.

But he'd taken no action to accomplish any of these things.

How long could he continue like this?

Voices coming from outside caught his attention. The front door swung inward as Eleisha walked inside with Philip on her heels.

"Wade, tomorrow will you see the new *Rambo* movie with me?" Philip asked before the door closed behind him. "Eleisha won't go."

Wade blinked. "There's a new *Rambo* movie? Who's playing Rambo?"

"Stallone."

"Stallone? That can't be right. The guy's sixty years old."

Philip turned to Eleisha. "Tell him I'm right. You saw the preview with me last week."

"What?" Eleisha was pulling off her jacket with a distracted expression, as if she hadn't been listening. "Oh, yes, Philip's right."

Looking at her face, Wade forgot all about Rambo. He could tell when something was bothering her.

The three of them had been together such a short time, but they knew each other better than most people who'd coexisted for a lifetime. They had looked into each other's minds and down the paths of time and personal experiences, seen fears and loves and private corners.

"What's wrong?" he asked.

Glancing back at him, she dropped her jacket on a chair, opened her mouth halfway, and then closed it again. For once, Philip seemed to forget about his own desire for entertainment, and he walked closer to her, his head towering over hers.

"Eleisha?" he asked.

Just when Wade thought he'd grown accustomed to

their physical appearance, he'd look at them together like this and feel surprised all over again. Their pale, softly glowing skin made them both seem timeless, yet there the resemblance stopped. Eleisha was probably not what a typical American would consider beautiful. But she was alarmingly . . . pretty. Born in a different era, she was small and slender with a mass of wispy, wheat gold hair that reached the top of her jeans. Sometimes, just the sight of her left Wade speechless.

Philip, on the other hand, looked like someone on the cover of *GQ* posing for Calvin Klein's fall fashion line, and without meaning to, he tended to make Wade feel diminished. They were both tall, but where Philip's tight muscles showed through his shirt, Wade's build leaned toward thin. Wade's white-blond hair stuck out in different directions, as he wore it fairly short, but he often forgot to see a stylist for months.

His feelings about Philip were conflicted. He didn't always exactly *like* Philip, but they were deeply connected by circumstance, and they knew each other far too well.

Eleisha glanced up over at Wade, almost as if she was nervous. "I need to show you both something, and I don't know what you'll say."

She walked halfway over to the staircase, lifted the top of one of the steps, and took out an ivory envelope. Wade had no idea that step lifted up to create a hiding space. When had Eleisha discovered that? What had she hidden there?

She hesitated a moment longer, and then said to Wade, "Do you remember a few nights after . . . after

Julian found us and we drove him off, that night when I tried to get you to start looking for a job here?"

He winced. "Of course I remember."

"This came that same night."

She handed him the envelope, and he opened it, reading the brief handwritten letter inside.

You are not alone. There are others like you. Respond to the Elizabeth Bathory Underground. P.O. Box 27750, San Francisco, CA 94973.

He was confused, having no idea what this meant, but before he could speak, Philip walked over and ripped both the letter and envelope from his hand.

"What is that?" Philip asked. He scanned the note and then raised his eyes from the paper to Eleisha's face. "A month ago? This came a month ago and you didn't show me?" His voice had lost its normal light, amusement-seeking tone. He sounded angry.

"Philip—" Eleisha began.

"It's a trap!" he nearly shouted, his accent growing thicker. "Sent by Julian." He looked at the envelope. "This is addressed to you. Here! By hiding this, you put yourself in danger! You put Wade in danger."

Philip often behaved as if he needed to protect Wade—which was neither flattering nor comforting.

"It's not Julian," Eleisha said. "Look at the handwriting."

"You aren't to answer this," Philip ordered. "You leave it with me, and you don't go hunting alone until I say so."

"I already answered it," Eleisha said quietly. "And then she wrote back, and then I wrote back . . . and then she wrote back. We've been corresponding every week."

Philip's expression darkened into rage, but before he could explode, Wade asked, "She?"

"Yes, just look at her letters." Eleisha hurried back to the staircase and drew out a small stack of ivory envelopes. Wade could barely believe she had been keeping this a secret. He thought he knew all Eleisha's secrets. She gripped the letters in one hand and held her palm up toward Philip. "Wait. Just hear me out. Her name is Rose, and she is like us. She lives somewhere in San Francisco, but she won't tell me where. She's frightened, too."

Digging through the envelopes, she pulled out a letter. "Here, Philip, come look at this one. She says that Julian could not have killed every vampire in Europe. She believes there must be others, only they are hiding . . . like she's been hiding. She thinks they're afraid of him, and she's been waiting, just waiting, for someone to fight back. When she learned we'd survived an attack and driven him off, she knew the world had shifted. She needs our help!"

Philip listened to this outburst without a word, but then he walked slowly over to Eleisha, staring down at her with eyes so hard that Wade would have backed up—but Eleisha didn't.

She stood her ground. "Look at the letter, Philip."

"And how did she know where we are?" Philip asked, ignoring the letter. His tone dropped low. "How did she know we drove off Julian?"

Eleisha's voice wavered. "She hasn't told me that. But this isn't a trap."

She turned to Wade, stretching out her hand. "Just read this one."

He was still reeling that she'd kept all of this from himself and Philip, but he took the letter and, scanning a middle paragraph, he could almost hear the polite, desperate voice behind the words. Without even asking, he flashed what he read into Philip's thoughts.

. . . but the house you stay in now is not suitable. You must find someplace larger, someplace to fortify where you can protect yourselves and me and anyone else we might find. I wait to hear from you. I have waited so long, even before I knew your name.

He looked up, thinking on the initial note. "The Elizabeth Bathory Underground?"

"That's what she calls it . . . or hopes to call it. It's an underground we'll create so we can look for others and help bring them in, keep them safe from Julian. Rose thinks the name is subtle enough to escape obvious notice but still offers a clue. Elizabeth Bathory was a countess from the sixteenth century who—"

"I know who she was," Wade cut in, frustrated by this sudden shift. "She murdered young girls to bathe in their blood, and she became linked into the history of vampires. That isn't what I meant. How could you get so involved in this without warning us?"

Eleisha looked at the floor. "I don't know. I liked writing to Rose, and I was afraid you'd ask me to stop . . . and I want to find her, Wade. I need to find her."

His frustration faded. He shared an empathy with both of his companions. He knew Philip reveled in having company after existing alone for so long—because of Julian. Philip's greatest fear was being alone again.

But Eleisha was more complicated. In 1839, Julian had realized his father, William, was dying of Alzheimer's disease—which had no name yet, but Wade recognized the symptoms while reading Eleisha's memories. In desperation, Julian turned his father, only to condemn the old man to eternal dementia. To cover his mistake, Julian turned Eleisha in order to create a permanent caretaker for William, and he'd put them both on a ship bound for America. Eleisha had spent nearly one hundred and seventy years caring for William, but like Maggie, William was gone now, too, turned to dust.

Eleisha missed caring for him. She possessed a need to be needed—which might explain her affection for Philip.

Now she wanted to look for lost vampires?

"You are not going *anywhere*," Philip snapped. "And you will stop sending these letters." He paced halfway across the room, muttering, "I have to think. I have to think what to do now."

"I don't need your permission," Eleisha said.

He stopped pacing and looked at her in surprise.

"I am going find Rose and offer her a safe place," she went on. "I want your help, and Wade's, but I'll do it alone if I have to."

Wade had never seen the two of them like this, and the look on Philip's face was beginning to worry him. Stepping toward Eleisha, Philip drew his lips up over his teeth in a snarl.

"You don't think I can stop you?"

"No." She shook her head. "Because if you do, I won't forgive you."

She might as well have slapped him. Releasing a sound between rage and anguish, he turned toward the door. "Then go by yourself! Walk into a trap by yourself!"

"It's not a trap! Just look at her letters!"

"This woman is terrified of Julian," Wade managed to put in.

Philip ignored both of them and stormed out the door.

Predictably, he got as far as the front porch before he stopped and turned halfway around, his pale face gone white.

"Whatever happens, if someone else knows we are here, we have to find a new place." He paused as if the next words pained him. "She spoke of finding a place we could fortify. If we do this . . . *if* we do this thing for you, we'll have to begin there."

For a few seconds, no one spoke. Then Eleisha said quietly, "I think I've already found one. I haven't seen it myself yet, just photos."

Wade's mouth fell open. More secrets? "What? Where?"

"Back home," she said. "In Portland. Let me book plane tickets, and I'll show you."

Wade stared at her as if she were a stranger, but then he realized this was the first time he'd heard her use the word "home" in over a month.

"Book the tickets," he whispered hoarsely.

At the moment, he didn't want to know any more.

chapter 2

Julian Ashton had fled to his family estate in Wales like a victim, like a coward—or at least that's how he viewed it.

His gift was fear, and he was accustomed to inducing the emotion, not to experiencing it himself. The only thing he feared was a telepathic member of his own kind, and he had destroyed the last one a long time ago.

He felt no remorse for this. He had taken simply necessary action and ensured his own survival . . . until now.

For centuries, his kind had existed by four laws, and the most sacred of these was "No vampire shall kill to feed." They'd retained their secrecy through telepathy, feeding on mortals, altering a memory, and then leaving the victim alive. New vampires required training from their makers to both awaken and hone psychic abilities, but Julian's telepathy had never surfaced. He had lived by his own laws, and so the elders began quietly turning against him. His maker, Angelo Travare, had tried to hide this news from him, but he *knew*. He heard the rumblings, and he had acted first, beheading every vampire who'd lived by the laws, including Angelo—who would have turned against him sooner or later. Angelo had hoped that Julian would eventually develop his powers, but this was a false hope, and Julian knew it.

He began to see a new path, a world without laws.

Vampires without telepathy—without any training by a maker—were no threat to him. On some level, he almost viewed them as kindred spirits.

Then . . . a month ago, without reason or warning, Eleisha, once his servant, had suddenly manifested psychic abilities so powerful she had forced her thoughts into his and taken over his mind, his body, his free will.

To make matters worse, she seemed to have won the protection of Philip Branté!

Eleisha had warned Julian off and then let him go, but he knew this was far from over.

Even after a month of hiding out in Cliffbracken, where he had always felt secure, his hands still shook at the memory of her thoughts pushing inside his. He had been completely helpless to stop her.

Of course she knew nothing of the past, of the elders, of the laws, but Julian's world had shifted, and he was uncertain what to do.

What would happen as her power grew stronger?

Since returning, he'd spent much of his time in the main floor study, but earlier tonight, he had made his way down into the depths of his decaying family manor, and he paced the hard mud floor of what had once been a dungeon, back in the days of his grandfather.

He was in the guard room, surrounded by small cells.

Why had he come down here?

Something had called him, something from the past. Julian was not one to dwell on mistakes or sins, but a small part of him had never quite left this room, never stopped eating away at him for what he'd done here one night in 1839.

He walked over to the nearest cell and looked inside. It was empty. He turned and looked at the floor of the guard room.

Empty.

He was alone, and yet he could still see the shadows, still hear the ghosts.

Closing his eyes, he let his mind drift back until he heard his mother, Lady Katherine, screaming and beseeching him to help his father, Lord William. Julian had cared nothing for his mother. She was a cold-hearted, self-centered woman. But watching his father sink deeper and deeper into dementia had proven too much.

He remembered the feeling in the pit of his stomach as he sank his teeth into his own father's neck and then cut himself, forcing his father to drink, to take all the blood back.

He remembered the horror of realizing what he'd done as Lord William dropped to the floor drooling and gibbering, locked forever in undead madness.

Then he'd locked his father in a cell, in the same dungeon his ancestors had used to make their enemies suffer.

But even down here, Lord William had not been far enough away, not nearly far enough.

The following night, Julian dragged Eleisha down into the same dungeon. He turned her and put them both on a ship bound for New York.

He had stolen her life and condemned her.

And now, after all this time, she had become telepathic, like the vampires of a past era.

What would she do as she dwelled on the memories of what he'd done to her? And how was he to know when she finally came after him?

He grew sick with fear, his own gift turning in upon itself.

He had to take some kind of action.

Pulling his gaze from the cell, he walked back through the guard room and down a short corridor to a secret passage that led to the stairwell going up.

Unable to rest his mind, he had been poring over one idea after the next regarding how to keep track of Eleisha's location. As he could not yet bring himself to leave Cliffbracken, he had few options, and none of them appealed to him.

But the same one continued to resurface in his mind. He'd flatly refused to even entertain the idea the first time it occurred to him, and he pushed it away. But every time it came back, he considered it a few moments longer . . . until one night, two weeks after returning here, he had used his cell phone and Visa card to order several newspapers from America.

Moving up the enclosed stairwell, he stopped on the first landing and then emerged onto the main floor of the manor, stepping out into the study.

The furniture, books, and shelves were covered in dust.

He still engaged a few servants to care for the place, but he'd ordered them to stay out of this room.

He'd gone too far into preparations for any prying eyes.

Reluctantly, he walked over to the round oak table, where his father had once consumed afternoon tea while dealing with the house accounts.

But at night, his mother had used this same table for different purposes.

Julian tightened his lips in distaste.

She and a few of her bored female acquaintances had become fascinated with magical arts and contact with the dead. In the span of a few years, they spent a small fortune on books and charlatans who claimed to be mediums.

However, as with most things, his mother lost interest in this pursuit, and her number of séances grew fewer and fewer. When Lord William began to lose his memory, Lady Katherine stopped inviting guests altogether.

But the occult books still remained here in the study.

A few that had provided him with general guidance were stacked upon the table.

Lives of the Necromancers: Or, an Account of the Most Eminent Persons in Successive Ages, Who Have Claimed for Themselves, or to Whom Has Been Imputed by Others, the Exercise of Magical Power by William Godwin.

Along with *Dialogues of the Dead* by George, First Baron Lyttelton.

But two books lay open. The smaller book—written in German—had given him more specific instructions regarding what he needed to do:

Geister Auffordern by Gottbert Drechsler.

The larger had proven most useful. It was so old that he could not find a publication date, and the cover was worn so thin, some of the letters weren't clear. He couldn't make out the complete title, but the words resembled *Medius Excessum Universum*. The Latin text inside was easier to read, and the book proved to be a startling treatise on the fates of souls trapped between worlds.

Three fat candles stood beside the books, and a new thermometer lay above them.

He hated all this . . . foolishness, as it reminded him too much of unnatural powers such as telepathy.

He remembered despising his mother for attempting to fill her life with such empty trifles. Of course she had never succeeded in summoning a ghost. She had no true connection to the dead, and she wasn't capable of understanding much of the material she'd read—especially the German.

But he did.

From what he had gleaned, only potential "summoners" with a connection to the dead could successfully call a spirit from the other side. In some accounts, this had included a person who had died briefly and been brought back to life. Another account in Drechsler's book involved a summoner who had been born with a kind of supernatural sense that allowed her to connect with those who had passed over. People like her were rare.

But Julian believed that he also possessed a connection. He was one of the living dead.

The last object on the table was a copy of the *Seattle Times* lying open to expose the obituaries.

He'd been scanning various papers, ignoring the numerous mundane deaths by car accident or cancer or heart disease, occasionally stopping upon a murder victim, but then passing the entry by.

Finally, three nights ago, he'd come upon a brief article—rather than a standard obituary—that made him pause longer.

Sixteen-year-old Mary Jordane of Bellevue, Washington, met a tragic death Tuesday night when she overdosed on her mother's prescription medications, combining Ambien with OxyContin. Her parents, Matthew and Laura Jordane, were attending an art exhibition in Seattle. After taking the medication, Mary attempted to call her father's cell phone several times, unaware he had turned it off. She called 911, but the paramedics did not arrive in time, and she died en route to Overlake Hospital Medical Center. She is survived by her parents and her grandmother, Estelle Goodrich.

The article went on recounting mundane details. Julian studied the accompanying photo, which appeared to have been taken at school by a class photographer. Even posed, her face was angry, defiant, and unhappy. She had short, spiky hair dyed magenta and a nose stud.

Although Julian practiced the purity of isolation, he knew something of human nature, and he could read between the lines. This girl was addicted to attention and had probably worn her parents thin, forcing her to create larger and larger dramas. Julian did not believe she'd ever intended to commit suicide. She had overdosed and then called her father, knowing her parents would run home immediately.

Her plan failed.

This was the ghost he wanted.

She did not wish to be dead, suggesting a good chance that she remained on the bleak middle plane, trying to get back to this one. If so, he could manipulate her. He could use her.

Gathering the candles and the thermometer, he left the table and moved over to the threadbare Indian rug in the center of the study. He sat on the floor and arranged the candles in a triangle. Pulling a lighter from his pocket, he lit the candles and then laid the thermometer beside himself on the rug.

From what he had read, what he was about to attempt required no telepathic ability whatsoever, simply a connection to the dead. There were risks, but he was prepared.

Staring at the candles, he tried to clear his mind. At first he failed, dwelling on Eleisha's suddenly manifesting psychic ability, wondering how this came to be, wondering if the same thing could happen to Philip, whom he'd terrified and driven into solitude. What would Philip do if he ever gained power over Julian?

Even worse than Eleisha.

But Julian forced himself into a state of numb emptiness as he focused on the candles, on Mary Jordane's name, on the image of her face, on achieving a connection.

"Mary Jordane," he said aloud, and then he closed his eyes, picturing the middle plane of existence, the in-between place where lost souls wandered.

"Mary Jordane," he repeated more loudly. "I ask you to come to me. Hear my voice."

Julian never made requests. He gave orders. This practice of *asking* her to hear him felt alien.

At first, nothing happened, but he continued focusing on the image of her face, and he called her name over and over. The temperature in the room began to drop. He had built no fire, so it was cold already, but Julian could feel the difference. He didn't need to look at the thermometer.

Then he sensed a presence—nothing concrete, just a feeling. He opened his eyes, staring at the three candles, keeping everything from his mind except for the image of Mary Jordane, but he did not ask her to manifest yet.

"Are you there?" he asked without looking up. He needed to maintain his focus.

No one answered.

"Are you Mary Jordane?"

"Ask me to show myself and you'll see," said a female voice, sounding as if she was standing in the room.

He raised both hands. "Not yet."

Several of the texts had warned him that malevolent ghosts could masquerade as the person being called—seeking entry into the world of the living. He did not fear ghosts, but he wished to be certain he'd found Mary.

"How did you die?" he asked. "Let me feel how you died."

Nothing happened and the moments kept ticking.

Then he began to feel ill, nauseous and dizzy. The sensation was made worse by the fact that he had not felt such things for two hundred years. The floor rushed up, and he narrowly avoided hitting the nearest candle. He was sick, floating on wave after wave of nausea, and then he grew tired.

"Stop," he said hoarsely. "Stop now!"

His head cleared. He had found Mary.

"Show yourself!" he ordered. "I call on you."

The air in front of him, just across the edge of the carpet, wavered and began to fill with color. A few seconds later, a transparent girl was staring back at him in surprise.

She looked younger than sixteen, skinny with a hint of budding breasts, wearing a purple T-shirt and a black mesh overshirt, torn jeans, and Doc Martens boots.

"I can see you," she gasped, as if she could still breathe. "How did you do that?" Her accent was common, like typical American trash. He was repulsed by the sight of her. He would not employ one such as her to scrub the floor of his kitchens.

She turned around in awe, taking in the study. "I'm here. I can see everything."

Now that he had succeeded in summoning this spirit, he was somewhat at a loss. The last thing he wanted to do was speak with her. He did not even care to speak with underlings here at the manor and preferred to pass down his orders in writing.

Mary stopped, looking at the shelves and candles and the antique table. "Wait. . . . Where am I?"

"You are in Wales," he managed to answer.

"Wales? Where is that?"

Good God.

"They told me," she babbled on. "They told me if you called me to appear, I could cross over to this side. I never thought . . ." She faltered, taking in the sight of him.

"Who told you?"

"The others. They were jealous when you called my name."

But her words were spoken somewhat absently as she moved closer to him, studying him. He cared little for his own appearance anymore. He was a large man with a bone structure that almost made him look heavy. His dark hair hung at uneven angles around a solid chin. His feet were bare tonight. He wore black slacks and a loose shirt that hadn't been laundered in weeks.

"I don't know you," she said, sounding like a pensive, confused child. "The others . . . they thought maybe my mother hired someone to find me. Someone to help me cross over. And that's why I didn't know your voice. I didn't think I'd ever get back."

As she said this, he knew what to do.

"I require your services," he said.

"My what?"

"You're from the Seattle area. I need you to find out if someone is still there, and tell me where she is, what she does, where she goes."

Mary's demeanor changed, and she looked him up and down dismissively. "I don't think so. I'm going home."

Finding this conversation more and more difficult, he said, "Yes, I will let you go home eventually. But you must do as I say first."

Her transparent features twisted, making her nose stud rise slightly. "Screw that. I don't even know you."

He wasn't certain his gift would work on a ghost, but he let the aura of fear flow outward, filling the room. "I summoned you here," he said coldly. "And I can send you back with a word. Would you like to go back?"

Deep satisfaction washed through him at the sudden anxiety on her face.

But she surprised him by asking, "Is Wales a long way from Seattle?"

"Yes."

"Then how do I get there?"

He blew out the candles and stood up. "You're inside a stone manor, a large dwelling. Wish yourself outside, somewhere on the grounds."

She looked at him with disbelief. Then she glanced away and her expression grew intense. She vanished.

He waited a few moments before attempting the most crucial part. If he could not succeed in his next attempt, the entire summoning was a failure.

"Mary Jordane!" he called loudly.

She instantly appeared before him. Her mouth fell open. "What the . . . ?"

The sense of relief was sweet. She was his slave.

"Were you standing outside the manor?" he asked.

"Yeah." Her eyes were wide.

"I called you. I can call you to my side from anywhere at any time. And I can send you back to the lost souls, to the in-between plane, and leave you there forever. Do you understand?"

She didn't answer, but her eyes were locked into his. The reality of her situation was beginning to sink in.

"But if you serve me," he went on, "if you do as I ask, when my task for you is finished, I will release you and let you remain in this world. You can haunt your family, your old school, anyplace you please, and remain here among the living. Is that what you want?"

Slowly, she nodded. "Just how am I supposed to find someone I've never met in Seattle?"

Was she attempting to stand up to him? He knew that others might admire her spirit. He did not.

"Because ghosts like yourself are drawn to dead," he answered. "Eleisha is undead, a vampire."

"Like you?"

"Yes."

At least the girl wasn't completely stupid, and she

appeared to be catching on more quickly than he initially expected. She must have sensed he wasn't alive almost as soon as she materialized.

"You simply have to focus upon a landmark in Seattle that you already know," he said. "From there, I think you'll be able to sense her."

"Someplace like the Seattle Center?"

"Yes."

"Okay . . . I know where that is. And if I do what you say, you won't send me back? When I'm done, I can just go home?"

If it were possible, he would have smiled. She might be trash, but she would serve him.

Three nights later, Eleisha stood between Wade and Philip in northwest Portland as they all gazed upward.

"You've got to be joking," Wade said in disbelief. "A church? Can you step inside?"

Philip didn't say anything.

Surprised that Wade would even entertain such old superstitions or trepidation about holy ground, Eleisha glanced over at him. "Of course we can. Don't be ridiculous."

Although both men had tried to pry hints from her, she'd refused to say a word about their destination, and after leaving the airport, she'd simply handed the taxi driver an address. She had seen this building only in photos, but standing in the churchyard, with the night-blooming roses winding up the tall, wrought-iron fence, she knew they had come to the right place.

The church was two stories high, constructed of red brick.

It looked like a haven.

She pulled the gate shut behind them and latched it. Then she fished a set of keys from her bag. "Let's look inside. It's been empty for a long time."

Wade's astonishment grew. "You've got the keys? Why isn't the real estate agent meeting us here?"

"I talked her into . . . Just come inside. I'll tell you everything."

"Eleisha," he insisted. "Agents don't give potential buyers the keys."

She ignored him and hurried up the steps to unlock the front doors, which were newer additions made from thick metal.

Philip stopped briefly to examine the doors. She looked back at him, and he nodded.

She turned on the overhead lights. "The deacons' committee decided to leave the power on so any buyers could see that all the wiring works."

They stepped into what had once been the main sanctuary, but now the altar was bare and all the pews had been ripped out, leaving only a large room with spiderwebs and a musty red and tan carpet. Half-oval stained-glass windows lined the walls, and Eleisha turned in a circle to see each one, soothed by the greens, blues, and yellows in the depictions.

"This was built in 1902, and it's been on the market for over two years," she said. "The congregation outgrew it, and they commissioned a new church." She looked at Philip again. "The walls are two feet thick, and there are only two doorways on the ground floor to the outside: this front one we just came in and a single back door."

He still hadn't spoken, but again he nodded and began studying the structure of the high-set windows.

Wade came in only a few steps. "You aren't seriously thinking of buying this place? Of living here?"

"Just leave your suitcases and come this way," she said, dropping her bag and moving behind the altar to a side door. The door led into a hallway where she faced two other doors, a stairway to the left leading down, and another stairway at the end of the hall leading up. Eleisha had studied the floor plan for hours and knew the layout by heart. She turned on the hallway lights.

"These two rooms are offices," she said, opening the closest door.

Wade peered inside at a pleasant room with hardwood floors and cream walls.

"There's a three-bedroom apartment in the basement, along with an industrial-sized kitchen on the other side," she added.

For first time since walking through the gate, Wade turned and seemed to be seriously listening to her. "A three-bedroom apartment?"

"Yes, the place was designed so the pastor and his family could live inside the church. But come upstairs with me first."

Without waiting for a response, she walked down the hall and up the stairs, emerging into another hallway, this one with a red-and-tan carpet like the sanctuary's. Three doors lined each wall, and she flicked on the light and moved onward, opening doors as she went.

"Most of these were Sunday school or meeting rooms, but they're empty now. We could turn one of them into a room for Rose."

The moment those words left her mouth, she regretted them. Both Philip and Wade had agreed to come to Portland and see this mysterious "place" she had in mind, but so far, neither of them had expressed sharing her determination to find this woman who'd written asking for their help. And although she'd meant her outburst back at Maggie's, that she'd find Rose alone if need be . . . the truth was she wanted Philip and Wade to be part of all this.

Finding a proper safe house was the first step. But she needed to pull them in one step at a time.

Wade and Philip walked the floor, looking inside all six of the bare rooms. Neither one responded to her mention of Rose.

Finally Philip said, "Too many exterior windows. We'll have to seal most of them up."

Wade stared at him. "You're standing outside a Sunday school room, and that's all you can say? 'Too many windows'? Have you missed the irony here?"

Philip shrugged and put his hand against the wall. "Old buildings are best. This is an *église solide*."

Eleisha had picked up enough French from him to know he'd called the place a sturdy church. Excitement began building inside her. He was clearly considering the idea. Regarding this part of her plan, though, she hadn't worried too much about convincing Philip.

Spending four weeks at Maggie's was probably the longest stretch he'd stayed in one place in decades. Before becoming entangled with Eleisha, Philip had not been a cautious hunter—leaving bodies wherever he dropped them. And he'd hunted more often than he needed to, so he was constantly on the move. No, he would feel no hesitation to leave Maggie's. He didn't care where he lived as long as Eleisha and Wade lived with him.

Wade was a different story. He didn't like making decisions, and he was a big fan of "thinking things through"—which she viewed as a euphemism for sitting on the fence.

She nearly ran back to the stairs. "Come on. Let's see the basement."

Not waiting for them, she jumped off the bottom step into the hallway and jogged to the stairs leading down, emerging into a sitting room. Overhead lighting down here was more sparse, as the place must have contained lamps before. She moved to the apartment's small kitchen and switched on a light. Then she walked back into the sitting room.

Even dimly lit, the sitting room was lovely, with soft yellow walls and white molding around the floors and ceiling.

When she turned around, Wade and Philip were standing quietly behind her. "It only has one bathroom, but the bedrooms are over there," she said, pointing through an old-fashioned archway. "And there is a small family kitchen that way. The big congregation kitchen is on the far side of the building."

Wade cooked sometimes—when he didn't order

pizza—and Eleisha and Philip sometimes made tea. They could not eat or digest food, but their kind could absorb tea and even small amounts of wine.

She stood tense, unable to read either of her companions. From the moment she had seen the photos, something about this place had called to her . . . as if calling her home. She felt safe here. Welcome. Wanted. Like the building had been abandoned for too long, and it needed them.

"What do you think?" she asked Philip.

"It's good," he said simply.

"Wade?"

He shook his head in frustration. "This is too big a decision to make right now. Shouldn't we look at other places? Shouldn't we take more time to consider?"

Was he trying to convince himself or her? If she chose to, she could allow a little of her gift to seep out, to seduce him, to make him see she felt safe here so that he would do anything for her. But she wouldn't do that. She wanted his true agreement.

"I don't want to go back to Seattle," she confessed, deciding to try honesty. "I don't want to go back to Maggie's. I don't want to look at any other places. This is the one, Wade."

He stepped closer, his white-blond hair falling forward into his eyes.

"Eleisha . . . ?"

"Don't you miss Portland?" she asked. "Don't you miss it here?"

Why she should love Portland and not Seattle was nonsensical, and she knew it, but for weeks now, the pull to come back to Oregon had grown stronger. The wish to leave Maggie's house had grown unbearable. That house held too many reminders. Maggie had existed there, decorated the place, made it her own. And William . . . he had died in that house. Eleisha tried, but she couldn't live there.

Philip walked across the sitting room and dropped down near the outlet of what appeared to be a cable hookup. The empty apartment still looked like something from 1902, but it had been updated.

"If we aren't going back," he said, studying the hookup, "we'll have to buy a new TV and DVD player. Wade, you can set the player up for me."

Wade blinked. "Not going back? Not ever? What about our stuff?"

Philip looked back at him. "What stuff? We brought most of our clothes along, and everything else was Maggie's."

That was true, and Eleisha had been banking on at least one of them reasoning this. She mentally searched for an opening to drop the next bomb.

Wade provided it.

"Well, it's not far to dawn," he said, sighing. "We should at least call for a cab and find a hotel. Even if we decide to buy this place, it's not like everything is going to happen overnight. We'll have to negotiate an offer, get the church inspected, get it appraised, and set up a closing date to sign papers. Do you both want to live in a hotel for a month?"

"No," Eleisha answered quietly.

His forehead wrinkled as he looked at her.

She held up the keys. "I leased the building for thirty days."

"What?"

"The deacons' committee is so motivated to sell that they agreed to some unusual requests . . . and I paid them four thousand dollars to let us have the place for a month. I told them we'd need to see if it suited us, but that was a lie. I knew once I got here, I wouldn't want to leave."

Philip stood up, and even he appeared surprised by this announcement.

"Come and look," she said, letting Wade walk ahead of her through the archway toward the bedrooms. She showed him each room in turn. They were charming, with more white molding and slanted ceilings. All three of them contained new beds made up with new sheets, blankets, and pillows.

"I'm using the same real estate agent who's representing the deacons," she said. "That means if she sells to us, she gets to keep both commission fees. So . . . she was willing to go slightly beyond the call of duty. We don't need to go to a hotel."

Philip was waiting in the hallway. He glanced through a door at the nearest bed. "I'll get our suitcases from upstairs. Wade will want his deodorant and toothpaste."

He turned around and left.

Eleisha watched him go, waiting until he was up the stairs—keeping her back to Wade. "I'll handle the negotiations," she said. "We don't need a loan. I can sell some stock and buy the place with cash."

She couldn't bring herself to look at Wade.

"Please," she whispered. "Please say we're home."

He was quiet for a little while, and then he said, "Okay."

*   *   *

For the last few nights, Julian had felt almost . . . calm.

Mary had managed to locate Eleisha within twenty-four hours and returned to report that Eleisha was living in a house on Queen Anne Hill with a "hot vampire" and a "skinny blond guy." Julian mulled over this information carefully, knowing that the house had belonged to Maggie. It surprised him that Philip would ever consent to staying in one place that long, as he had a tendency to leave bodies lying around. Julian knew almost nothing of the blond man Eleisha had referred to as "Wade," but the very thought of her and Philip existing in the same house with a mortal was baffling.

Even Eleisha had never exhibited behavior quite *that* bizarre.

Regardless of these mysteries, only one fact mattered. Mary had confirmed that Eleisha was still in Seattle. So, neither Philip nor Eleisha seemed to be coming after him, and they were both safely across the ocean on another continent.

That was all he cared about for now: that they stayed away from him.

So, although having to listen to Mary grated on his nerves, she had managed to bring him some peace—even though she'd whined like a child when he ordered her back to Seattle.

It infuriated him that he couldn't just banish her back to the other lost souls.

But he'd neglected to mention that her servitude might be required for a long time, as it was possible he'd need to keep permanent tabs on Eleisha. He thought it best not to give Mary such information yet;

better to control her with a mix of fear and the hint of promises.

In the end, at least she'd obeyed him and gone to keep watch. As he had not seen her in several nights, he assumed all was status quo.

Tonight, he was feeling so liberated, he even left the study and wandered into the dining hall, looking at the massive walnut table, surprised at himself for suddenly thinking of the old days when the manor was alive with people and servants and banquets and hunting parties.

Such events had lost their glitter for him after he was turned. He'd tried coming home several times back then, but he could feel only contempt for the petty mortals at the table—even the nobles.

Yet he had never lost his connection to this place, to Cliffbracken. Legalities had been somewhat tenuous after his mother died in 1842, while his father was still considered "missing." Julian hired a lawyer to go through proper channels to have his father declared dead, but this took seven years.

Then everything came to him, the entire estate, and later, in 1881, he used a law firm to help him pretend to sell the estate to a historical society . . . which in truth was made up only of himself.

But this way, the manor did not appear to have only one owner for an unreasonable amount of time. No one ever came here except for a few servants, and he changed them every ten years or so.

The dining hall was silent, and he walked through to the other side and down a stone corridor leading to the mudroom, where piles of boots had once been stacked and wriggling spaniels had run through on wet paws.

Julian had not been in here for years.

Why would he come here?

I'm hungry.

How long since he had fed? Too long. His subconscious must be telling him that it was time to leave the manor for a few hours, drive a proper distance, and go hunting.

Yes, with Eleisha well accounted for and safely ensconced in Maggie's old house, there was no reason he shouldn't expose himself and get out for a while. He needed blood, and a fresh kill would do him good. Perhaps he could find a small blond girl and make her suffer.

Feeling even better, he was about to leave the mudroom and go upstairs to change his clothes, when the air shimmered before him, and Mary appeared with a panicked expression on her transparent face, magenta hair sticking out in several directions.

"They're gone!" she cried. "Don't be mad at me!"

All the relief of the past few nights drained away. "What?"

"They were gone last night, but I thought . . . I thought they'd come back. Today I got so scared I went inside their house. Their clothes are gone and the heat's turned off, and I don't know where they are."

"Stop!" he ordered. She wasn't making any sense. "You have been watching them. How could they leave without you knowing?"

She appeared to be biting the inside of her mouth—which was impossible and provided an offensive image—and she reached up to twirl a strand of her short hair. "Don't be mad," she repeated. "I just left for a little while. I just wanted to see some . . . other things, and when I got back they were gone, but I didn't worry till tonight." She paused. "I thought I should tell you now and not wait till you called me."

Anger and fear began growing in the pit of his stomach. He stepped forward, wanting to strike her, to knock her off her feet.

He couldn't.

But he could send this stupid bit of trash back where he found her.

Her eyes widened. "I'll find them!" she cried. "Don't send me back. I'm getting good at moving from place to place. I swear I can find them."

He forced himself to calm down, to think. He did not trust himself to speak for a moment, and then he said tightly, "Just where would you begin to look?"

"Well . . . aren't you scared they might come here? Show me the closest airport on a map. I found out I can wish myself places by looking at maps."

"And how did you realize that?"

She fidgeted. "Practice," she answered evasively. "So I can help you better. But if I can't find them around the airport, you'll have to tell me where to go next. If Eleisha's not here, where would she go?"

Julian's thoughts turned inward. Where would she go? She'd lived in New York with Edward Claymore for over seventy years upon arriving in America, but then she had gone to Portland. For some reason, she preferred it there and she'd stayed.

"I'll get some maps from the study," he said slowly.

"Try sensing anywhere near the manor first, and then Cardiff International Airport, and if you can't find her, go back to America and try Portland, Oregon."

Relief passed across Mary's face as she realized he wasn't going to banish her. "I'll find her."

chapter 3

By two nights later, several things had happened in Eleisha's world.

First, through Rose's address being absorbed into her consciousness, Eleisha had named their new home, and she spoke the name so often that Wade was also referring to the church as "the underground." He joked it was rather like Tara from *Gone With the Wind*. But Eleisha compared it more to terms like "headquarters," in old spy movies.

Second, the deacons had gladly accepted her offer on the property. She'd waived the right to the sale being complete pending an inspection, and a bank appraisal wasn't necessary because she planned on buying the place with cash.

Now, she just needed to sell some stock and have the money available.

Unfortunately, her broker was on vacation in Costa

Rica and wouldn't be back in the States for six days. But the closing date to sign paperwork wasn't set for three weeks, so aside from feeling in limbo, she wasn't concerned.

She'd written a long letter to Rose, telling her everything about the underground, including the wrought-iron fence and night-blooming roses, how the place felt like home . . . how it had been abandoned and seemed to need someone. She could tell Rose things she could never tell Philip or Wade. Now, she would simply have to wait for a response before knowing the next step. Eleisha understood Rose's caution—as Rose didn't know if she could trust them either.

Last night, Eleisha had taken a taxi east to set up orders at several furniture stores, while Wade and Philip had taken the public Streetcar downtown to pick out a new television and DVD player. They'd brought a DVD player home, but the flat-screen TV that Philip wanted was temporarily out of stock, and they would have to wait a few days for delivery.

So now, with little else to do, Wade and Eleisha had set to work cleaning the inside of the church. Wade might be terrible at making decisions, but once a decision was made, he threw himself in with both feet. At the moment, he was busy scrubbing the upstairs windowsills.

Philip had discovered a hardwood floor beneath the outdated carpet in the sanctuary, and so he was ripping up the carpet.

Eleisha was trying to get the sitting room in the downstairs apartment ready for a delivery of furniture from Crate and Barrel. Scrubbing and sweeping, she felt almost like a housewife, dressed in a pair of Wade's old sweatpants and a flannel shirt, with her hair in a knot on top of her head. She found the idea humorous. Her. A housewife. How long since she'd set up a house?

Had it been 1912?

Yes, that was the last time . . . really, the only time.

When she'd landed in New York in 1839, so lost and confused, another vampire, Edward Claymore, had taken her and William under his wing. Edward had protected her and trained her to hunt. But he'd never felt a need for a "home" and always kept them living in lavish New York hotels. In the end, Eleisha had struck out on her own, come here to Portland, and bought a house for herself and William. Yes, that was the last time she had set up a home.

It felt good to be doing so again.

She finished wiping the last cobweb from a corner. The room was clean. What now?

She decided to go upstairs to see how Philip was progressing. Emerging from the door behind the altar into the sanctuary, she found him sitting on the floor in a pile of moldy carpet remnants, gazing at nothing.

Most uncharacteristic.

Dust floated in the air. Soft illumination from the streetlights outside filtered through the stained-glass windows, glowing in greens and yellows off the side of his face.

"Are you okay?" she asked.

He looked up at her. When he spoke, his accent sounded thick and he started mixing English with French. "I want to talk. *Sérieusement*."

He wanted to talk seriously? She tensed, hoping they were not going to have another showdown over Rose. She was definitely not feeling up to a fight with Philip.

"What?" she asked cautiously.

He stood, went over to the altar, and picked up a manila folder. "Come and look."

His expression was so intense, it frightened her. What could be so important that Philip wasn't even complaining about the lack of fun or about all the hard work of prepping their new home?

She hurried over. "What is it?"

He crouched down and opened the folder, spreading out its contents. Eleisha found herself looking at the newest editions of *GQ*, *Men's Vogue*, and a small collection of photos of famous male actors. Brad Pitt was on the top of the stack.

Philip picked up the *GQ*. "Look at the men here and then tell me. What do they have in common, eh?"

If he had spoken in Russian, Eleisha would not have been more confused. "I don't understand what you're—"

"Look! What is the same about them all?"

She glanced down at the magazine as he paged through it for her.

"They're all shallow and self-absorbed?" she ventured.

"No!"

She flinched. He was really upset about something.

"Their hair," he said. "Now, look at this *Vogue*. Not a single man has long hair like mine." He lowered his voice to conspiratorial tones. "I am passé."

For nearly thirty seconds, she almost couldn't believe what he was saying. In the past month, she had lost her purpose in existence—her William. Then she and Philip had faced down Julian, abandoned Seattle, and found a new home so they could bring in a frightened vampire who had somehow escaped Julian's killing spree in the nineteenth century, and Philip was worried about his hair?

"It's your fault," he went on. "All your talk of new music and new movies, and I did not know until now that my hair makes me look like some shabby eighties rock star."

Eighties rock stars did not run around wearing shirts by Hugo Boss. . . . Well, maybe some of them did.

"Oh, Philip." Eleisha sank down beside him, realizing there was more going on here than vanity. The world at large kept moving faster and faster, and living alone for so long, he hadn't been able to keep up, and he'd never seen himself through any eyes but his own. He was becoming more self-aware due to his newfound companionship. "What if you get it cut, and you don't like it?" she asked. "It might not grow back."

She'd discovered this fact within a year of being turned. Although any flesh wound she'd received healed quickly, other aspects of her body worked differently. At first, her hair and fingernails had continued to grow, but then they stopped.

"Here," he answered, digging through the stack of actors' photos, holding up a head shot of Viggo Mortensen from *A Perfect Murder*. "What about this? It's still down below his ears."

"Where did you get all these pictures?"

"From other magazines. Wade took me to a book-store called Powell's last night. It is very big."

A part of her still could not believe he'd been labor-ing over anything so trivial, but if he was this con-cerned, she wanted to help. Philip had fought Julian for her, protected her, stayed with her when she needed him—when he could have left and gone anywhere in the world.

"Well . . . I've never been to a hair salon," she said, "but Wade has. He might be able to suggest one."

"Wade!" Philip was aghast. "He goes to Supercuts. No, I've read articles, and I know something of this. I should not pay less than two hundred dollars, and I should only see a gay stylist. I can risk no mistakes."

His expression was so troubled.

Torn between wanting to comfort him and wanting to hit him across the face with a loose floorboard, Eleisha said, "Okay, we'll get a phonebook, and we'll start calling, and we'll find you an overpriced gay stylist."

He rocked back on his heels, clearly relieved. "*Bien.*"

She could hardly believe this was the same man who'd recently kicked Julian out a window.

Julian paced the filthy study at Cliffbracken, dragging a sword over the Indian carpet.

Mary had not returned to him, and every few hours, he was gripped by an almost overwhelming impulse to call her back. But he feared pulling her away too soon—in case she was close to locating Eleisha.

What could be taking so long?

He hated anything outside his own control.

The only way he could gain an advantage over Eleisha was by catching her unaware, before she could invade his mind. If she was coming after him and he had no idea where she was, catching her off guard was impossible. His only option was to stay locked inside the manor—where he knew every inch and every sound—until Mary brought him a report.

But he was hungry . . . starving.

Walking to the door, he cracked it. Even from here, he could feel warm life force drifting down the halls from the kitchen.

One of the servants was still working.

Back in the days when Lord William and Lady Katherine ran the estate, they employed a small army of servants. But at present, Julian retained only three people: a handyman, whose job was to repair anything visibly falling apart, and two cleaning women, who could hardly handle a manor this size but managed to keep the main floor in fairly good order. All three of them lived "in house," but he never saw any of them. They had been sent out here by an agency in Cardiff and knew how to remain invisible.

Still gripping the sword, he stumbled from the library, down through the dining hall, into the corridor, turning right before he reached the mudroom, and made his way to the kitchens—as the pull of warm blood drew him on.

He heard a woman humming just a little off-key.

He stopped in the shadows of the doorway.

She stood by the table putting loaves of fresh-baked bread into large Tupperware containers. None of the servants had ever dared ask why he required no meals, but of course they had to feed themselves.

This woman looked to be about thirty. Her brown hair was woven back in a loose braid. She wore jeans and a wool sweater. Few servants wore uniforms these days even in the great houses, but here, any semblance of such formality had passed away.

Julian didn't even know her name.

He wished she looked younger and that she had wheat-gold hair, so he could pretend she was Eleisha and make her suffer.

Without speaking, he allowed some of his gift to seep out, to drift into the kitchens, and she looked up in alarm, seeing him there in the doorway.

Even without his gift, he knew the sight of him would frighten her. He hadn't bathed or changed clothes in weeks, and he was holding on to a sword.

"Sir . . . ?" she stammered, stepping away from the table. "I'm sorry. I did not know you were out of the . . ." She didn't finish the sentence and backed toward the other doorway on the far side of the room. Her breathing was ragged.

He emanated the full power of his gift and watched in satisfaction as the alarm on her face changed to terror and her mouth locked in an O shape.

She froze.

He dropped the sword and strode toward her, grabbing her shoulders, turning her around, and slamming her against the table. She could not even scream as wave after wave of fear passed through her.

With his feet planted on the floor, he lifted her a few inches and bent her backward over the table, pinning her with his chest, basking in the terror and warmth her body emitted. He was starving, but he didn't want this to end just yet, so he cut off the power of his gift, banishing her induced fear and letting her feel panic of her own accord . . . of him.

The glaze in her eyes cleared and she began struggling wildly.

"No!" she shouted, trying to push him away, and then she screamed, "Liam! Liam, help me!"

Julian didn't care if she shouted for help, and he doubted anyone would hear her. The others were probably upstairs at the other end of the manor. Her breasts were pressed against him, and he enjoyed the feel of her struggles for a few more seconds, and then he drove his teeth into her throat, draining blood so fast that she stopped screaming.

He knew that he was supposed to see her memories as he drained her, that others of his kind saw the entire lives of their victims in the fleeting moments before their death. But Julian saw nothing.

He just reveled in the blood, in the sweet strength of life force flowing down his throat.

Her struggles grew weaker. He drank until her heart stopped beating.

Then he dragged her body through the kitchen by one arm—stopping long enough to pick up the sword. He dragged her all the way into the study, through the passage leading to the old dungeon, and he dropped her in the guard room a few feet from the spot where he'd drained his father.

Neither of the other servants even knew this part of the manor existed.

He felt better, stronger.

Gripping the sword tighter, he headed back up the passage into the study. He had blood on his shirt, and he could feel smears on his mouth. Thinking more clearly now that he'd fed, he decided to go to his own chamber upstairs and clean himself up. But as he walked toward the doors, the air in front of him shimmered, and Mary suddenly appeared, transparent magenta hair glowing in the lamplight.

"I found them," she gasped, again making unsettling sounds as if she could still breathe. Sometimes, he wondered if she knew she was dead.

"They're in Portland," she rushed on, "staying in some old church."

She seemed about to say more when she saw the blood on his face and shirt, and she stopped.

Julian could feel some of his uncertainty draining away. Eleisha was still on another continent.

Philip led the way off the public Streetcar and stepped down onto Eleventh and Couch. He made sure Eleisha was following, and then he started walking toward Twelfth Street, as earlier this evening, Eleisha had mentioned going to the Whole Foods store parking lot.

He was sick of hunting in parking lots.

He was sick of feeding in cars.

He was sick of drinking from wrists and leaving victims alive. He used to revel in hunting. Now the whole ordeal felt foreign and unnatural and unsatisfying.

But he could not speak such thoughts to Eleisha.

If he did, she might not forgive him.

And he would rather feed from wrists and alter petty mortal memories for eternity than lose Eleisha.

That was the reason he'd come here, following her on this foolish quest to buy a "safe house," after which she would locate this coiled serpent who'd been writing to her, seducing her with lies. Julian was behind this. He had to be. Who else knew Maggie's home address? Who else knew Eleisha's name and could connect those elements? No, Julian was leading Eleisha into a trap, and since Philip couldn't stop her from rushing down this path, he was forced to follow and protect her.

Five nights had passed since she'd written to Rose from Portland, and now they were stuck in a waiting period, uncertain what the next step would be.

Eleisha fell into step beside him. Tonight, her hair hung loose, and she wore a white tank top over a chocolate brown broomstick skirt. He sometimes teased her and called the latter a "hippie skirt," but he liked the way it flowed when she walked.

"This is my favorite part of the city," she said. "I watched it develop over the years."

Apparently—and he still found this hard to believe—she had lived in the same house here with doddering, decrepit William from 1912 to 2008. How was that possible? He would never have submitted to such an existence. To make matters worse, she seemed to miss her old life. He did not understand her.

But that didn't matter. She made him feel things he'd never experienced, things he couldn't name. She fed him something he never even knew he was hungry for.

And tonight, he had more reason to be pleased with her.

He liked his new hair.

True to her word, Eleisha had found a stylist named Ricardo, so flaming he might have set off the ceiling sprinklers. He tutted and tutted over Philip's "magnificent" hair and swore he wouldn't touch it with a pair of scissors. But in the end, he'd charged three hundred dollars for the haircut, and Philip now looked much more modern ... like the photo of Viggo Mortensen. He was very pleased.

"Do you like my hair?" he asked.

Eleisha tilted her head back and rolled her eyes. "Yes, Philip. I've told you over and over: I like your hair. Women will swoon at your feet. Now focus on hunting. You need to control the situation better this time."

She was heading for the parking garage.

He stopped.

"Can we not try something different?" he asked. "Are you not bored with cars?"

For nearly two hundred years, his only entertainment had been hunting in every possible variety of ways, and as powerful as his feelings were for Eleisha, she had managed to make it a tedious chore.

She turned around and frowned in confusion. "Well, we can't leave an unconscious person in the street. They might get robbed ... or worse."

How could she possibly be such a sheep?

An idea struck him, something to make this more fun. Why hadn't he thought of it before? "You want me to try harder . . . to do this without your help, no? Then we make it a game."

"A game?"

"Yes, I will think of someplace clever—difficult—to lure a mortal. I drink and alter memories to give a reasonable explanation, no matter where the mortal will wake up. Then you must think of someplace more clever."

"Philip, we just need to feed. I don't think it is such a good—"

"Then I won't learn!" he argued. "I will be too bored to try."

She stepped toward him. "You'll make sure the place is safe?"

He almost always got his way with her in the end. The situation with this mysterious letter writer was the only time she hadn't given in.

"Of course," he said. "Follow me. I have an idea, and you will never top it. My gift is better for this game."

He led the way to Fifth Avenue and walked into Macy's.

Reluctantly, Eleisha followed him through the menswear section, through the cosmetics department, and over into lingerie.

"What are you going to do?" she asked quietly, already alarmed.

"Go over there," he answered, pointing to the nightgowns and slippers, "and pretend you don't know me. I have to look like I'm alone."

For the first time in a month, he was interested in hunting again. Maybe this would work. Maybe if

Eleisha played this game with him, he could take some pleasure.

Within moments, he spotted a pretty redhead wearing a pink dress and tan sandals. Pink was a bad color on her, but otherwise, she appealed to him. She was looking at bras.

He took a black lace bra off the rack and moved up behind her.

"Pardon me," he said, and he let his gift begin to flow.

She stiffened and then turned around, staring at him. Up close, she was quite lovely, with ivory skin and a few tiny freckles.

"I am buying a present for my sister," he said. "Can you help me decide?"

She glanced at the bra in his hand. "You're buying that for your sister?"

He smiled and let the power of his gift increase. "Maybe not. But I am buying a present."

Her eyes were getting bigger as she focused on his face, as if she couldn't believe he was real.

He picked up a cream lace bra by Vanity Fair. "This one is good too. Come with me to the dressing room," he whispered. "We can see them in a better light."

She followed him without a word, without a question, as if it was the most natural thing in the world to follow a complete stranger into the dressing room in the Macy's lingerie department. He checked inside first, to make sure the corridor between the stalls was empty. To his glee, he could hear several women trying on clothes behind the doors, but no one could see him. Their veiled presence gave this part of the game more spice. Looking down at the red-haired girl, he put a finger to his lips, urging her to silence, and led her inside a stall. He closed the door.

Let Eleisha try to top this!

The girl was breathing hard and watching his face expectantly, and then suddenly Philip's sense of fun drained away. Alone with her, he was overwhelmed by a desire to hunt in the same fashion he always had. To put one hand over her mouth, bite down savagely, and drain her until she stopped moving. He wanted to feel her fear, to feel her struggle, to see all her memories, and feel her despair in the moment she realized she could not stop him and that she was going to die.

But he could not do this.

Eleisha might come in and find the mess.

So, instead, he reached out with his thoughts and entered the girl's mind.

"You are so tired," he whispered. "Sleep."

He caught her as she dropped, and he positioned her carefully on a small bench attached to the wall. He fed from her wrist this time, focusing on keeping her asleep, taking no joy in feeding at all. The blood tasted like memories of bland water to him, almost like nothing. He saw a few flickering images of a dirty kitchen, a mother smoking a cigarette, a dented Honda Civic . . . a boyfriend named Ricky.

Philip took only what he needed, and then he used his teeth to connect the holes—as Eleisha had taught him. Looking around the dressing room stall, he saw some decorative square boards painted purple and nailed at equal intervals up and down the door. Quietly, he reached out and jerked one loose, exposing the nail.

Then he reached into the girl's mind again, erasing

her memory of meeting him and replacing it with one where she entered the stall, cut herself on the nail, and fainted from the blood and pain.

Then he slipped out, left the dressing room, and went to find Eleisha—still standing among the nightgowns and slippers.

"Everything okay?" Her tone suggested worry.

"Yes, go and look. She's still alive and not lying alone in the street."

"I don't need to look. Did you alter her memory?"

"Of course!"

She reached out and touched his arm. "What's wrong then?"

"Nothing."

She tried to smile. "So it's my turn?"

He tried to smile back. "Yes, your turn."

Rather than make the hunt more fun, his game had only made him hungrier for what he'd lost.

As they walked back onto the dark street outside, he knew he would need to go hunting alone—and soon.

Wade sat on the floor of the empty sanctuary, looking at the open letter in his hand. Eleisha and Philip had gone hunting, and for the first time in five nights, she'd been too preoccupied to check the mailbox.

But after she left, Wade checked it.

The first thing he'd seen was a DVD he'd ordered for Philip, and then he saw the letter lying there beneath it. He recognized the handwriting.

He'd stuffed it inside his shirt and then gone back inside with no intention of opening it, and he found ways to keep himself busy. The new television had finally arrived, so he hooked everything up, noting how homey the sitting room in the downstairs apartment was becoming. He much preferred Eleisha's taste in furniture to Maggie's, as Eleisha tended to choose pieces that were functional and comfortable as opposed to impressive. She'd ordered a sage green couch with a lot of pillows. She also liked little tables and lamps to read by.

But no matter how hard he tried, he could not stop thinking about the letter.

He went back upstairs, through the sanctuary and then outside, through the gate to the street, looking up and down. Eleisha was nowhere in sight. If only she would come home, he'd hand the letter over, and then he was certain she'd let him read it. But to open her mail? Something addressed to her? That felt wrong.

He walked slowly back to the sanctuary, closed the doors behind himself, and sank down onto the floor.

He felt torn between Eleisha and Philip. He didn't have to read their minds to see where they stood. Eleisha trusted Rose completely. Philip clearly believed this whole arrangement was a trap.

The problem was, Wade had no idea which of them was right, and he wasn't used to leaning upon his own instincts. All his life, Wade could read minds. Other people could not feel him doing this, so they couldn't stop him. He was never invasive without a reason, but he'd been a police psychologist, with tough calls to make every day. Knowing what was going on inside somebody's head was a unique advantage in offering diagnoses.

However, Eleisha and Philip could feel him inside

their thoughts, and if they chose, they could keep him out . . . and the three of them had set up some ground rules anyway.

No, if he was going to protect Eleisha, and himself, from a trap, he was going to have to rely on his own judgment. What if he didn't read the letter, didn't know what was in it before giving it to her, and his caution resulted in her being hurt?

Reaching inside his shirt, he took the letter out and opened it. Even while doing this, a part of him felt it was wrong, and another part felt that it was the only right thing to do.

He read.

Eleisha,

I cannot tell you what your letter meant to me. The church . . . the underground, sounds like a haven and a fortress.

There are so many things I long to say that cannot be written down on paper. You keep promising the danger is over, that you brought Julian to his knees and sent him away. But you speak of things you do not understand . . . could not understand.

I still tremble on the nights I must leave my apartment.

You have shown trust in me, and it is my turn to show trust in you. Because of you, I believe that we do not have to exist alone anymore. I reside at:

2743 Jones Street Apt. 2-A, San Francisco, CA

I will expect you soon.

> *With hope,*
> *Rose*

Wade sat staring at the page, and a feeling he could not explain washed over him: that Rose was the wisest of people, that she could be absolutely trusted, that her words rang true.

He lowered the letter and looked away. The feeling passed.

What was that?

He shook his head to clear it.

Then he heard Eleisha's voice outside, and he shoved the letter inside his shirt again. The front doors opened.

Mary materialized just inside the churchyard, around the back, keeping well hidden among the rosebushes. In her current state of existence, one thing that surprised her was than *anyone* could see her if she changed locations without knowing exactly where she would appear . . . and she ended up materializing out in the open.

She'd scared the hell out of a couple of old ladies at the Seattle Center before realizing they could see her— and then she blinked out again. But she was learning tricks to avoid this.

She hadn't told Julian, but she was learning how to manipulate her abilities far beyond the scant instructions he'd given her.

For instance, she'd found that she could materialize right inside the walls of a building. This didn't hurt her, and no one could see her. The problem was that she couldn't see or hear either. But she was discovering new ways to spy and eavesdrop without being spotted, and she was gaining a much stronger grasp on wishing herself into "nothingness" or a state of limbo where she was invisible to people until she either wished to materialize again . . . or Julian called her.

She thought of this as being able to "blink in and out."

She'd also learned that she had a powerful advantage over the other spirits who'd remained here in what she called "the real world." From what she understood—by talking to other ghosts—spirits of the dead could exist on three different planes: 1) the real world of the living, 2) the gray in-between plane, and 3) the afterlife. She had no idea what the afterlife looked like, as she had never seen it, but during her time on the gray plane, she'd come to believe the vast majority of ghosts ended up there, as she once could have . . . had she been willing to leave the in-between plane of the spirits who refused to accept death, who still longed to find a way back here, back to the living.

While first hunting for Eleisha in Seattle, she realized she couldn't yet tell the difference between various forms of the dead. So she'd ended up finding several other ghosts. They weren't common here in the real world.

But the few she'd met had all been trapped here the moment they died by strong ties to either a person or a place, and many ghosts spent their time in the relaxed state of "nothingness" beyond the sight of living people. However . . . being tied down to a person or place, they could not move with the ease that she could, even if they wished to. As of yet, she hadn't met a single spirit who'd crossed over from the other side, like she had.

She was unique.

She liked it here. She could go anywhere. See anything. She wasn't tied to anyone.

Well, that wasn't true. She was tied to Julian. Bastard. He hated her. She could see it in his dirty face. But when he threatened to send her back, she believed him. She was terrified of going back to that ugly gray plane of nothing, with only other ghosts like herself who shouldn't be dead . . . who knew they *couldn't* be dead, who struggled and fought and wept to find a way to get back here.

She was here.

And she wasn't leaving.

Once she was done with Julian's tasks and he released her, she was going home to her parents. They were never abandoning her at home again. They were never getting rid of her.

She'd considered popping in on them several times but decided against it just yet. She wanted to wait until she had her freedom first. Then, boy, would they be surprised. This was all their fault! They left her to go see some stupid art opening, not even asking if she wanted to go. They never asked her if she wanted to go with them, and her dad was selfish enough to turn his phone off so she couldn't even call. They'd practically murdered her. They'd be sorry soon.

Looking around, she realized she was alone outside the church and floated up a few feet to look in one of the stained windows. Peering through a piece of yellow glass, she could see the blond guy sitting on the floor of the empty sanctuary, reading a sheet of paper.

He suddenly looked up and crammed the paper in

his pocket. The front doors opened and Eleisha and the other one—Philip—walked inside.

Mary had to find a way to listen. Julian was getting sick of her just reporting on their whereabouts, and he had started demanding she give him reports on what they said to each other. Ugh.

She put her face against a piece of red glass and let the side of her head pass through just enough so she could hear what was being said.

No one would see her against these thick, colored windows.

"Of course you won," Eleisha said, opening the front doors. "It was no contest. The best I could do was lure a 7-Eleven clerk into a back room."

She'd cut her own hand and then gone into an empty convenience store and turned on her gift, and the clerk had fallen all over himself to help her. Philip's success had been much more clever and creative.

But she hoped he would not wish to play his game again, and she could not understand why he'd been so quiet afterward. She chatted to try to cheer him. She was half-tempted to try reading his mind, but he'd feel her and push her out if he was hiding something private. What could he be hiding? She had agreed to his "more fun" change of plan tonight. She'd done exactly what he wanted.

Then she stepped inside the church and was surprised to see Wade sitting on the floor of the empty sanctuary.

He stood up. "Philip, I've got the DVD player hooked up to the TV, and a movie came in that I think you'll like, an early nineties action film called *Universal Soldier* with Jean-Claude Van Damme. Lots of machine guns and some good hand-to-hand fight scenes."

Philip took a step toward him, the dark look on his face vanishing. "Oh, Wade . . ."

He stopped. Philip didn't know how to express gratitude. It wasn't that he didn't feel it; he'd just lost the ability to express it long ago.

"Will you watch it with me?" he asked.

"Sure, just go downstairs and get the film put in, and I'll be right down. I want to talk to Eleisha for a minute."

A tense pitch in his voice made Eleisha pause and look at him. Philip bounded off down the stairs, and she waited until he was out of earshot.

"What's wrong?" she asked.

Wade tightened his mouth in indecision, and then he blurted out, "A letter arrived from Rose today. I read it."

As he said this, he pulled a crumpled letter from his shirt and held it out.

Rose sent a letter! And so quickly.

"What did she say? Did she tell us what to do?" Eleisha took the letter and scanned it, exclaiming, "An address! She wants us to come, and she's trusted us with her address."

Her mind drifted into the future, of finding Rose in her apartment, bringing her here, making a room for her, building their community . . .

"Aren't you angry?" Wade asked in surprise.

"About what?"

"That I read her letter, and it was written to you."

"I don't mind. I already showed you all her letters. I only wish Philip would read them. Then he'd understand."

Suddenly, Wade tensed up again. He reached out and took the letter from her. "That's right. Philip hasn't actually read any of these, has he?"

"No, except that first short one. I wish he would."

"Eleisha, what is Rose's gift?"

The question threw her. Why would he ask that? She shook her head. "I don't know. We never talk about things like that."

"Is she telepathic?"

"I don't know that either, but if she's not, then she's still killing to feed and you'll have to teach her how to wake her abilities, like you woke mine and Philip's. You will, won't you?"

"Of course I will."

She smiled. "I knew it. You'll be saving so many lives."

He stared at her. Had that never occurred to him before? That by teaching her, by teaching Philip, he was saving mortals who would have died at their hands?

A plan, a vision, had been growing in her mind for weeks now. Sinking down to the floor, she motioned for him to sit as well.

Slowly, still staring at her, he followed, sitting crossed-legged with his knees close to hers.

"We shouldn't just stop with Rose," she whispered. "What if she's right and there are others like her, alone, like Philip was? We can find them. We can bring them here, and you can wake their telepathy, and I can teach them to hunt without killing. We can build a community here."

She was frightened, telling him this, wondering how he would react.

Currently, Wade's life lacked purpose, and he needed a purpose. But Eleisha also knew she'd been somewhat deceptive lately, first by hiding her communication with Rose for a month, and then hiding her plans to buy the church—and then springing it on him while he stood in the basement . . . and now trying to win his agreement for her own vision, for her hopes.

"That's what you want?" he asked. "To build a community here? For you and me to find hidden members of your kind and teach them to feed without killing?"

At a loss for words, she nodded.

He looked away, but he wasn't angry. She could see him thinking on her words, and she just sat there for a while, letting him think.

"Are you with me?" she asked finally.

He looked back at her, studying her face.

"So . . . what do we do now?" he asked.

"First, we go to San Francisco. We get Rose."

Julian was alone at the manor. When he woke up a few nights past, both the remaining servants were gone. He could not feel their warmth from anywhere on the estate.

The revelation annoyed him. He'd have to contact the agency again. If he was going to reside here, the main floor should be kept clean.

But for now, he rather enjoyed having the entire place to himself, and he wandered outside, among the abandoned stables. He'd spent more time on the estate this past month than in the previous hundred years. He owned a town house in Yorkshire, but he'd come to prefer the south of France these past few decades.

Yet now, he felt safe only here.

It had been so long since he'd had anything to fear that he'd forgotten the cold safety of Cliffbracken. Foolish really; with the possible exception of his familiarity with the entire place, he was no safer here than anywhere else. But he could not bring himself to travel again. Not yet.

He kept mulling over the same questions.

Why would Eleisha buy a church in Portland and move into it . . . like a home?

And what would make Philip stay with her?

And if Philip had been living in Seattle for an entire month, and then Portland for a week, why weren't the papers filled with stories of ugly murders?

And who was this mortal staying with them, and why hadn't Philip drained his blood weeks ago? Philip despised mortals.

None of it made any sense.

Eleisha was planning something. He knew it.

He had ordered Mary to bring him more detailed reports, and he hoped the selfish girl understood him. In many ways, she had proven herself useful, but her presence grew more and more grating. She had no manners at all. He longed to banish her, to send her back and to listen to her scream all the way to the other side. But he couldn't.

He left the stables and tramped toward the manor. Reaching the back door to the mudroom, he pulled it open. Tonight, he was dressed in canvas pants and a black wool sweater and rubber boots. He was about to take off the boots when the air shimmered and Mary appeared.

She began babbling the second she materialized.

"They found another vampire! Eleisha has been writing to her, and they're all going to San Francisco!"

Julian froze, halfway bent over.

He stood straight and stepped into the mudroom. "Stop!" he ordered, but an unwanted tightness was growing in the pit of his stomach. "What are you saying?"

Mary floated close enough that he could see her nose stud in detail. "Eleisha's been exchanging letters with somebody named Rose in San Francisco. They were talking about gifts and hunting and if Rose knew how to feed without killing." She paused. "This is all important stuff to you, isn't it? You know what it means."

Julian stumbled back and almost fell against the wall. He caught himself, but the dim room was growing darker, as if his vision didn't work. This was worse . . . so much worse than anything he'd imagined.

Slowly, he walked back to the study, not bothering to see if Mary followed. He walked across the shabby carpet to a shelf of his own books, where he pulled down a large leather-bound volume:

The Makers and Their Children.

His own maker, Angelo Travare, had written it over a course of centuries . . . including fine details on every vampire existing in Europe by the year 1825. This was how Julian found them all, how he knew for certain he had destroyed them all—all the ones who had sought to kill him because he would not . . . he could not feed without killing by altering the memories of his victims.

He needlessly paged through the book.

He already knew there was no one listed named Rose.

Three thoughts emerged from the roar in his mind.

First, Eleisha had found someone who'd slipped through his net.

Second, if this vampire in hiding had been created before the purge, then she knew the laws that Julian's predecessors, the elders . . . the makers, had lived by and taught to their children. She would view him as a sinner and an aberration, and if Eleisha was seeking out other vampires, bringing them together, the laws could reemerge and he could become *the hunted* again.

And third, he could no longer wait here to see how this played out. He would have to investigate on his own.

chapter 4

Two nights later, Eleisha sat between Philip and Wade as their plane approached San Francisco International. Wade had been unusually quiet for the entire flight, and Philip had been agitated—as he did not care for flying. Apparently, a few years ago, he'd gotten aboard a Boeing 747 that ended up being delayed for three hours, and as a result, he'd landed in Germany right at dawn. He'd managed to get off and hide in the back of a janitor's closet before falling dormant, but the experience had put him off flying, and he resented being asked to get back on a plane so soon after the recent flight from Seattle to Portland.

"See, it's all right, Philip," Eleisha said, pointing out the window at the city lights. "We're landing right on time."

She arranged their arrival for just past midnight.

He nodded once and didn't answer.

At least having to deal with Wade's and Philip's moods had kept her mind off tonight's impending meeting. She was well aware that she might be over-romanticizing the "rescue" of Rose, and Eleisha was hardly a romantic. Although she believed Wade was becoming interested in her larger plans, she also knew that he thought she was only acting out of some sort of pathology because she missed William, but Wade was a professional psychologist, and he often tended to point to one main reason for someone else's behavior.

Yes, of course Eleisha missed William, but she longed to undo the damage Julian had inflicted on his own kind. She also wanted a community, and she didn't believe that any survivors of Julian's killing spree should have to hide alone. She didn't have just one reason. She had many.

"Flight attendants, prepare for landing," said a voice over the intercom.

Eleisha gripped the arms of her seat. She didn't mind flying, but she had never cared for landings.

"Do we find a hotel tonight or go straight to this address you have?" Philip asked. He always avoided using Rose's name.

"I think we should go straight to her apartment. Is that all right?"

"None of this is all right. I am only here because you forced me."

She looked the other way, but Wade didn't seem any happier than Philip. They would both feel better soon, once they had met Rose. Then they'd realize this was no trap, that Rose needed their help.

"The wheels are about to touch," Wade said. "Hold on."

Eleisha felt unsettled for only those few seconds right as the plane landed when suddenly everything felt too fast and loud. She closed her eyes and felt the plane begin to brake. After that, she was fine.

The plane rolled up to the gate, and soon after, everyone aboard filed out. Eleisha was annoyed that they still had to go to baggage claim. She had wanted to travel light with everyone bringing only a small carry-on. But Wade and Philip had both insisted on packing suitcases and checking them in. She might have expected this of Philip, but not Wade.

The airport wasn't too crowded, and they made their way to baggage claim fairly quickly. But once Wade had his suitcase in his hand, he looked around.

"I need to find a men's room," he said.

Philip lifted his own bag, tilted his head, and pointed back the way they had come. "I saw a sign by the arrival board. Over there."

"I'll be right back," Wade said. "You go outside and try to get us a cab."

He hurried away, carrying the suitcase, and Eleisha watched him go.

She didn't like this. "What is he doing?"

"I don't know."

Eleisha could always tell when Philip lied.

Other people from the flight were bustling around them, grabbing suitcases off the carousel and then hugging friends or relatives who'd come to meet them. She decided not to press the point in the middle of baggage claim, and they walked out the nearest set of glass doors to the ground transportation area.

Philip approached a cab to see if the driver was otherwise engaged, and Wade came trotting through the doors. Without bothering to ask, Eleisha pushed her thoughts into his, and before he could stop her, she caught a clear image of him in a stall of the men's room fishing his Beretta out of the suitcase and strapping the holster under his canvas jacket.

He almost tripped at the sudden mental invasion. In seconds, she was at his side.

"Eleisha!" he said aloud. She was breaking their pact about asking permission first.

"You brought your gun?" she hissed in his ear. "In your suitcase?"

"They wouldn't have let me carry it on the plane," he answered dryly.

"You won't need it. Julian won't come anywhere near us."

"We don't know what we're walking into, and you seem to have lost some perspective."

She stared at him, hurt. Those were harsh words coming from Wade. Why couldn't he and Philip see that Rose was no threat . . . and neither was Julian anymore. Not to her. She had terrified him into leaving her alone.

She turned away from Wade.

Philip was motioning them over. They loaded their bags into the taxi and climbed into the backseat, suffering in the awkward silence. Eleisha handed the driver Rose's address.

Normally, Eleisha liked to look out the window at

new places, but the ride was so tense, she simply sat there, dwelling on unpleasant possibilities. If Wade was carrying a gun, what might Philip have in his suitcase? At least he hadn't stopped in the men's room, too. But she was beginning to wish she'd left both of them back home at the underground.

For such a long ride, the time seemed to pass quickly, and before she knew it, they were stepping onto the curb of Jones Street on the outskirts of Chinatown.

Philip looked about with unguarded interest. Even this late, the streets were alive with lights and people. Eleisha stood facing a decaying apartment building, but an Asian shop owner just down the block was signing for a delivery of open boxes of bok choy. At this hour?

"There," Wade said, pointing at the apartment building. "We need to go to the second floor."

This was the first thing he'd said since leaving the airport, and his voice was tight. Eleisha moved to block both her companions from moving forward. At this point, she would have preferred them to stay out here, but Philip would never agree. So she said, "Rose is a lot more scared than either one of you, and we're walking into *her* home. You remember that."

Philip glared at her but didn't answer.

She walked into the building and up one flight of stairs. If Wade pulled that gun, she'd knock him unconscious.

Moments later, they were standing in front of apartment 2-A. The hallway smelled stale and brown paint peeled in flakes off the outer frame. Eleisha raised her hand to knock and then suddenly lost her nerve. With no phone number, she hadn't been able to call. How would Rose feel about the three of them just . . . arriving here.

Another thought occurred to her. "Wade, don't try to reach out telepathically yet. If she doesn't know about our abilities, you'll just frighten her."

Philip reached past her head and pounded on the door.

"Philip!" she said. "Stop it." Then she leaned closer to the door. "Rose, it's me. We've come to get you."

Nothing happened for almost a minute. What if she had gone out? She wasn't expecting them.

Then a calm voice, with the hint of a Scottish accent, said, "What is your name?"

"It's me. Eleisha."

The door cracked and then opened.

And Eleisha was finally face-to-face with Rose. After all their letters, they were standing two feet apart. The first thing she felt was surprise. She did not know why, but she had pictured Rose as petite with gray hair. The woman before her was slender but nearly as tall as Philip. She had long brown hair with a few silver streaks. Her eyes were deep brown with flecks of yellow. She wore a white sleeveless rayon dress that reached the floor and silver hoops in her ears.

"Eleisha?"

The second that word left her mouth, Eleisha knew everything was as it should be. Rose was wise and truthful and needed their help.

Rose looked out past Eleisha to the two men.

"This is Philip and that is Wade. I told you all about them," Eleisha said quickly.

"Yes."

Stepping to the right, Rose allowed them inside her home. Eleisha glanced back to make sure her companions weren't going to do anything stupid. But Wade's tense caution seemed to have vanished. His eyes followed Rose with an expression of astonishment.

Philip looked puzzled but not dangerous.

"You are real," he said.

Rose closed the door as Eleisha took in the sight of the apartment. Although the walls were badly in need of paint, the main room was filled with polished antiques: low tables, porcelain lamps, and several Victorian couches with wooden arms and burgundy upholstery. The lampshades were covered with sheer pieces of silk materials. Small crystals hung down the walls, creating prisms of colored light. A small television sat upon a 1930s radio cabinet in one corner.

The living room ran directly into the kitchen, separated only by an archway, but the counters sported brightly colored pots of every herb Eleisha could remember from her youth in Wales: lavender, oregano, basil, parsley, thyme, sage, valerian, yarrow. . . . She lost count of the pots.

"I am real," Rose answered Philip, "and we must make plans."

Again, Eleisha was hit anew by the certainty that anything Rose suggested would be the correct decision.

Wade reached out to steady himself on the arm of a Victorian couch, but Philip shook his head—hard—and snarled. "Turn it off!"

"Philip?" Eleisha asked. What did he mean?

"Now!" Philip ordered Rose.

Rose watched him for a long moment and then took a step back. The feeling of absolute certainty inside Eleisha faded, and she found herself looking at nothing more than a handsome woman with long brown hair.

"Wisdom," Wade whispered. "Her gift is wisdom." He studied Rose. "Your victims have faith in your judgment?"

Philip shook his head in what seemed to be derision.

But Rose flinched at the word "victims," and Eleisha hurried toward her. Many of her feelings over the past few weeks were beginning to make more sense now, but she didn't care if Rose instilled false faith. They all wielded their gifts like weapons. Philip was no one to judge.

"Eleisha, stay back," he ordered.

She froze in place, fearing he would take action if she ignored him. This was not going at all as she'd hoped.

"You are working for Julian," Philip told Rose. "I know it."

For just a blink, Rose's serene composure flickered. "Working for . . . How dare you?"

"Then how did you know of Maggie's address in Seattle?" Philip demanded. "How did you know Eleisha was living at that house? How did you escape Julian in the first place? I don't know you, and I have never heard of you." He moved closer, his eyes narrowing. "You serve Julian, don't you? You are his slave."

"Philip!" Eleisha gasped. Is that what he'd been thinking all this time?

Without answering him, Rose looked down at Eleisha. "I was not expecting an interrogation." Her voice was calm, but her eyes gave away her fear. Truly, after the letters they shared, she had not expected Eleisha to bring a hostile male vampire inside the apartment.

Eleisha did not know what to say, and so she fell back upon honesty. "He's only trying to protect me and Wade. Just tell him how you found us . . . how you found me. Then everything will be all right. He'll be on your side, and trust me, you want Philip on your side."

Rose blinked. If she'd been living alone since Julian's killing spree in the mid-nineteenth century, this whole scene must feel like foreign ground.

But she seemed taken aback by Eleisha's blunt outburst. "You have shown trust in me," she said. "I will show trust in you."

Then she looked upward and said, "Seamus, show yourself."

The room grew cold. The air near Wade shimmered, and a transparent young man appeared from nowhere. Wade jumped backward in alarm. But the young man was glaring in open hatred at Philip.

"You bastard," he said in a thick Scottish accent.

He had the look of someone from the distant past, like a painting in a museum, with shoulder-length brown hair and wearing a loose hand-stitched shirt over black breeches. But he also wore a plaid blanket over one shoulder, held fast by a belt. His knife sheath was empty.

A ghost?

Wade's mouth hung open in shock, and Eleisha stumbled backward. A real ghost? She had come to view the reality of vampires as a fact of life, but it had never occurred to her that other forms of the dead might exist here as well.

"Seamus is my nephew. He found you," Rose said, her serene composure returning. "It is a long story . . . hours in the telling, but I can swear that neither one of us has ever even seen Julian, much less done his bidding."

Philip wavered, watching the ghost. He did not seem stunned by this revelation. He looked back at Rose. "Who made you?" His voice was not so threatening.

She drew herself up to full height. "Edward Claymore."

Eleisha grabbed the back of a couch, her head spinning. "Edward? No, that isn't . . . He would have told me."

Regret colored Rose's pale face. "Oh, my dear, I did not mean for any of this to spill out on the floor tonight. I did not expect . . . I was not prepared to . . ." She trailed off.

Then Wade finally said something. "You don't have to talk at all." He appeared to still be recovering from the sight of Seamus.

Philip glanced over at Wade. "Too soon."

"No," Wade answered. "I don't think you'll trust her until you've seen her past."

Rose was watching them both in cautious puzzlement. "My past?"

"Whatever they want, don't do it. We don't need them," Seamus said. "Any of them."

Eleisha was shaken by Rose's claim about Edward. It couldn't be true, but why would Rose lie?

"What are you suggesting?" Rose asked Wade.

Eleisha agreed with Philip that it was much too soon to expose Rose to telepathy, but she also agreed with Wade that this standoff would not end until some foundation of mutual trust was established—and she had to know about Edward. He could not have kept such a great secret, not from her. Could he?

She reached out and grasped Rose's hand. "Come and sit on the carpet with us. If you think back, all the way back, and then begin remembering your own life, we'll be able to see your memories. No, don't be scared! It's all right. Just sit here." She drew Rose over to an open space in the center of the room. "Philip, come sit down. Wade, can you act as her guide?"

"Rose, no!" Seamus shouted.

She held her free hand up to silence him and sank down beside Eleisha, her eyes searching Eleisha's face. "You can see my memories?"

"If you drop any mental barriers and think back, remember what happened, we can all see them. After that, Wade can keep your memories linear. But . . . it can be painful, like reliving it as it happened. Are you willing to try?"

Rose offered one slow nod.

Wade dropped down on the floor, cross-legged, and then Philip finally joined them, glancing a few times at Seamus. But Philip's expression was curious and intense, and he seemed to be losing his conviction that Rose was working for Julian.

"Just think back," Eleisha said softly, "as far as you can."

Carefully, she reached out with her thoughts and connected to Rose's mind, finding access easier than she expected. Then the room dimmed, and that was the last conscious act she remembered for several hours.

chapter 5

Rose

Rose de Spenser had always been considered a strange child: big-eyed and serious and old beyond her years.

Perhaps it was because her mother died giving birth to her.

Perhaps it was because her great-great-great-grandfather had been French—and everyone knew the French were mad.

Perhaps it was because she stepped into the role of housekeeper for her father and brother by the time she was seven.

But whatever the reason, most people agreed that Rose was odd.

She was born in Loam Village, just south of Inverness, Scotland, in 1790, but were it not for the fact that Mary, Queen of Scots had become a young widow all the way back in 1560, it's quite possible Rose would have been born—with a different face—on French soil . . . or never been born at all.

Queen Mary had been living in France for most of her life when her husband, Francis, suddenly died, and having no more use for her, the French royals sent her back to Scotland in 1561, along with a large retinue of servants and stewards.

When Rose was a child, her brother, Gregor, had sometimes mused that their migrating ancestor had been one of the noble envoys accompanying the queen, but her father insisted this was not the case. Although little else was known about Alain de Spenser, he had been only a minor wardrobe steward in the queen's retinue. This was not important. What was important was that he'd remained in Scotland, married a local girl, and founded a line of de Spensers.

Having some access to Scottish land owners, Alain's eldest son made a name for himself in estate management—and he founded the family trade.

By the time Rose was born, her people had been living in Scotland for more than two hundred years, and yet she was still singled out for her French surname.

She grew up cooking and cleaning and sewing for her father and brother, knowing the only way she'd ever get rid of her surname was by marrying into another family, but this idea hardly appealed to her. She liked her home, she loved her father and Gregor, and most important, she was poignantly aware that marriage led to pregnancy and pregnancy often led to death.

But she was fascinated with the process by which

people arrived into this world—another element her neighbors found odd. She could always be found snooping around when a village baby was about to be born.

Her father made certain that she and Gregor were well versed in their letters and numbers, but Rose showed little interest. She loved herbs and gardens and animals, and she always seemed to know when one of the local women was close to giving birth.

Then one day, when Rose was fourteen, their closest neighbor, Miriam Boyd, came pounding on the front door. She was pregnant and had gone into labor while her husband was away. Gregor ran for the midwife, while Rose took Miriam inside and put her in a bed.

Later, Rose considered this the most important day of her life because on this day, she finally caught Betty's attention.

Betty was at least sixty years old—ancient in their world—and had been delivering babies since she was seventeen. Rose longed for her notice. Shortly after Betty arrived at the house that day, she could see how capable Rose was and began giving her instructions.

Rose wiped Miriam's sweating face and held her hand when she screamed, and Betty allowed Rose to remain for the entire birth: a wriggling, blood-covered baby girl. Rose was in awe of Betty's power, of her knowledge, of her position among the people.

In addition, Rose's father was so relieved that the birth had gone safely—and Miriam hadn't died in his house—that he paid the birthing fee himself.

Betty was a woman earning her own living.

Rose followed her outside.

"You have the gift," Betty said.

"Teach me more."

And Betty did.

But things changed, as things must, and the following year, Rose's father developed a sharp pain in his right side one night, which grew agonizing in a matter of hours. Rose and Gregor did everything they could to try to help him, but he died two days later. This loss was hard, and the house fell quiet.

Gregor, who was five years older than Rose, took over his father's position, managing two separate estates. The nature of her brother's profession kept him away from home a great deal, but she managed his absences by continuing to increase her skill and knowledge as a midwife—and Betty grew a little weaker each year.

Then Gregor met a fresh-faced young woman called Briana, and the house magically came alive again. Briana was built like a small bird with a long, black mane. She laughed and smiled and sang. Rose welcomed Briana into their home when Gregor married her in 1806, and the couple was expecting a child soon after.

Rose was only seventeen when her nephew, Seamus de Spenser, came screaming out into the world, and she was the first person to touch him with her hands, to hold him and wash him, and to experience something besides the satisfaction of a safe delivery. She looked into his eyes and knew that he was her blood and kin.

Two years later, Seamus' sister, Kenna, arrived, and Rose delivered her as well. The house had become full . . . and happy once more.

One night, Betty died quietly in her sleep, leaving Rose to take her place.

Years passed.

Life fell into a comfortable routine of meals and work. Gregor still handled two large estates—but he somehow managed to be home more often—and Briana kept the house. Rose earned a reputation as the most skilled midwife between Inverness and Elgin. She even purchased a pony and cart so she could travel farther in her profession. It pained her whenever she lost a woman or a baby, but childbed was a dangerous place, and she did her best to save everyone she could.

Her record was even better than Betty's.

Besides daily work, the de Spensers also enjoyed each other's company and celebrated holidays together in grand fashion: Christmas, Easter, Imbolc, Beltane, Lammas, and Samhain.

Kenna was the small image of Briana in looks and manner, but Seamus had little in common with either of his parents. He showed no interest in his father's profession and spent a good deal of his time watching other men in the village train horses.

Then, one day, shortly after Seamus turned nine years old, he came running into the house, breathless with excitement, his shaggy brown hair in a tangled mess.

"Mother! Rose! Get Kenna and grab a few coins. A troupe of actors has arrived. All the way from London! They said they're going to do Desdemona's death scene in the market square. Hurry! They're setting up now."

Briana looked up from the dough she was kneading

and laughed. "Calm yourself, boy. And what do you know of Desdemona's death scene? Those actors are not going anywhere soon." But then she seemed pleased at the idea of an afternoon's entertainment. "Rose?" she asked. "Shall we take the children?"

The mood was infectious, and Rose bundled up Kenna while Briana washed her hands, and they all trekked off into the village.

"Oh, look," Rose said, pointing at the brightly painted wagon and makeshift stage. Seamus ran ahead, pushing into a place out front, and not to be outdone by her brother, Kenna let go of her mother's hand and ran after him.

"Mind your manners!" Briana called. "Don't be pushin' folks."

Rose had a difficult time bringing herself to discipline Seamus. She loved him so much and he was just . . . high-spirited.

"Briana! Rose!" Miriam Boyd called to them. "Come and find a place here with us."

The air crackled with the excitement, almost like a festival, or at least an event outside the daily routine.

A vendor who traveled with the troupe was working at a cart near the stage, selling questionable-looking meat pies, and some of the villagers were buying them as fast as he could take their coins.

"Don't let the children eat any of those," Rose said with a slight frown.

"Of course not," Briana said, trying to see over the crowd. "I wish I was as tall as you."

The crowd fell silent as the stage's makeshift curtain parted. A woman in a long blond wig and wearing a pale blue gown lay sleeping on a bed. Othello stepped out into view, tall and impressive with his blackened face and leather armor and fur robes.

But he nearly tripped, as if his boot caught on a board. His eyes were glassy, and a feeling of unease began building inside Rose.

"It is the cause, it is the cause, my soul." The actor's voice rang loud and deep, reaching the very back of the crowd. "Let me not name it to you, you chaste stars!"

He took another step and faltered again. "It is the cause. Yet I'll not shed her blood. Nor scar that whiter skin of hers than snow, and smooth as monumental alabaster."

He unsheathed his sword and dropped it. The audience was enraptured, but Rose spotted a few lines in his makeup. She focused her eyes, trying to see his face more clearly, and she realized he was sweating in the cold day.

Her feeling of unease grew stronger.

"Yet she must die, else she'll betray more men." Othello's voice rang out. He wavered during the next line. "Put out the light, and then put out the light."

He collapsed onto the stage, his head hitting the floor with a thudding sound.

For the span of a few breaths, the audience remained quiet, thinking this part of the show, but then the woman on the couch rose up and cried, "Henry?"

She ran to him, and the crowd began to murmur in confusion. Seamus was at the edge of the stage, his face concerned, and he grabbed the side to swing himself up.

Rose's feeling of unease exploded into fear as she remembered his earlier words at the house.

All the way from London.

"Seamus!" she shouted, shoving her way toward the stage. "Don't touch him!"

Rose was strong, and she reached the stage in seconds, but Seamus was already kneeling beside the sweating, unconscious actor.

"Don't touch him," she repeated. "Get back."

"What is it?" Briana asked, rushing up behind and grabbing Kenna, lifting her off the ground.

"Fever," Rose answered.

Two days later, the actor died.

Four days after that, Seamus fell ill, along with others in the village. Soon after, half the town was moaning and sweating. In the de Spenser house, only Rose did not contract the sickness. She worked day and night to care for her family.

In a matter of weeks, a quarter of Loam Village was dead. Nearly everyone had lost family members, but the de Spenser house was hardest hit. Gregor, Briana, and Kenna all passed over, leaving Rose and Seamus too shocked to even mourn.

Worse, Seamus blamed himself.

Rose had survived the untimely death of her father, but this was almost too much to bear, and at the same time she was forced into dealing with business matters—as there was no one else. Seamus was too young to take over his father's profession, and yet he inherited the house and his father's money. Old Quentin, one of the village elders, helped Rose to sort these matters, and she was surprised to learn the size of her brother's wealth. She and Seamus would want for nothing . . . except for their lost family.

Sometimes, later, looking back, Rose did not know how she and Seamus survived the cold, empty sorrow of those first few years together. She loved him, but she was not his mother. She was not even the mothering kind.

Still, she did her best.

They were both comfortable that he never called her "Mother" or even "Auntie," and he always called her "Rose."

She went on working as a midwife, and he took over some of the household tasks. She continued teaching him his numbers and reading and writing—as his mother had. Day by day, they slowly created a life together.

In his early teens, he talked her into going to a horse fair, and she let him buy two half-wild colts. He brought them home and put countless hours into training them, and then sold them to a young lord in Inverness for a decent profit.

He had stumbled upon his own path, as a horse trader.

One morning, Rose woke up and made their tea and walked out to watch him patiently training his newest acquisition, a lovely dappled gray. She smiled.

"I'll get breakfast," she called.

Two hours after washing the dishes, she had her first conscious painful thought that day of Gregor, Briana, and Kenna. But then she realized this was the first morning since their deaths that half the morning had passed before such pain hit her.

The next day, she did not suffer their loss until midafternoon.

And she knew she would recover.

At seventeen, Seamus had grown taller than Rose. He was strong and honest and sure of himself. Between his house and his inheritance and his growing reputation as a horse trader, he was considered by far to be the best "catch" in the village, and several families approached Rose with possible offers.

But she heard none of it.

If Seamus wished to hook himself to a girl, that was his choice, not hers.

As of yet, he'd shown no interest in taking a wife.

Perhaps he was like her, and he never would marry.

Staring into the looking glass one night, Rose wondered what had become of the girl who felt such joy at bringing him into the world, holding his squirming warm body to her breast. At the age of thirty-four, her face showed no lines, but her long, brown hair held streaks of silver.

Just as when she was a child, she knew some of the villagers were beginning to view her as strange. A peculiar spinster, obsessed with new babies, but wanting none of her own.

Why had she never married?

Perhaps because no man ever stirred her.

That all changed one night after supper when Seamus suddenly announced he felt like going to the pub.

"The pub?" she asked. "When did you ever feel like going to the pub?"

"Tonight." He smiled. "Come with me."

She picked up his plate. "There must be some crowd

from the horse fairs visiting?" she ventured, teasing him. "Some men you want to buy a colt from cheap? Or maybe it's a girl you're chasing?"

He shrugged. "A few men from the horse fairs. I see nothing wrong with sharing a pint and starting a conversation."

She laughed and got her cloak. In truth, a pint and a little company appealed to her tonight. Spring was just around the corner, and the gray days of winter would soon be past.

She did not remember what she and Seamus chatted about that night as they walked into the village proper and down the main path toward the Black Bull—one of only two pubs in Loam. She remembered going inside, feeling the welcome warmth, closing the door while removing her cloak . . . and then hearing a voice from somewhere across the room behind her.

"This ale is first rate tonight, Gareth. What did you do, wash out the mug first?"

People laughed.

His accent was smooth—English, not Scottish. The sound of it melted into her skin as she turned around slowly to find its owner.

A man she'd never seen before stood by the bar, chatting with the pub's owner, Gareth. The stranger was neither tall nor short, with a medium build. He had dark brown hair and green eyes that she could see all the way from the door. He wore polished boots, new breeches, and a white shirt. His black jacket hung over his arm. Although well-heeled, he was not particularly handsome—at least not by Scottish standards—and yet everyone in the place was watching him, listening to him. She should have been warned by this, as the English were not well liked this far north.

But even Seamus stopped and stared.

"Ah, Edward," Gareth said. "You insult me. You know I never wash my mugs. Kills all the flavor!"

Edward. That was his name.

She moved deeper into the room. He looked her way and froze. His green eyes locked into hers. His gaze slid upward, to the top of her head, and then down her long silver streaks. She could not read his expression, but he seemed so . . . interested.

He glanced quickly at Seamus and turned back to his banter with Gareth.

Rose's heart was racing. She tried to recover.

"So, where are your horse traders?" she asked Seamus.

He looked around and then pointed. "Over there. I may have to pry their attention. Who is that Englishman?"

"I don't know." Several tables were empty. "I'll just sit here awhile. You go and do your business."

"You don't mind?" he asked.

"Go on."

In truth, she needed to gather her wits. Every time Edward spoke, his voice seemed to penetrate right through her skin. Seamus made his way toward a small group of men, and she sank into a chair, grateful for a moment to herself.

But a moment was all she had.

Then she heard Edward say, "Gareth, would you introduce me to that lady?"

She looked up. They were coming to her table!

Other patrons murmured disappointment as Edward left the bar.

Dressed in a faded purple gown with brown laces and her hair hanging down her back, Rose hardly felt like a lady. Her thoughts were wild. Whatever would she say? But why did she care? In all her life, she'd never cared what others thought of her.

"Edward Claymore," Gareth said, arriving at the table with a sweep of his arm—like some foppish gentleman. "May I present Rose de Spenser, Loam Village's own midwife. And a good one, if I may say."

"De Spenser?" Edward repeated, his voice landing like music on her ears. "French?"

"No, sir," she managed to answer.

Up close, she realized he was handsome, with fine features, and he was so charming, so polite. She'd never noticed nor favored such qualities in a man, but right now, she could barely breathe. He sat down.

"Away with you, Gareth," he said cheerfully, offering no offense. "I wish to speak with fairer company than you. Bring us some wine."

Seamus looked over and stood halfway up. She shook her head at him and motioned him back down. He frowned but turned back to his companions.

Other villagers glanced their way and murmured in low voices, probably wondering why this well-to-do Englishman chose to bestow his company upon Rose. But she did not care. She stared at Edward. For a short while he simply stared back.

"Well," he said finally. "This is unprecedented. I am at a loss for words."

"You seem to have plenty to me," she answered.

He smiled. "Yes, quite. Getting me to talk is normally easy. Shutting me up is the challenge."

Unable to stop herself, she smiled back. "Gareth spoke no title with your name, but you dress like a lord."

He was taken aback by her blunt statement. Perhaps the English did not speak so openly. Yet he also seemed unable to stop making jokes and lowered his voice. "If you must know, I am a spy for the king, here on a secret mission to compare the taste of Scottish cheeses to English ones and steal your secrets."

Rose did not respond to this evasion, nor did she blink, but sat watching him with her large serious eyes.

Gareth brought them two cups of wine, looked at them both curiously, and then went back to the bar.

Slowly, Edward's expression lost its humorous glow, and she felt the tingle on her skin fade away. When he spoke again, he sounded more like any other man.

"Good God," he said, as if slightly shaken. "You want a real answer, don't you?" He paused. "No, I am not a lord. I serve a Scottish noble named John Mc-Crugger. Have you heard of him?"

She shook her head. She knew little of nobles. They rarely touched her world.

"I am his manservant," Edward went on. "But my master is away, and I am free to do as I please for now. Does that make you like me less?"

"No, it makes me like you more. At least you perform honest work."

He laughed, and for the first time, it sounded genuine. "Honest work. Heaven preserve us."

When she did not laugh in response, he looked at her intently. "Most of the time, I am very alone. So are you. I can see it."

"I am not alone," she answered. "I have my nephew, Seamus." She pointed to him. He was speaking heatedly with the visiting horse traders.

Edward's gaze did not follow her hand but rather moved to the silver streaks in her hair. "But you've lost someone . . . something painful happened."

Rose had never spoken of those nights where Kenna, Briana, and Gregor died in turn. How could this man see inside her? Without knowing why, she wanted him to know. "Yes, something that left me broken for a long time."

He leaned forward and sipped his wine, waiting quietly, and Rose began to speak, keeping her voice low, so only he could hear, and she told him everything from the night her father died until that morning when she made it well past breakfast without remembering everyone she had lost.

He did not interrupt. He just listened.

When she finished and fell silent, he waited in silence a little longer and then said, "I understand loss. . . . Not my family, but I have lost more than I can say."

She looked at him, puzzled, and without warning, he fell back into his cheerful, charming pose. Her skin tingled again when he spoke.

"Well, you have managed a great feat of magic tonight," he said. "I have not thought about myself in nearly an hour! Unbelievable."

In spite of being soothed by his voice, Rose felt a

sudden pang that he'd banished one of her few moments of real intimacy with another person. She blinked and did not know what to say.

Then Seamus looked over at them, and his eyes narrowed at the sight of Edward still sitting at her table. He left the horse traders and came over, ignoring Edward.

"It's late, Rose. We should go home."

She was unsettled, her stomach rolling, but she managed to ask, "Did you strike a bargain?"

"I've arranged to have a look at a few colts." He tossed his head toward the door. "Let's go."

His tone carried authority. When had he become a man?

She didn't wish to leave, but she knew the magic of the night was over—gone. Whatever link Edward created between them to help her talk, it had evaporated. She stood up.

"Thank you for the wine," she said.

His green eyes were startled and sad. "You are most welcome."

She followed Seamus to the door.

That night, she lay in bed for hours, thinking, rolling. She could not sleep. She knew Edward was only passing through the village, but it cut like a knife that she would never see him again.

The following afternoon, Seamus left to go look at some horses, and Rose was glad to have the house to herself. Her experience the night before had left her shaken, uncertain. Somehow, she'd managed to go her whole life without getting lost in a man's eyes.

And now, she could barely eat for the churning in her stomach.

Fool!

She scolded herself.

A polished man had paid her a little attention, and she was swooning like a maid.

But no, she felt more than swoons. He had allowed her to let out the pain, to speak . . . and he had listened.

Well, he was probably three villages away by now. As she had recovered from death, she could recover from a few moments of vivid life. She just needed time.

So she busied herself by scrubbing the kitchen floor and preparing some loaves of bread to bake. The sun set and dusk fell. She tried to eat some leftover mutton stew but made sure she left enough for Seamus. Hopefully, he would be home soon tonight with a new colt or two. It was always pleasant to watch him begin a fresh round of training.

She was just settling down by the fire to mend one of his shirts when a knock sounded on the door.

Who could that be? To the best of her knowledge, none of the pregnant village women, even in the outlying areas, were close to their time yet. She hoped someone was not delivering early, and she ran to the door.

Her breath caught when she saw who was standing on the other side.

Edward Claymore.

He and Rose were the same height, so she could look directly into his eyes. His brown hair was windblown, as if he had been traveling, but his expression held her attention the most: confused, even desperate.

"Rose," he began in a familiar manner, as if he had known her a good deal longer than one night. "Forgive me. I . . ." He stopped.

Her heart pounded in disbelief. He was here. She stepped back and opened the door. "It's all right."

He walked past her, not even looking about at the pleasantly furnished sitting room. "I left, but I had to come back. I wanted to see you again."

"And why is that?"

"I don't know."

His voice held no music or charm tonight, and her skin did not tingle at his words, but she preferred him like this, as if he was showing her a side of himself he shared with no one else. Could this be real? Did she affect him as he affected her?

She had no idea what to say. Words had never been her strength.

"Are you hungry?" she asked lamely. "Would you like to sit by the fire?"

"Why am I here?" he whispered, and he did not seem to be speaking to her. The confusion on his face spread, only now he seemed alarmed as well.

She feared he would leave, and she had no idea how to make him stay.

"Last night," he said, looking at her hair. "You made me feel as I haven't felt in a long time. You made me forget."

She did affect him the same way! Is this why people married each other? Did they meet someone who caused turbulence in their stomachs and chests, and then feel a need to make a permanent bond?

"Edward," she said, reaching out and grasping his pale hand, drawing him over to a low couch by the fire. Words were wasted now. She did not know what to do but believed that he did. Pulling him to sit beside her, she touched his face.

To her surprise, he grabbed her hand and stopped her. His grip was strong. "Don't," he said as if warning her.

But he was wrong. And if he would not act, then she would. She moved closer to him, and this time, he did not stop her but simply watched her with fascinated green eyes. She leaned over to kiss him, wondering what his mouth would taste like. He remained frozen for a few seconds and then began to kiss her back, letting go of her hand and holding on to the small of her back.

His mouth opened slightly, moving against hers, softly first and then harder. She responded, running her hands up his chest, finally understanding why women risked so much to experience these moments. She never wanted this to end.

He pushed her back against a thick pillow, and she tried to hold him closer, to kiss him harder, but she could *feel* something building in his tense body, in the fierce movement of his mouth.

He took his lips off hers and buried his face in her throat.

She had never experienced anything like this. Why had so much time passed before they found each other?

"Edward," she whispered.

Everything would be different now. She knew it.

The tension in his tight body was still building, and she wanted to help him.

"What do I do?" she whispered. "Tell me what to do."

He didn't answer, and then he made a sound she'd never heard from a man, almost a snarl.

She tried to shift beneath him to see his face, but he grabbed her shoulders, held her down, and drove his teeth into her neck. The pain was shocking as she felt her flesh and sinews ripping.

He was drinking, swallowing her blood.

She didn't scream but bucked wildly to throw him off. His hands were impossibly strong, and terror passed through her as she began to grow weak from blood loss.

"Edward!" she cried.

He stopped, frozen. Then he pulled back, and his face twisted into horror. "Oh. Rose, I didn't mean to . . . I didn't come here to . . ."

His mouth was smeared in dark red, and her blood was soaking the pillow beneath her head, running from her torn throat in a steady stream.

She was dying. She did not feel fear or rage, only sorrow that her visions of Edward had been an illusion. He was a monster—not a lover, not a husband.

The front door opened, and Seamus walked in.

"Rose?"

He stopped, as if unable to take the scene before him. Then he cried out in anguish, pulling a knife from the sheath at his belt and rushing forward.

"No," she tried to say. "Seamus, don't!" But the words were too soft and gurgling.

Even in her weakened state, Rose never did understand why Edward hesitated, but he didn't move until Seamus was upon him, slashing at him.

The world was dimming, but she could hear Seamus cursing and slashing. Allowing her head to loll, she saw Edward moving at lightning speed, grabbing Seamus' knife hand, turning it, and plunging the blade into his chest.

Seamus' eyes grew wide, and then he collapsed onto the floor, gasping a few times, and then no more. His eyes were still open.

Edward staggered backward, staring at Rose and Seamus in shock, as if he could not believe what had just happened.

But neither could Rose.

She thought she had found love, and she'd let a killer into their house, and now her Seamus was gone.

Blood running from her throat, Rose pushed herself off the couch, falling next to Seamus. At least she could die beside him.

Edward knelt beside her. "I didn't mean for this to—"

"Get away from her!" a voice boomed.

Rose looked up to see Seamus standing over them. He was alive! Whole. But then she realized she could see through him, and his body was still on the floor.

"Oh, no," she whispered. This time, her words were clear.

He had died a violent death and come back instantly in the fire of passion as a ghost, tied to the house or tied to her, and she was dying by inches. What if she did not come back as well?

"Edward," she whispered. "Don't let me die. Don't let me leave him all alone. Please. He's lost everyone. Don't let me die!"

Seamus took a swing at Edward, but his fist passed through Edward's body. Seamus cried out and swung again; this time realization was dawning on his face as he saw his own body on the floor.

Edward looked at the door and back to Rose.

"Don't let me leave him all alone," she begged again, her words almost inaudible. But he could not save her, and she knew it. She cursed herself for letting him into the house.

His face twisted in anger, and then suddenly, he tore the veins of his own wrist with his teeth and shoved his wrist into her mouth. "Drink it," he said, his mouth close to her ear. "Take it all back, and you won't die."

Seamus screamed in rage and helpless frustration.

The grotesque nature of Rose's actions did not dawn until later. She could only think of Seamus, and she drew down, sucking dark fluid from Edward's wrist as the macabre scene in her sitting room grew even darker.

He leaned closer. "Don't go out into the sunlight ever again, or you will burn. When you get hungry, remember you can only feed on blood. Do you understand? You must feed on blood."

She could just barely hear him over the roar growing in her ears.

Then the world went black.

*   *   *

"Rose! Oh, my God, Rose." A pause followed. "Quentin! I don't think she's breathing."

Slitting her eyes, Rose realized that Miriam Boyd was kneeling beside her, sobbing. People were moving about inside the house.

Old Quentin was inspecting her throat, his wrinkled face gone pale with shock. Seamus' dead body still lay on the floor beside her.

"She's alive," someone said.

"We heard Seamus yelling," Quentin said. "Who did this?"

"Edward Claymore," Rose whispered. She felt no regret at exposing him for a killer. She felt no sorrow for Seamus. She felt nothing.

Well-meaning friends put her to bed. They took Seamus' body to prepare him for burial, and she let them. Then she surprised everyone by asking them all to leave.

"No, Rose. Your throat looks bad, and you need someone here," Miriam said.

"Please. Everyone go."

Reluctantly, perhaps thinking she needed to mourn alone, her neighbors left.

She got out of bed and went downstairs. Many years ago, her grandfather had placed iron brackets on each side of the door and created a heavy wooden bar. But no one in her family had ever needed to use it. She lifted the bar and used it to block the door.

"Are you here?" she asked.

"I am here."

She turned around to see Seamus standing behind her, dressed exactly as he'd been when he came home, except that his sheath was empty and she could see right through him.

He stared at her as if she were a stranger. "How can you be alive?"

"I do not think I am."

A week passed, and she did not leave the house nor unbar the door.

Several neighbors came to knock, but she would not let anyone in. She called through the door to Quentin that she wished to be left alone. She did not attend Seamus' funeral. She knew what they were all thinking, that the death of her last kin had broken her mind, left her mad.

Perhaps they were right.

She and Seamus were trapped inside. She slept all day and woke only at night. The magnitude and sorrow of what had happened slowly hit Seamus in a series of stages. At first, he seemed lost in denial. On the third night he asked her.

"How did Claymore come into the house, Rose? Did he just walk through the door and catch you unaware?"

"No," she answered flatly. "I let him in. I wanted him to come in."

He raged at her, blaming her, and she did not rebuke him.

On the fifth day, he stopped raging and asked, "What are we going to do?"

"I don't know."

She grew hungrier each night. Edward's final words constantly echoed in her ears.

Do not go out into the sunlight ever again, or you will burn. When you get hungry, remember you can only feed on blood. Do you understand? You must feed on blood.

Most country people loved to whisper tales of ghosts, fairies, changelings, vampires, and even of spirits who drained the living. Rose had never taken much interest in such legends, but now wished she had.

Her own lack of emotion was *wrong*, and she knew it.

But her body no longer functioned as a proper living thing. She did not eat nor drink nor require the privy. Her mouth produced no saliva. Her heart did not beat.

Yet she hungered.

On the eighth night, she slipped out of the house and went to the stable. At present, Seamus had no colts in the stalls, but Rose had forgotten to feed her pony. She found hay and a fresh bucket of water on the floor of his stall. Someone had been caring for him. Probably Quentin. She harnessed her pony and climbed into her cart.

"Where are you going?" Seamus asked, materializing in the doorway.

"I must go out. I will come back."

"Where?" he demanded.

She was starving, growing weak and desperate. "Move or I will drive the cart through you."

His eyes widened at both her words and tone, and he vanished.

She could not care for his feelings, not just now.

Looking back later, she truly did not even know what she was doing, or how she had the sense to leave Loam Village and drive a good distance away. But for the first time in her life, she felt uncomfortable, almost frightened by the broad night sky, and she longed for the enclosed safety of the house. She felt much too . . . exposed out here.

In spite of this newfound fear, she intended to go all the way up to Eagan Village, about two hours east, but then she saw movement on the road up ahead, and she came upon a young man standing on the ground, examining his horse's hoof.

Again, without knowing why, she felt a need to gain his absolute confidence, and she pulled up her pony and asked, "Do you need help?"

He stiffened and then straightened, turning his head to see her. His face was awed, just as the villagers in the pub had looked while listening to Edward.

"My horse picked up a stone," the young man said. "He's limping."

Rose climbed down from the cart, watching the man. She could almost see him glowing with warmth, with life. She could hear his heart beating. She could see the pulse in his throat.

"My brother is a horse trainer. Let me see," she said, letting her voice soothe him, assure him that she would know what to do.

Without hesitation, he knelt down and picked up the horse's hoof. Rose looked at the embedded stone. "He'd best not walk or he'll go lame," she said. "Tie him up and come with me. We'll bring the blacksmith from my village to pull the stone."

He did not even ask her about her village or how far it might be. He seemed lost in the wisdom of her words as he tied up his horse. His heartbeat grew louder, and she was fighting herself not to lunge at him. A creek gurgled beyond the trees to the left of the road.

"My pony is thirsty," she said. "Come and help me water him first."

The young man asked no questions and helped her lead the harnessed pony to the creek. Rose crouched down, and the man crouched beside her. She reached out to touch his face as she had touched Edward's . . . and he let her.

The next action felt natural, and without conscious thought, she pushed him back against the grassy bank and drove her teeth into his throat—as Edward had done to her.

He bucked once in shock, but she held him down, draining and drinking.

Blood and warmth and life flowed into her mouth, down her throat, filling her with strength. She saw images in her mind, sheep and dogs and green fields and a girl named Missy. She drank and drank until she could take no more.

Then she sat up.

The hunger was gone, but suddenly so was the hollow emptiness. Looking down, she felt shame and regret. She touched her own throat. The wound was entirely healed.

"What are you?" Seamus asked from behind her. "What have you become?"

Even transparent, his face was a mask of horror. She could not blame him.

But she didn't answer. Instead, she looked down at the young man on the grass. His heart was no longer beating. She dragged him a few paces to the creek and dropped his body into the current.

"We are cursed, Rose," Seamus said quietly.

"Yes," she agreed. "I think we are."

A year and a half slipped by.

Rose had recovered from the death of her father and then the deaths of Gregor, Briana, and Kenna, but she would never recover from the actions of Edward Claymore.

She and Seamus hid in the house by day and through most of the nights. They were both dead and yet tied to this world. Some things did improve. After a time, Seamus came to understand her need to feed in order to survive, and as he loved her—and she was his only companion—he focused his blame and judgment upon Edward, not upon her.

To pass the time, she read him books, or they spoke of the past, or he offered her suggestions while she altered the house to suit her present condition better, such as reinforcing and covering all the windows.

Her neighbors accepted that Seamus' death had been the last straw to drive her into darkness, and for the most part they left her alone, although Quentin always cared for the pony. Sometimes they left her buckets of milk or meat pies on the front step, which she could not consume. Rose wished she could feel gratitude toward them for their kindness, but her emotions were slow in returning.

She fought to go as long as possible between feedings, sometimes starving herself to the edge of her strength, but the hunger always won in the end, and she would forget her shame and regret.

At least twice a month, she slipped out and drove far from the village. No one even knew she had left the house. She never got over the new fear of being out in the open. And the shame always returned as she looked down into a dead face and torn throat, but she could not stop herself the next time she grew hungry.

Then, in the spring of 1826, Miriam knocked on the door one evening. She had not tried to visit in many months.

"Rose," she called. "A letter came for you today, from New York. Can you open the door for me, and I'll just slip it in?"

Rose waited, tense, inside the house. A letter? From New York?

But she could not bring herself to unbar the door, as she was hungry and feared being so near to Miriam.

"I'll just leave it here on the doorstep," Miriam called. "You can find it later."

At these words, a rush of gratitude did pass through Rose, surprising her. Perhaps she was healing to a point?

She waited until Miriam's footsteps sounded well down the path. Then she unbarred the door and saw a white envelope on the step. It was addressed to her. She grabbed it, taking it inside and barring the door again.

The return address was in Manhattan but did not contain the name of the sender. Her hands shook as she unsealed the flap. Inside, she found a one-page letter and two hundred pounds in paper notes.

*   *   *

Dear Rose,

You have no reason to listen to me nor heed my advice. But I left you in ignorance, telling you nothing of our world. There are others like you and I, existing all across Europe, and one of them, Julian Ashton, has gone mad and is killing his own kind. My own master is dead, and I have fled to America . . . but only because Julian let me go, and I still do not know why.

So far, with the exception of myself and two other vampires, Julian is beheading anyone he finds. You are not safe in Scotland. I swear that I've told no one of your existence, but if rumors of blood-drained bodies reach Julian's ears, he will come for you.

You must keep your existence a secret. Take the money I've enclosed here, go to Aberdeen, and buy passage on a ship to Philadelphia. You will be safe there. Write to me when you have landed, and I will send more money. Leave tonight. I fear too much time has passed already. I would have written sooner, but I've only just arrived. Please, Rose, go to America. If you stay in that village, Julian will destroy you.

Your servant,
Edward

Her hands still trembled. After what he'd done to her, done to Seamus, how dare he write such a note, feigning protection . . . and to send money!

"Do you believe him?" Seamus said in her ear.

She jumped, not aware he had materialized right behind her, reading the letter over her shoulder.

But his words jolted her mind off Edward's act of writing and onto the content of the letter.

So far, with the exception of myself and two other vampires, Julian is beheading anyone he finds.

Vampires.

There. He'd written it down.

She had never allowed herself to speak the word nor write it, but now that he had, it seemed real. She was a vampire.

She was part of a world she knew nothing about.

There are others like you and I, existing all across Europe.

And one of them had gone mad and was killing his own kind.

"We must do as he says," Seamus insisted. "Leave tonight. Too many people have died or disappeared because of you! Even if we don't receive outside news anymore, the villages must have set up a militia. The stories must be spreading."

His reaction surprised her, that he should be so quick to do anything Edward suggested.

"You think we should leave our home?" she asked. "My father's home? And his father's? No, Seamus."

"What if he's right?" Seamus shouted, his transparent hand pointing at the letter. "What if this Julian cuts off your head?" He sounded desperate.

He did not want to be alone.

"I do not think we can stay here anyway," he rushed on. "Sooner or later, someone is going to see you leaving one night. I believe people are already wondering what you eat . . . locked away in here. You cannot stay forever."

"Go to America?" she asked. "A place we've never even seen?"

"He said you'll be safe there."

The weight of the arrival of Edward's letter suddenly hit her. She had never been farther from home than Inverness or Elgin. The thought of leaving the enclosed safety of the house brought fear up into her throat.

"Seamus . . . I don't even know the way to Aberdeen. I don't know how to book passage on a ship to Philadelphia."

Rose, who had always considered herself quite brave, realized she possessed a deep fear of unknown places, of not knowing exactly where to go or what to do when she got there.

"I'll help you," he said. "I know the way to Aberdeen. Father took me twice when I was a boy."

Arguments and hesitation and fear ensued, but in the end, Seamus won. Rose packed her clothes and all the money in the house, and they slipped away in the night. Aberdeen was a crushing and crowded place, and once there, Seamus could not materialize in public to communicate with her. Between trips with his father, and later in his horse trading, he had done a good deal more traveling than she had, and she wanted his advice, but she managed to book herself passage on a ship bound for America, and she even arranged for a windowless cabin with a stout door.

The thought of an enclosed space brought some comfort.

Half of her was numb and the other half was screaming that this journey was wrong.

How could she leave Loam Village? How could she leave her home?

But she never saw Scotland again. The sea journey was a nightmare. She starved herself inside her cabin as the ship rocked on the high waves. One night, she grew so desperate from hunger that she managed to draw off a sailor alone, feed, and push his body over the side. Occasionally, men fell overboard at sea.

But she and Seamus arrived in Philadelphia to a busy crowded world, an alien world. How had Edward done this? She wondered over and over why he had gone to so much trouble to warn her of the danger Julian posed. She wondered why he had not asked her to come to him in New York . . . and yet she had no desire to see him.

He had murdered Seamus and destroyed her life.

Still, after securing herself in a hotel, she wrote to him:

Edward,
   We are here in Philadelphia. We have arrived.

                                                              Rose

She could not bring herself to write more, but she did not wish to leave him wondering what had become of her. Why? Perhaps because besides Seamus, she had no one else, and some part of her did not wish to forever sever the connection with Edward. She included her current address. Three weeks later, a letter arrived.

Dear Rose,
   I am relieved. I have a contact in France, and she tells me the situation in Europe grows worse. I do not

know how Julian is managing to behead so many vam-
pires who are older and more powerful than himself,
nor do I know how he is finding them.

Please keep your existence a secret. Do not go back
to Europe, and I believe you will be safe.

I have enclosed four hundred dollars in American
money.

Your servant,
Edward

Rose found the letter detached and informational.
He spoke of vampires she'd never met and a conflict
she had no part of. She also felt that he wished to say a
great deal more but would not.

She tried to exist in Philadelphia.

She tried to be good company for Seamus.

She began writing more lengthy letters to Edward,
mainly about Philadelphia and their various hotels and
nightly activities. She did not write often, perhaps
every six months. Time felt different to her now.

He always wrote back. He kept her informed of everything he learned of Julian's bloody actions, and her
fear of a mad vampire she'd never met began to grow.
In spite of everything . . . everything he'd done, she
could not help being grateful to Edward for helping her
to leave Scotland.

The years passed.

Seamus learned to move about in the world a bit
more freely, never allowing himself to be seen by anyone besides Rose, but he never liked the feel nor the
sights of Philadelphia, and when she sought out books
to read to him, he began asking for accounts of other

places in America. He was especially fascinated by accounts of the West Coast, and Rose began to fear he might wish to relocate again.

The adjustment from Scotland to Philadelphia had been almost too much for her, and she had no desire to ever go through such events again. She learned to use her "voice of wisdom" well during hunting. Edward called it her "gift."

Although she had no affection for Philadelphia, she had learned her way around well enough to hunt at safe distances. In addition, though she would never admit it aloud—or possibly even to herself—she had grown comfortable with the thought of Edward just up north in New York, far enough never to see him . . . but not too far.

But Seamus began asking for more and more books about the west, on gold hunting and horses and new cities cropping up and the adventures taking place there, and by 1870, he began focusing his interests on California.

His obsession began to make her feel more and more alone. As if she had no one to truly talk to—except Edward. And Edward often reiterated the importance of her living alone, remaining in secret. These reminders caused her to think on his existence as well, always staying in hotels, even more alone than herself. At least she had Seamus. She did not feel sympathy for Edward but rather empathy for the hollow, changeless existence they shared. In a moment of weakness, one night in a letter, she expressed these thoughts to him.

He did not answer for a month, and then a letter arrived that shifted Rose's view of their world. The letter was raw and emotional and nothing like Edward had ever written before.

Rose,

Your words shame me.

That you think of me at all with any semblance of charity or concern breaks my heart. I must confess to you now, like a killer seeking absolution from a priest he has wronged.

I have hidden a secret from you for years.

I did not think it possible for our kind to feel guilt, suffer from regret, but I have suffered for my actions that night in your house so long ago. . . . Not for turning you, but for leaving you with no knowledge of what you had become or how to survive. You know nothing of your own kind, but for one of us to make a vampire and then abandon you as I did is a sin. Yet so is making a vampire in the heat of the moment, and I feared what my master would do if he found out. . . . I was a coward.

Then after he was destroyed, it seemed too late for me to make amends to you. I did what I could by sending the warning. I could not even bring myself to look at you. Now, it is far, far too late for amends.

Thirteen years after you arrived in Philadelphia, something happened in Wales, and I never wrote a word of it. Julian turned his father, William, a senile old man, thereby condemning him forever to a state of dementia. The next night, Julian turned a servant girl to care for the old creature, and he put them both on a ship and sent them to me.

I have been living with these two, with this secret,

for decades. I could not bring myself to tell you. The old man wears upon me, but the girl, Eleisha Clevon, has given me something I never thought to find.

Redemption.

I have trained her, cared for her, and she needs me.

Finally, tonight, reading your last letter for the twentieth time, I feel that I can tell you that I suffered for abandoning you. I would never sink to ask your forgiveness.

All I can do now is try to make up for the past through my care of Eleisha. Do not fear that I am alone. Do not waste such thoughts on me. Only know that I have suffered remorse you cannot imagine for abandoning you so long ago.

Edward

Rose stared at the letter. Then she crumpled it and threw it into the fire. Did he think these confessions brought her comfort? Did he think she cared that he had suffered for his crimes against her? And now, he had been lavishing his care, his training, on a Welsh serving girl, and he expected this to give him absolution for destroying her life and murdering Seamus?

She was numb.

Slowly, she walked from the sitting room into her bedroom. Seamus was in there, looking at drawings.

"Rose," he said. "Come look at these pictures of San Francisco. You would like this new city. The streets are simple, but people are pouring in to settle here. Could we at least see it?" His face was so hopeful and yet hesitant. He knew how she hated to travel, feared to travel.

"How would we get there?" she whispered.

"By train. The track to the coast was just completed last year."

"All right," she said softly. "I'll book a train ticket."

"Truly?"

"Yes."

Seamus was all she possessed of value now. Her illusions of some connection to Edward were just that . . . illusions.

Once more, the trip was a nightmare, and she vowed never to go through this again.

Upon arriving, Rose sent a two-line letter to Edward telling him of their relocation.

He wrote back, sounding shocked and hurt, wanting to know how he had offended her, but she never answered. After that, he occasionally sent money but did not write. Financially, her needs were few, and due to him, she had barely touched Seamus' inheritance.

Although she never expected to, Rose found some peace in San Francisco. The people and energy in the air suited her better than Philadelphia. The place was rather primitive at first, but by the late nineteenth century, it had become an international city.

Much of the city was damaged by an earthquake in 1906, but rebuilding followed almost immediately.

In 1908, she bought an apartment on the second floor of a lavish building. Finally, a home of their own.

By now, hunting was easy due to more accessible transportation and the strength of her gift, but she never ceased to feel shame after a kill or to continue her efforts to go as long as possible without feeding.

Seamus also liked the city, but even so, as the years passed, he was given at times to melancholy about the state of his existence: endless, unchanging, no one for company but Rose. She could hardly blame him but had no idea how to help.

She and Edward maintained a polite silence.

Remembering their home in Scotland, she took up some of her old interests, such as herb gardening, and she tried to create some semblance of a home for Seamus.

Then in 1913, a letter arrived.

Rose,
   She has left me. She has gone to Oregon.
   To my disgust, I am lost. I am alone. I don't know what to do.

                                            Help me.

To Rose's shock, she was hit in the face by blatant pity.

How strange, how unexpected to feel pity for Edward. But she did. If there was one thing Rose understood, it was loss, especially the loss of someone she loved. She wrote back, and she offered him comfort.

She told him that he would heal in time.

But he did not. He only grew worse. Later, she counseled him to move to Portland—where Eleisha had settled.

He took her advice.

Then his letters stopped.

Over the years that followed, sometimes Rose wondered about Eleisha and William and this "contact" that Edward mentioned in France, and she wondered how many of their kind still existed. But she knew all their survival depended on living quietly away from Julian, on not gaining his attention, and in her case, on living in secret . . . or at least this was what Edward had convinced her.

She and Seamus continued to make it through the nights, with little changing besides the city exploding around them in population and development. The building they lived in grew old, but she could not bring herself to move, not again. It was both a kind of prison and a home at the same time.

In the early spring of 2008, as morning arrived, she was just falling dormant in her bed when something happened.

Her mind exploded in pain, and images of Edward burst inside her brain, along with the memories of everyone he had ever fed upon. In between his victims, she saw the same image over and over of a lovely dark-blond girl in her teens, with a serious face and hazel eyes. The pain was searing, and it went on and on. . . .

"Rose!" Seamus was beside her bed. "What's wrong? Stop screaming. Someone will break the door down."

The pain faded and then vanished.

"What's wrong?"

"I think Edward may be dead," she answered flatly. "I think I felt him die."

His transparent mouth fell partway open. "Did Julian find him? Kill him?"

"I don't know."

Rose waited. She waited in fear, and a part of her mourned for Edward. Nothing happened for six weeks, and then although the sensation was much weaker, she was hit with the memories of another vampire, an exotic woman with dark hair who also passed images of the blond girl with hazel eyes, and of many victims, and of a bright city with its own carnival . . . and the Space Needle. Seattle.

To Rose, it felt as if the vampire was dying.

Back in Scotland, when Julian was still killing vampires in Europe after she'd been turned, she had never felt this, seen anything like this. Perhaps she had been too young in her undead state?

A few nights later, she felt another death, an old man, and she saw almost nothing in his memories but the girl with hazel eyes—and of feeding on rabbits.

Someone was killing vampires.

"Seamus, can you go to Seattle? Try to find out what's happening?"

"Without you?" he asked. He never strayed too far from her side. He said he felt tied to her.

"It isn't safe for me to go anywhere now. I should not leave the apartment."

He nodded. This was true.

And so he tried. He found out that once he'd reached a general vicinity, he could sense the undead. He found Eleisha and Philip in Seattle. He was outside the Red Lion Hotel when Philip kicked Julian out the window. He learned where Eleisha was staying and read the address on the house. But the longer he was away from Rose, the weaker he grew.

He focused upon her and rematerialized in the apartment and told her what he had seen, what he had learned.

Once again, she knew something in their world had shifted.

Instead of hiding, instead of living alone, somebody was fighting back against Julian. If Eleisha and Philip could defend themselves, they could defend others. But could she trust them? She did not know. She did not even want to give them her name. She remembered an account she'd read of a Hungarian countess dubbed a "vampire" for her practices. This story was well known and should offer enough of a hint. But she wanted to offer more . . . a hint of her goals, the whispers in the back of her mind of others like herself who might be trapped in hiding.

Rose opened up a post office box.

Then she went home and sat down at the antique desk while Seamus stood anxiously behind her, and she wrote:

> *You are not alone. There are others like you. Respond to the Elizabeth Bathory Underground. P.O. Box 27750, San Francisco, CA 94973.*

chapter 6

"No . . . no more!" Eleisha cried, pulling out of Rose's mind.

Eleisha had fallen forward onto the floor, supporting herself on her forearms.

All she could see was Edward's face, and she was having trouble separating Rose's memories from her own. She *was* Rose. She felt everything Rose had gone through.

And to see Edward again, larger than life, his smile, his green eyes, to hear his laugh . . . She managed to partially disentangle her thoughts.

He had used her to try to heal himself.

She tried to push herself up.

"Eleisha!" Philip's voice cut through the haze.

She felt his hands latch onto her, one on her arm and the other around her waist, as he pulled her up against his chest—which was hard and cold. He held her tightly.

She tensed for a moment and then pressed her face into his shoulder, gripping his shirt with her fingers.

Rose was making choking sounds from the shock of having relived her own life. Eleisha wondered why Rose had ever given her even an ounce of kindness.

She should hate me.

"What's wrong?" Seamus was asking in alarm. "What happened?"

Only Wade kept his head.

Eleisha could hear his feet on the carpet, and she shifted her face slightly to see him hurrying toward Rose.

"It's all right," he said. His voice was shaky, as he had relived all the same events, and coming out of these deep journeys was never easy. But Wade had been reading minds his whole life. He knelt beside Rose. "It's over."

"What was that?" she said in a choked voice. "How did you do that?"

He didn't answer. This was not the time to try to explain his ability to help others channel linear memories. Eleisha could manage as a guide up to a point, but not as well as he could.

"Put both palms against the floor," he said. "You're back in the apartment, in the present."

The sight of his calm efforts made Eleisha ashamed for hiding in Philip's chest, and she tried to pull back, but he tightened his arm.

"Let go," she said.

"That was too much," he said. "Too much for you."

For her? What about Rose?

"I'm all right."

He relaxed his hold and she sat up, looking at Rose, who stared back. Rose had known about her all this time.

"He never told me," Eleisha said.

Rose was becoming more composed, but Seamus kept looking back and forth between all of them in confusion.

"I know," Rose answered.

All of Edward's sins came crashing down on Eleisha: what he had done to Rose, to Seamus, and then his abandonment, and his heartless letter of how he was trying to make up for this tragedy by caring for her. How could he? And how could he not tell her? She had been his companion for nearly one hundred and seventy years. If only she had known.

She would make it up to Rose, all of it.

"How did Edward die?" Rose asked suddenly. "Did Julian kill him?"

Eleisha flinched. "No, he killed himself. I think he got tired of living."

Rose glanced away. "What about the others?"

"Maggie and William?" Eleisha glanced at Wade, uncertain how to answer.

"No, Julian didn't kill them, but that's a long story," he said. "And we're all pretty wrung out. I think . . . we all have questions that can wait."

This was certainly true. From what Eleisha had seen, Rose didn't even know why Julian had murdered some vampires and left others, like Edward, alone—because Edward hadn't known Julian was hunting only telepathic members of their kind. Rose didn't even know that she possessed the ability to feed without killing. They still had a good deal to talk about.

Eleisha tilted her head back to look up at Philip. "Do you believe she is not working for Julian now?"

He nodded stiffly, but she couldn't tell what he was thinking. What had Rose's memories made him feel? She was tempted to look inside his thoughts but held herself back.

She climbed to her feet and went to Rose, still lost in disbelief that Rose did not hate her.

"You and Seamus don't have to be alone ever again," she said. "We'll leave tomorrow night. Go home to the underground."

Rose's eyes widened. "Tomorrow night? That's too soon. And what of Julian? How will you protect us?"

"He doesn't even know we're here. But it doesn't matter. He's not a threat," Eleisha insisted. "He won't come near me. I swear."

Why did no one believe her? She had *felt* his terror, his conviction to flee from her and never come back. She had been inside his mind.

"Why is tomorrow too soon?" Wade asked, frowning.

"I had no idea you would come tonight," Rose answered. "I've lived here for a hundred years. I have arrangements to make before we can leave."

But Eleisha could hear a hint of fear behind her calm voice. Traveling . . . journeys . . . unfamiliar places frightened Rose.

"Of course," she said quickly, looking back at Philip.

But he nodded again.

Only Wade seemed uncertain. He'd been expecting a short trip.

She's frightened, Eleisha flashed to him. *She needs time.*

He looked at her. "Should we find a hotel?" he asked.

"I have room here," Rose said, climbing to her feet, her legs still trembling. "Couches and a spare bedroom I never use. Apartments were more spacious back when I bought this place."

Talk of couches and spare bedrooms seemed safe in the midst of all they had shared. But Eleisha could not release the memory of Edward's mouth on Rose's the night he turned her. Eleisha had never thought of Edward as a man, someone with passions or drives. She knew for certain he'd never felt that way toward her. To him, she had been a child, a doll to dress up. Rose was hardly either of those things. Did Edward fear feelings that might be too real? Perhaps guilt wasn't the only thing that kept him from ever seeing Rose again.

"Are you sure you want us here?" Wade asked. "You might feel invaded."

Eleisha felt a rush of affection for him. Such a statement would never occur to Philip, but Wade almost always considered the feelings of others.

Rose glanced with hesitation at Philip, and then her eyes fell upon Eleisha. "You are welcome to stay. Change is a welcome thing here."

Seamus had remained quiet through most of this. Perhaps he felt helpless to stop the flow of events.

Eleisha thought on his life, too, cut off so soon, leaving him in a state of endless limbo.

He was watching her. Then she realized he had not been seen by anyone but Rose since the night he died. Maybe new company would not be so unwelcome?

"How long will you need, Rose?" she asked.

Rose hesitated. "I am not sure. A few nights at least."

And now we are five, Eleisha thought.

Wade woke up to a silent apartment in the late afternoon. He was lying on a Victorian couch. Disoriented for a moment, he blinked and sat up, trying to remember where he was.

The previous night came rushing back.

For the first time, with a few moments to himself since arriving, he suddenly realized that he *wanted* to help Eleisha in this venture. Rose was exactly what Eleisha described her to be—frightened, lonely, and blind to her own potential. He could help her, train her, and teach her to feed without killing. He could help Eleisha create the underground and then help her find others like Rose. He could do more good in this venture, save more lives, than he could in a hundred years working as a psychologist for the Portland police.

He could do something that no one else could.

As he looked around the faded sitting room, it struck him as sad, like a flower that had once been lovely but was close to losing its petals. He got up and walked into the kitchen. This room was more cheerful with its colorful pots of herbs. There was a kettle on the stove, and he found a few dusty tea mugs, but the other cupboards and the refrigerator were empty . . . as if the very presence of a kitchen was a lie.

He went back out into the sitting room. The place was so quiet.

Vampires slept all day.

The door to Rose's bedroom was closed.

Philip and Eleisha had taken the guest room. He understood this, as they both liked to feel hidden away somewhere during their dormancy. He walked over and cracked their door, just to check on them.

The room was dark, and it took a moment for his eyes to adjust. For some reason, the sight awaiting him sent a jolt through his body.

Philip was lying on the bed, on his back, wearing only a pair of jeans. Eleisha wore sweatpants and a tank top, but she was curled up against him with her head on his shoulder, her long hair tangled across his throat. Their chests did not move. They did not breathe.

They both looked dead.

Even dead they shared a connection he could not penetrate—with either of them. They were his only companions now, and yet he often felt like the outsider.

Still, he knew them, understood them better than they realized, although he kept such revelations to himself. He *knew* how it felt to feed on human blood, to kill to survive.

He had experienced this from Eleisha, Philip, and now Rose. He had felt the sensation of sinking one's teeth into a human throat, watching memories, and drinking blood. But the act was starkly different for all three of the vampires he had lived through.

Philip reveled in killing.

Eleisha had found it regretful.

Rose felt open shame.

At this thought, a small portion of his resolution to become closely involved with Rose wavered.

He turned his eyes to Philip.

Yes, Rose appeared to be the lost victim that Eleisha had described, but was Philip's caution wrong? None of them really knew Rose yet, she had certainly shown the ability to shut her remorse off when she grew hungry enough, and she had avoided getting too close to mortals she cared about for fear of feeding on them.

Wade could never forget he was a lone mortal among a growing number of the undead.

He straightened, pushing doubt away.

He would not abandon this path. In spite of his agreement with Philip's caution, Eleisha's passion to find others like herself and have him teach them to feed without killing provided a stronger pull.

It gave him purpose.

Suddenly, he realized he was hungry.

He walked back to the couch and put on his shoes. Then he headed for the front door.

"Where are you going?" a hollow voice challenged.

He half turned to see Seamus' transparent form standing outside the guest room door. As accustomed as Wade had become to the reality of vampires, the sight of this Scottish ghost still left him unsettled.

"Out to find some food," he answered. "I haven't eaten since yesterday."

The suspicious expression on Seamus' face vanished. "Oh, I'd forgotten you would need to . . ." He trailed off.

Wade turned fully from the door, not quite sure what to say as he realized Seamus wasn't used to anyone being awake in the apartment during daylight hours. How alien this all must feel to him.

"Your aunt did the right thing," he said finally, "writing to Eleisha."

Seamus looked away from Wade and back through the guest room door. "I think so, too . . . now. I think it's good she came, and you as well." Then his eyes narrowed. "Except that *she* trusts *him*!"

At first, Wade wasn't sure what this meant. More on impulse than a conscious decision, Wade reached out telepathically, not certain he could read a ghost but trying to pick up any thoughts. He sensed nothing, as if Seamus wasn't there.

He took a few steps back toward the guest room and saw that Seamus was looking at Eleisha sleeping on Philip's shoulder.

"Oh, you mean Eleisha trusts . . ." Wade struggled for words. "Of course she trusts him. He'd throw himself in front of a bus for her."

"He's a killer."

"Eleisha has killed, too, many times. So has Rose."

"They're not like him."

Well, that was true, and Wade could offer no argument. But Seamus was going to have to accept Philip if he wanted help from Eleisha and Wade. Philip came as part of the package—and he wasn't a killer anymore.

Wade debated explaining how Eleisha and Philip fed now, but he knew Seamus was still reeling from an onslaught of radical changes in less than twenty-four hours.

"Why do you stay with them?" Seamus asked, his Scottish accent growing thicker and his voice growing sad. "You need not."

Wade wasn't certain how to answer—or even if he should answer. "Normal people don't enjoy my company," he began, "once they find out I see everything they're thinking. Even if I promised not to . . . no one could know for sure. I had a friend once who could feel my thoughts and keep me out . . . but he's gone now. I fit in with Eleisha and Philip. They're like me."

That wasn't completely true, and he was forever caught in the betwixt and between, but Eleisha and Philip accepted him. More important, they valued him.

"You should go and eat," Seamus said. "There is a bakery two blocks away on Taylor Street. I've only seen it closed when Rose is . . . out at night, but it looks like a decent place."

Wade smiled.

Seamus had not lost his humanity.

Eleisha woke as dusk settled.

The guest room door was cracked open, and she could hear the sound of pans rattling from somewhere out in the apartment. When she tried to sit up, she found her hair tangled around Philip's throat, and she reached to pull it free.

He grabbed her hand.

His amber eyes were open, and he was looking up at her.

"I need to go out for a while," he said quietly. "Can you stay here with Wade?"

"Why do you need to go out?"

"To buy some things."

She pulled her hand away, freed her hair, and sat up. She could think of only a few items he might wish to buy. "You don't need Paul Mitchell hair products for a three- or four-night stay, Philip. Why didn't you bring your own?"

He moved over and climbed off the bed. "I just need to go out. Will you stay with Wade? I don't want him here alone."

He reached for his shirt, and she studied the white cigars burns covering the back and top of his shoulders. Their kind healed from flesh wounds quickly, but they retained any scars from mortal life—and apparently, Philip's father had not been the nurturing type.

"You sound strange," she said. "What's wrong?"

"I don't want Wade left alone."

Was he worried Rose would hurt Wade? After reading Rose's memories last night, she thought Philip would completely change his attitude toward the situation, but he seemed just as angry and hesitant now as before. How could he not pity Rose for what she'd been through?

But as he pulled on his boots, Eleisha only said, "Of course I'll stay. You won't be long?"

His expression softened. "I won't be long."

He walked out. She climbed off the bed and followed him partway. But he didn't even look around to try to find Wade to say good-bye. He just left, closing the front door quietly.

Puzzled, Eleisha padded off toward the kitchen, where she found Wade frying eggs and talking to Seamus.

"No, seriously," Wade was saying. "As a kid, I lived on a farm in North Dakota, with cows and chickens."

"And horses?" Seamus asked.

"Sure, horses."

They both fell silent as they noticed her in the open archway between the sitting room and kitchen.

"Where's Philip?" Wade asked, spatula in midair.

"He went out. He said he needed to buy some things."

Seamus stared at her.

Then Eleisha heard the sound of a door opening, and she turned to see Rose come from her room wearing a long sage green dress and gold earrings, with her hair brushed to a shining luster.

Eleisha became poignantly aware that she was still wearing a pair of Wade's old sweatpants and the pink Hello Kitty tank top she'd slept in all day . . . and her hair was a wild mess.

Suddenly the whole scene felt awkward.

Vampires didn't invite overnight guests. This "morning after" moment was foreign and uncomfortable.

But as Rose walked over to join her in the archway, she did not even notice Eleisha's attire. She was looking at Wade in what appeared to be wonder.

"Eggs," she whispered. "Where did you get the pan?"

"Went shopping," Wade answered, pointing to some paper bags on the counter. "I saw you had a kettle and mugs, so I picked up a few kinds of tea and washed out the mugs. Eleisha likes a cup when she wakes up."

Rose walked in and looked inside the shopping bags. "Here, let me get the water boiling. Eleisha, come sit at the table."

And the strained moment was gone.

Eleisha walked over and sat down a few feet from where Seamus appeared to be standing. Rose bustled about, finishing Wade's eggs and making tea, and the image was so natural that Eleisha almost forgot their quartet was made up of two vampires, a telepathic mortal, and a ghost.

They just seemed like four people enjoying an evening in the kitchen.

With a stab of guilt, Eleisha was suddenly glad Philip had gone out. He would hate this. He would have ruined it.

She sat quietly as Wade dropped down into a chair beside her with his eggs and a croissant he'd pulled from a bag. He was eating with a plastic fork and talking to Seamus about horses.

Rose put a cup of tea in front of Wade and handed one to Eleisha. Then she took a sip from her own. Eleisha knew that she should say *something*. She pointed to a purple pot. "Is that saffron? I haven't seen that growing in many years."

Rose nodded. "I don't know why, but growing all

the herbs has helped fill my nights, as William did for you."

Wade stopped talking to Seamus in midsentence and looked at Eleisha. "You told her about taking care of William?" he asked in mild surprise.

Eleisha glanced away. "Yes, in our letters."

Of course Rose had heard something of William from Edward, but Eleisha had not known that before. Secrets within secrets. Perhaps it was going to be difficult to stick to safe subjects. But Wade only yawned, as if he was tired, and took a long drink from his mug and turned back to Seamus.

"I hope you won't mind an upstairs room at the church," Eleisha said to Rose. "I almost started decorating one for you, but I didn't know what you'd like. I'm sure I would have gotten it wrong."

But this caused Rose to wince, as it probably reminded her of the impending journey to Oregon. Eleisha searched for some way to change the subject again. It felt so good to be sitting here with Rose and a cup of tea. She didn't want it to end.

Wade yawned again.

His eggs were gone, and he tried to stand up from the table and wobbled slightly.

"Are you all right?" Eleisha asked, standing to help him.

"Yeah, I'm just tired."

His eyes looked glassy.

"Let's move him to a couch," Rose said.

Eleisha helped him to a low burgundy settee. "Didn't you sleep at all today?" she asked, growing more concerned.

"Yeah, Leisha . . . I slept."

His white-blond head rolled back and his eyes closed.

"Wade!"

"It's all right," Rose said quietly from behind her. "He'll just sleep for a few hours."

Eleisha whirled around. "What did you do?"

"Just gave him something to make him sleep."

"You drugged his tea?"

She couldn't believe it. Philip had been right. Rose was an enemy. How was that possible? Eleisha positioned herself in front of Wade, wondering if she should try using her gift or look for a weapon. Or she could try taking hold of Rose's thoughts, as she had with Julian.

"It's all right, Eleisha," Rose said again. "I would never hurt your friend, but I need to show you something, and he cannot see it. We need to go out tonight . . . by ourselves."

As these words landed smoothly on Eleisha's ears, she believed them. Of course Rose was right. Rose was wise, and she would never hurt Wade. She just had to share something with Eleisha.

Philip took a taxi to Fisherman's Wharf.

Reliving Rose's memories last night had been too much for him. Through her, he'd experienced real hunting again—a true feeding. But instead of satisfying him, the sensation only made him feel like he wanted to claw out of his own skin.

When he woke up tonight, only a few seconds ahead of Eleisha, he knew he had to leave the apartment by himself. It troubled him to leave her and Wade by themselves, but nothing would have stopped him from heading for the door.

Nothing.

"Pull over here," he told the cabbie when they reached Beach Street. He paid his fare and got out.

The lights and music of Pier 39 filled his senses, and he rejoiced in the sight of the busy crowds. Walking down the pier, he passed an endless variety of shops: souvenirs, chocolates, seashells, wine, T-shirts, novelty stockings . . . all bursting with tourists.

Then he reached a large, two-story carousel in the center. Colorful horses moved up and down to canned music, ridden by children gripping caramel apples.

Eleisha would like this.

He pushed the unbidden thought away. He did not want to think about her.

Hearing the sound of feminine laughter, he turned his head quickly. Three young women were standing outside a souvenir shop, carrying bags and talking in low voices, occasionally laughing more loudly.

Suddenly, Philip realized coming to Pier 39 presented a problem he had not considered: people rarely came here alone.

In the past, this had never hindered him, as he would simply kill anyone he needed to. But tonight he wished to do this quietly, which was why he'd come down to the waterfront.

He studied the group of laughing women: a tall one with a blond bob haircut, a chubby one—not far out of her teens—and a slender, dark-haired one wearing a T-shirt from the North Beach Museum.

He zeroed in on the last one.

The crowds continued to pass around, hiding him in the flowing mass.

How could get her alone? He could easily approach the trio and use his gift to draw her off, but if she disappeared, the other two could provide a detailed description of him.

He did not fear police, but any trouble at all would let Eleisha know what he'd done.

So he tried something new.

The dark-haired woman was not carrying a purse—and the other two were. Perhaps she did not bother with such things?

But he reached out with his thoughts, slipping them inside her mind. In her recent memories, he saw they had eaten in a café farther down the pier, and she had been carrying a mesh bag. She did not seem aware of his mental invasion.

Your bag. You left it in the café, he suggested, moving a little closer.

"Oh, damn it," she said suddenly, looking down. "I left my bag. I'll be right back."

She trotted off, leaving her friends to wait.

He followed her.

He had no idea where she'd left the bag, but it didn't matter. As she passed a fudge shop, he came up behind her.

"Excuse me."

He let his gift begin to flow.

She froze and then turned around.

"I have heard there are sea lions nearby," he said. "Can you show me?"

Her eyes moved up to his face, and she did not speak

for several seconds. Then she said, "Sea lions? Oh, yeah, I saw them earlier, that way." She pointed to the right.

"Are they far?" he asked, letting his accent grow thicker, letting more of his gift seep out.

Eyes fixated on him, she breathed in and shook her head slowly. "No, just over there."

"Show me."

She seemed to forget about her lost bag and her friends. Turning right, she led him down a passage between two buildings, through a set of doors, and out onto a long, fenced dock. Away from the carousel's music, he could hear water lapping against the shore.

As they left the crowds of the busy section of the pier, he rejoiced at the numerous shadowed nooks and crannies on the backsides of all the shops.

The young woman was leading him farther into the darkness toward the edge of the pier.

He heard sea lions barking, and he saw lights all the way from Beach Street glinting off the water ahead. Then he spotted a flight of stairs that formed a landing at the top of the first level.

"Here," he said, moving to stand under the stairs, beneath the landing. Without a word, she followed him. Several people passed by, but no one looked inside the dark hollow.

She was breathing quickly now. He pressed her up against the wall and kissed her, reveling in the warmth of her mouth and the pounding of blood just below her skin. He grew excited but fought to control himself.

It was a pity he couldn't let her scream.

He vowed that next time, he'd find someplace more private, someplace where he could take more time.

Moving one hand up, he took his mouth off hers, whispering soft words in her ear. She was gripping his waist, trying to pull him closer.

Then he covered her mouth with his hand, tilted her head back, drove his teeth into her throat, and turned off his gift.

He needed to feel her fear.

She bucked in panic and tried to scream, but he had her mouth completely covered and he was gulping in mouthfuls of her blood. Waves of her terror passed through him like a sweet memory he'd almost forgotten.

Visions of her life flowed past in his mind as he consumed her—consumed everything about her, as he should. He saw a grandmother with gray curls, a cat named Boomer, a green ten-speed bicycle, the trees of a college campus, a handsome political science professor named Dr. McFarland . . .

Her heart stopped.

He pulled his teeth out and just held her body against the wall, letting the life force soak in. He felt like himself again, whole and strong and satisfied.

This sector of the pier was nearly deserted, with no shops or attractions. He held her up easily with one arm, and he looked out. He could hear voices down by the sea lions, but he saw no one near. He walked over to the edge, and he quietly slipped the woman's body into the water.

She disappeared beneath dark waves.

Philip closed his eyes for a moment, and he saw

Eleisha's calm face looking back at him. He remembered the feel of her soft hair tangled around him when he'd woken up tonight.

He knew that he should feel remorse for his actions, for keeping this secret from her.

But he didn't.

Julian retrieved his baggage and then walked out of the San Francisco International Airport through a set of glass doors and into the cool night air. He was carefully groomed with his hair combed back, and he was wearing slacks, an Italian belt, a white shirt from Savile Row, and a black wool coat that reached his calves. He carried a light overnight bag in one hand and a long wooden box in the other.

He took a taxi to Nob Hill, to the Fairmont, where he had already reserved the Buckingham Suite.

He needed no one to help carry his luggage, so he got a key at the front desk and went straight to his room.

Opening the door, he walked across a parquet floor into a wood-paneled parlor with a fireplace. The suite was decorated in tones of dark rust and hints of yellow. Glancing across the parlor, he noticed a glass-enclosed balcony.

Fairly impressive for America.

But he didn't care.

"Mary Jordane," he called.

The air shimmered and her spiky magenta hair materialized, followed by the rest of her. She looked around.

"Geez," she said. "You've got even more money

than I thought." Then her eyes landed on the long wooden box in his hand. It stretched from his knee up past his shoulder. "What's in there?"

"You have work to do," he said coldly. "Find them."

chapter 7

Eleisha did not know what to say or even what to feel as she followed Rose down a dark street in the Mission District bordered by rows of run-down, empty-looking buildings.

Rose had *drugged* Wade and then used her gift to draw Eleisha away from him.

And yet . . . Eleisha still followed.

She could have done any number of things to stop this, to subdue Rose and run back to Wade.

But she didn't.

"It's not far now," Rose said, moving more quickly. "Just down this side street."

Eleisha stopped.

Rose looked back at her. "You've come this far. We have to trust each other."

How could Eleisha explain what she was feeling? She'd led Wade to San Francisco, and before twenty-four hours passed, Rose had already proven she could not be trusted.

"No, we don't," she answered.

"He is only sleeping," Rose insisted. "Seamus will stay with him, and in a few hours he will wake."

"You could have just asked me to come."

"I couldn't. You'll understand soon."

What could be so important that she would go to these lengths to get Eleisha off alone? In truth, Eleisha wanted to know. She took a few steps forward.

"This way," Rose said, sounding relieved.

They walked down a nearly black side-street, and Eleisha realized the buildings around them were abandoned warehouses. If they'd been two mortal women walking here at night, anyone with half a brain would have considered them quite foolish.

"You've done well with your Wade," Rose said suddenly. "He's a rare one. So kind to my Seamus."

Your Wade.

Eleisha hardly thought of him as her own. Still, somehow, Rose's open sentiments made her feel a little more grounded—a little less shaken about following her instincts.

"But Philip," Rose went on, her voice taking on a harder tone. "I don't know how you ended up with the likes of him. I don't think I want to know."

In spite of her resentment over Rose's methods in getting her here, Eleisha realized they were completely alone and could speak freely—beyond their letters. She had no idea when this might happen again.

"I know he can be a handful," she said, "but we need him."

Rose stopped walking. "A handful? That's how you see Philip?"

Eleisha blinked and did not know how to answer. After the memory share last night, she had not expected Philip and Rose to keep regarding each other in this hostile fashion. But if they were all going to start building a community together, something would have to change.

Finally she said, "With the exception of occasional, and short, periods with Maggie or Julian, Philip spent over a hundred and eighty years alone . . . and he hates being alone more than anything. Have some pity, Rose."

"Pity?" She sounded incredulous. She seemed about to say more and then changed her mind, walking forward again. "In here," she said.

Eleisha followed, putting aside the Philip argument for now and feeling herself growing almost lost in wonder over whatever it was that Rose needed to show her.

"What is this about?" she asked, following Rose up a questionable-looking flight of stairs. "Where are we?"

"This used to be a warehouse for grain and rice, but it's been long abandoned. I'm surprised any of these buildings are still here. I'm certain that soon some developer will tear them all down and put up a Starbucks, a Gap, and a Pottery Barn. Soulless bastards."

Eleisha glanced up at the back of Rose's head, wondering how she'd feel about Eleisha's plan to sell her shares of Starbucks in order to purchase the church.

The warehouse was so dark inside, it was difficult to

see at all. At the top of the stairs, they emerged into a cavernous room. Eleisha squinted, but she couldn't see all the way across to the back wall. The effect was unsettling. She felt exposed and in the open, and yet half-blind.

What was she supposed to see here?

Rose took a few steps into the vast, black room. "I don't think I felt any true hope until after you wrote back to me, and then suddenly . . . so many possibilities seemed real. That there might be others like us. That someone was willing to fight back. I know that I should have waited for you, I shouldn't have started on my own, but I couldn't help it."

Eleisha shook her head. "I don't understand."

Rose turned to face her. The white streaks in her hair glowed softly. "I started looking. I studied news reports, looking for anything that might give me a clue. And then . . . then I found recent stories about people in Moscow, Russia, being admitted to hospitals with unexplained blood losses. I sent Seamus to Russia."

Eleisha wavered, almost losing her balance, reaching back for the stair rail. Rose had been looking for other vampires on her own?

"You found . . . Wait," Eleisha stammered, "the stories were about *living* people admitted with unexplained blood loss?"

"Yes. The old ones, the ones who existed before us, they didn't kill to feed as we do. They didn't have to."

How could Rose possibly know that? Edward hadn't known, and Eleisha had been able to put some of the pieces together only in the past month.

"Who?" she demanded. "Who told you that?"

"I did." A clear masculine voice rang across the cavernous warehouse floor.

Philip climbed out of a taxi back on Jones Street, carrying a long wooden box. He had made one stop—one purchase—before coming back, but now he was feeling anxious to get up to the apartment to watch over Eleisha and Wade.

He didn't trust Rose, not even after reading her memories. Especially not after reading her memories.

She was nothing like Eleisha or Wade. They both *felt* things. They liked to please others. Rose did not care to please anyone besides herself. She was cold inside . . . not at all like Eleisha or Wade.

He walked quickly into the apartment building and took the stairs two at a time up to the second floor. Finding the door locked, he knocked.

No one answered.

He knocked again, louder. "Eleisha? It's me. Open the door."

Nothing.

Fear began swelling inside him, and he knocked a third time. Then he kicked the door open and looked around wildly, seeing Wade lying on a couch with his eyes closed—but still breathing. Philip saw no one else. He rushed over, dropping his wooden box and shaking Wade.

"Wake up! Where's Eleisha?"

Wade's eyelids fluttered briefly, and he murmured something unintelligible, but then his head lolled to the side. Using two fingers, Philip opened one of his eye-lids.

Wade was unconscious.

The fear swelling inside Philip exploded into panic, and he looked around. Eleisha was gone, and he had no idea what Rose had done with her.

"Seamus! Where are you?" He strode through the apartment. "You tell me where they are or I swear I'll . . ."

What? What could he swear? Seamus was already dead.

Panic and indecision flowed through him. He didn't want to leave Wade lying there helpless with the front door broken, but he had to find Eleisha.

This was his fault. He never should have left them in the first place.

Striding back to the couch, he leaned down, jerked open the wooden box, lifted out a machete, and pulled it from its leather sheath. He wouldn't leave Wade for long, but he had to start looking for Eleisha.

He dropped the sheath on the rug. Not even bother-ing to hide the machete, he walked out the front door.

Eleisha stood frozen in the warehouse as a figure moved from the shadows of the back wall and out into view, and he kept coming closer. Her eyes had adjusted somewhat, and she just stood there, watching him. He was not quite six feet tall, with a solid bone structure and muscular chest. His head was almost shaved, with just a shadow of light brown hair, like a soldier. His face was lean, and his nose had a slight bump in the bridge as if it had once been broken. He wore jeans, boots, and a loose flannel shirt. His eyes struck Eleisha the most. They were almost clear, with a hint of blue.

He was dragging a sword with his right hand.

"This?" he spat, looking Eleisha up and down. "This is your champion, Rose?"

His accent was British, not Russian.

Rose looked at his sword. "Robert, you don't need that."

Eleisha felt sick. She'd walked right into a trap. The contempt in the man's eyes was so thick she almost backed up.

From the moment Wade had fallen unconscious, the night had taken on a surreal quality, and she realized she was still dressed in his old sweatpants and her Hello Kitty tank top . . . with her hair a mess.

It didn't matter.

She'd had enough of this, and she let her gift seep out, slowly for a few seconds, and then in stronger and stronger waves, sinking it into both their minds.

She would have preferred a straight psychic invasion, as she had used on Julian, but she didn't know this man, and if he was telepathic, he could block her, and she'd lose any advantage. That was the drawback in fighting unknown members of her own kind. Anyone with telepathy could just block her entry—working with Wade had taught her that much. Instead, she called on reserves inside herself that she'd never sought before, twisting her gift with her newfound psychic ability, weaving subtle illusions inside their perceptions.

They saw her as helpless, frightened, in need of protection, only to a greater degree. She was someone to kill for. Someone to die for.

Rose turned around, her lips parted, her eyes wide.

But Eleisha ignored her and moved toward the man. What had Rose called him? Robert?

Pitching her voice to a near whisper, Eleisha murmured, "Swords frighten me. Please, put it down."

It fell from his hand instantly, clanging to the floor. She didn't know how to use it herself and wanted to kick it across the floor, but she feared breaking her connection to him. His eyes were locked on her face.

"I am so afraid," she whispered. "I need to run. You stay here and protect my way."

He shifted his weight to his right foot, wavered slightly, and repeated, "Protect your way."

But then . . . she felt something inside her mind, something pushing back. Robert stumbled forward, and he made a sound like a mortal trying to suck in breath. She could feel him pushing her out.

"Turn it off," he gasped.

She stepped closer, trying to hold on, wrapping her thoughts around his, making him see her as helpless, frightened, someone he must let run away.

I won't hurt you, he flashed into her mind. *Turn it off.*

His verbal thoughts were so clear—even clearer than Wade's—that she felt truth behind them. Who was he?

Still doubting herself, beginning to doubt her own instincts, she shut off her gift.

Rose staggered a few feet back, nearing the staircase.

Robert dropped to one knee as if released from some

physical hold, and he placed his palm against the floor. "Jesus, Mary, and Joseph," he said, looking up at Eleisha, the contempt on his face fading slightly. "Who taught you to do that?"

She just looked at him, studying his lean face and his nearly clear eyes.

"You're of the wild generation," he said, his tone growing more demanding. "*Who* taught you to do that?"

Wild generation? What did he mean?

Rose was gaining control of herself and hurried forward, holding her long green skirt in one hand. "Eleisha, this is Robert Brighton. Forgive me for not telling you anything before, but I swore I would not expose him. He has no reason to trust any of us . . . any more than we have to trust each other." She paused, standing close to Eleisha. "He agreed to see only you."

Eleisha looked at her, thoroughly confused now. Rose had not led her into a trap? Could it be that Rose was so determined, so desperate, to bring any vampires still in hiding together that she would do anything, go to any lengths just to manipulate meetings? Could Eleisha blame her? Isn't this what they both wanted? What they had planned and dreamed of in their letters? If that was the case, then perhaps Rose could be trusted—as long as Eleisha never forgot how single-minded she could be in this pursuit.

Without asking, Eleisha slipped inside Rose's mind.

You found him and drew him here? Through Seamus?

Rose's eyes widened again. *Yes, and a brief exchange of letters.*

Why?

If we are to build a community, we have to find the others. But I never thought to find one like him still in existence—

"That is impolite," Robert said. "And this is point-less. You have no knowledge and no manners. You plan for things of which you have no understanding."

Eleisha pulled out of Rose's mind and tilted her head to one side. In Philip's memories, she had seen detailed images of him living with Julian, John McCrugger, and his maker, Angelo Travare. Only after the beginning of Julian's killing spree did the vampires break up and travel alone. Had it been normal for them to exist to-gether before? This Robert Brighton had been hiding—just like Rose—but he had come out of hiding and traveled all the way from Russia to San Francisco, so no matter how much he protested, he must be desperate to rejoin his own kind.

"Why did you come here?" Eleisha asked him. "Did Rose tell you about the church? Do you want to come home with us?"

He seemed taken aback by her direct questions and paused. Then he shook his head. "Not if you keep com-pany with Philip Branté. He's feral. As blood brother to Julian, he was the only one with a chance to stop those horrors, and he did nothing, not that I should have ex-pected more. Angelo had already ruined him, taught him nothing, let him run wild, let him kill whoever he pleased."

Eleisha was getting sick of these vampires constantly

bashing Philip, but she froze, taking in Robert's words. If he knew Philip and Julian personally . . . then Julian must have known him, and he was clearly telepathic.

"How did you survive?" she asked.

Again, he seemed unsettled by her direct question, as if he thought her rude.

"I did not," he answered. "Julian believes he hacked my head off."

"What?"

"Eleisha," Rose interrupted, "this can all wait." She turned to Robert. "You can see the truth of my words." She pointed to Eleisha. "She fought Julian and won—sent him packing. Everything has changed. You must agree to meet Philip and Wade. There is strength in numbers."

His expression went still for a moment, as if he considered her offer, and then he took a step backward. "I'll not be in the same room with Philip Branté. He's feral. And a coward."

Eleisha turned around and headed for the stairs. "I don't care who you are. I won't listen to this."

Rose ran after her, catching her arm, leaning close to whisper, "Wait. He is old, with knowledge of our kind we could never find anywhere else. Please, Eleisha, convince him. He may be the only one from . . . before."

Eleisha stopped. How old was he? She'd believed that any survivors would most likely be like herself or Edward or Rose—turned either right as the killing spree began or after, with no opportunity for telepathic training or somehow off Julian's radar.

But she could not help being disgusted by this Robert Brighton's arrogance and contempt. If he was going to join them, he would have to accept a few truths.

She turned to face him. "You call Philip a coward?" she asked. "When you've been hiding in Russia? Yes, Philip is terrified of Julian. We all are. But he kicked Julian out a twelve-story window. Do you know why? To protect me. Don't you ever call him a coward." She dropped her voice lower. "I don't believe Julian will ever come near us again, but I can't promise anything will or won't happen. If you want your freedom, if you want to live with your own kind again, then you have to be willing to expose yourself and *fight*."

He stared at her in surprise.

"If not," she added, "you can go back to Russia and hide out by yourself. I'm sure the high summers are lovely there."

"Will you at least meet with them?" Rose rushed to say. "Can I set up a meeting?"

He didn't answer for a long moment, and then nodded stiffly, once. "Not here. Somewhere public . . . but not too public."

Rose closed her eyes. "Tomorrow night, just past dusk, at the Japanese Tea Garden. That should work."

She opened her eyes again and took Eleisha's hand as if anxious to be off now that they had completed her desired task. Eleisha allowed herself to be led down the stairs—beginning to understand the depth of Rose's resolution. But she still felt shaken by her own outburst.

As they neared the last step, she asked, "How old is he?"

Rose hesitated before answering quietly. "I don't know for certain, but I know he was a man-at-arms for Thomas Howard, Earl of Surrey."

"Earl of . . . ?"

Although she was of Welsh heritage, like all those from the Commonwealth, Eleisha knew basic English history—at least the major players. Thomas Howard, Earl of Surrey, had later become the third Duke of Norfolk. He was Anne Boleyn's uncle and had served in the court of Henry VIII.

That would make Robert nearly five hundred years old.

Wade's tongue felt thick inside his mouth.

He could hear voices on the edge of his awareness.

"The door is broken!" someone said in alarm. "Seamus, how did this happen?"

He felt soft fingers on his forearm. "Can you hear me?"

Forcing his eyelids to open, he saw the blurred image of Eleisha leaning over him. "Leisha?"

He was lying on a settee. How had he gotten here? The last thing he remembered was eating dinner in the kitchen. She helped him to sit up. He saw an open wooden box lying at his feet . . . with a leather sheath lying beside it.

"Who broke the door?" she asked.

"Philip did." A hollow voice with a Scottish accent came from nowhere. Seamus appeared behind Eleisha, his expression angry. "He came back and found the door locked, so he kicked it in."

Eleisha crouched down on the floor. "Oh . . . I'm sorry. Where is he now?"

"Out looking for you."

She got up, went over, and opened a window, closing her eyes. "I'll try to reach him. I don't think he would go far with Wade still in the apartment and the door broken."

Wade was still confused. How had he ended up on the couch, and when had Philip come back? He didn't remember anything.

Less than five minutes later, he heard the sound of booted feet running down the hallway, and Philip nearly fell through the broken door, carrying a machete.

"Eleisha!"

His eyes looked half-crazy, and Rose drew away from him, closer to her bedroom door. Seamus hissed. Wade stood up, but he was dizzy. What was going on?

Eleisha ran from the window to intercept Philip. "It's all right," she was saying. "Everything's all right. I'm sorry we missed each other. Where did you get that? Put it down."

Wade was trying to follow too many things at once.

"Don't tell me what to do!" Philip ordered, and he pointed at Rose with his free hand. "She drugged Wade, didn't she? Where have you been?"

Drugged Wade?

His head was beginning to clear a little, and he remembered bits and pieces: eating eggs, drinking tea, growing tired . . .

"I can't explain it with words," Eleisha rushed to say. "I need to show you." She took Philip's outstretched hand. "Come and sit. Just let me show you. Wade, can you make it over here?"

Philip still looked enraged and manic, but he let her pull him to a clear area of the room. "What?" he demanded. "Show me what?"

Wade stumbled over, still trying to gain his wits. Eleisha had dust smeared on her face and her tank top.

"Sit down," she said. "Let me in."

Sitting, Wade closed his eyes, and the shock of Eleisha's rapid mental entry almost made him fall backward. To see her memories clearly, he had to reach back, make the connection.

Then he was in the kitchen drinking tea earlier that night, seeing himself through Eleisha's eyes. He was Eleisha. She took him forward from there, and he forgot himself.

Wade did not know how much time has passed when Eleisha pulled out of his mind. His head felt clearer, but he gasped several times, reeling from everything she had just shown him. He'd felt it all, exactly as she had. Her doubts, her fear, the fierce use of her gift . . . her strength. Her realization of the depth of Rose's single-minded determination.

And Robert Brighton, a soldier from the sixteenth century.

Reality was still sinking in.

"No!" Philip shouted almost immediately, breaking the revelations of the moment. "An elder?" His French accent was so thick, the words were hard to follow. "You don't know with what you deal. We leave this place tonight!"

"Eleisha?" Rose questioned softly, still standing by her door.

Philip turned on her, his lips curling up in a snarl.

Eleisha grabbed his arm. "Philip, stop. Listen. . . ." Trailing off, she looked toward the guest room. "Come with me." She pulled him toward it—and again, he let her—taking him inside and closing the door. Wade could hear Philip's low, angry voice on the other side, followed by Eleisha's softer, comforting one.

Suddenly, Wade was completely fed up with Philip.

How nice, how very nice it would be to throw a temper tantrum, wave a machete around, and have Eleisha drag him off to the bedroom to calm him down. Maybe he should try it sometime and see what happened?

But Seamus and Rose were both watching him with uncertain eyes.

"He's mad," Seamus said. "You know that, don't you?"

Wade sighed and shook his head. "No, he isn't." He walked over to Rose. "Don't worry. Eleisha will get him to agree."

"How do you know?"

"Because she always does."

Eleisha spent the remainder of the night in the guest room talking to Philip, listening to him, trying to reach common ground and still do the right thing for everyone involved.

She felt bad for just leaving Wade out in the sitting room, after he'd been drugged and was still recovering, but somehow, she believed Rose would take care of him. Later, she heard the television come on and the occasional murmur of male voices over what sounded like an old western, and she knew he would be okay watching TV with Seamus.

She didn't want to leave Philip, and she didn't want to bring him out among the others yet. He was still too upset.

But there was more to his heated reaction to Robert's existence than fear for her and Wade. She just didn't know what it was, and she wasn't sure how to ask him.

When she felt dawn approaching, she said, "You should get comfortable. The sun will be up soon."

He took off his shirt and his boots and stretched out on the bed, staring at the ceiling. She climbed up on the bed next to him, kneeling to look down at his face. "You know this Robert . . . don't you?" she whispered.

"Angelo believed that John, Julian, and I should know of all the elders. He wrote a book called *The Makers and Their Children*, with their names and their histories. Julian knew the book better than me, but Angelo taught me things about Robert Brighton. I remember the name. I know he was a soldier."

"Did you ever meet him?"

He hesitated and then answered quietly. "Only once, not long after I was turned and I was still with Angelo. Robert came to visit . . . with his maker."

"His maker?"

"Her name was Jessenia, and she looked like a gypsy,

but she was not. They both hated me, would not be in the same room with me. I stood in a hallway outside a door, and I heard Jessenia tell Angelo that I should be destroyed if he was not going to teach me, and that Julian should be destroyed if he did not develop his abilities. I didn't know what any of this meant then. I didn't care."

Eleisha remembered Robert's harsh words about Angelo letting Philip run wild and kill whomever he pleased.

"Telepathy?" she whispered.

"I think so now. I think maybe they all hunted as you do, as you taught me, and they blamed Angelo for the way I hunted then."

His voice held an edge of pain. Everyone changed over decades and decades of existence. Eleisha knew that for all his temper and selfish behavior, he'd learned to care what others thought of him.

"But it's all different now, Philip. Once he knows you, he won't hate you anymore. And we can't just leave him to go on existing alone—not if he wants to join us. Besides, he can tell us so much about what really happened. We've been in the dark for a long time."

She could feel her eyelids growing heavy. Although the windows were completely covered, the sun outside must be rising.

Philip reached up and pulled her down against his shoulder. "Sleep."

By the following night, everyone's mood and attitude had altered somewhat. Although Rose and Philip didn't speak, they seemed at least resigned to tolerate each other. Eleisha couldn't help feeling relieved by this.

They arrived at the Japanese Tea Garden in Golden Gate Park just over an hour past dusk. Seamus was nowhere in sight, and she wasn't yet quite sure how his existence worked, so she didn't know if he was with them or not. Lights all around illuminated ponds and sculpted shrubs, but Eleisha continued to dwell on several things Philip had told her the night before.

For one, he'd mentioned a book in which Angelo had written down information about all the elder vampires. Doing anything of this nature had been expressly forbidden as far as Eleisha knew. Edward had warned her against writing anything down regarding names, addresses, and phone numbers—even though he'd broken that rule himself later. And Julian had sent short letters drilling this into her head.

But Angelo had created a detailed book of information. Was such an act acceptable back then?

Second, she couldn't stop thinking about Robert's maker telling Angelo that Julian should be destroyed if he did not develop telepathically. Eleisha had been led to believe—even by Philip—that Julian had "gone mad" and launched upon his killing spree. Was it possible that some of his fears were justified? Why would the elders care so much that he wasn't telepathic?

In the back of her mind . . . she might already know the answer: Because without telepathy, he couldn't alter a victim's memory, and so in order to feed, he would have to kill to protect himself from exposure.

"Did you decide on anywhere more specific to meet?" Wade asked.

"No, just here," Rose answered.

Although the night wasn't cold, both the men had intentionally worn their coats—with the slight distinction that Wade's came from Target and Philip's was Armani. Wade wore his gun out of sight, and Philip had hooked the machete's sheath to his belt and then buttoned his long coat over it. Eleisha had wanted to argue with both of them, but she didn't. Their agreement to this meeting was already too tenuous.

Now all four of them waited by a koi pond.

Wade pointed to Philip's hip. "I don't know why you bought that thing. I would have helped you get a gun."

Oh, lovely, Eleisha thought. They were going to engage in a discussion of weapons. That was all Rose needed to hear.

Philip shook his head. "I don't want a gun. This is better."

"Better? You have to be in close quarters to use that thing."

"I know how to use it. It won't jam. It won't misfire. It won't run out of bullets. It's better."

"Yes, but—"

"Wade, please," Eleisha cut in, glancing at Rose.

He followed her gaze and stopped talking. Eleisha walked over to sit on a bench. Philip paced in front of her, too agitated to sit, but he looked down at her. "I like your hair like that."

For some reason, she had dressed more carefully

than usual tonight, wearing a pair of new jeans, low-heeled boots, and a sleeveless white linen shirt. She'd brushed out her hair and pinned up part of the back, leaving loose wisps hanging around her face. She still wasn't sure why she'd gone to the effort. Maybe because she'd met Robert last night looking like a runaway teenager—and she wanted his confidence. Maybe because Rose always took so much time and looked elegant every waking moment.

"Are you certain he'll come?" Wade asked.

"Yes, he'll come," Rose answered.

Eleisha was suddenly nervous about facing him again, about the contempt she'd seen last night in his eyes—and she hoped he would not antagonize Philip. She knew so little, almost nothing, about this older vampire, what powers he might have that they did not.

"Rose?" she asked quietly. "Do you know what Robert's gift is?"

"No, I haven't felt him use it yet."

"It is the mirror image of yours, Eleisha," Philip answered.

"A poetic answer," said a low voice from their right. "How surprising."

Philip whirled toward the sound as Robert stepped from behind a meticulously shaped tree. He looked much as he did last night—except that he, too, was wearing a long coat. But as with Seamus, Eleisha couldn't help seeing his face as a painting from a bygone era, like something she might view on a museum wall.

She tensed, knowing these first few seconds were crucial.

Robert glanced briefly over Wade, Rose, and Eleisha, and then he locked eyes with Philip. To her surprise, he didn't look angry. He didn't even look arrogant. Rather, he looked . . . uncertain.

No one spoke.

After a while, Rose finally said, "Well, someone should say something, or the moment might turn socially awkward."

In spite of the tension, Eleisha smiled. "No," she answered. "We certainly don't want that."

Rose smiled back and moved over to Robert. She pointed toward their little group. "Robert, you've met Eleisha, and I believe you already know Philip. This is Wade. He is the one who trained Eleisha and Philip to waken their abilities."

Eleisha let her take over as the whole scene took on a surreal quality, as if Robert was an out-of-town guest meeting Rose's family. Even without using her gift, Rose's voice carried a tone of wisdom, of reason. Any mortals passing by would not have bothered glancing their way. Eleisha did find it strange that Robert didn't flinch at them having a mortal in their group—he didn't even seem to notice the difference. Julian would have found this unthinkable.

Robert nodded once to Wade, but he couldn't seem to stop looking at Philip's face and clothes and hair, but with doubt in his eyes, as if he was questioning Philip's identity. Why? Eleisha wanted to try to read his thoughts, but she dared not. He would feel her.

"You've been alone?" Philip asked him abruptly. "All this time?"

Robert's jaw twitched, and he offered a short nod.

"Me, too," Philip said, tossing his head toward Eleisha and Wade. "Until them. It's better with them. Like being alive again."

A flicker of pain crossed Robert's face. It passed. "But you're telepathic now? I . . . I don't expect you to *know* anything if a mortal trained you, but can you at least hunt safely?"

Eleisha winced at such a question being asked aloud in a public garden.

Philip said something in French so quickly she couldn't follow it, and then he looked around. "This place is too open, no? Come."

As if all was decided, he didn't wait for an answer and began walking for the front gates. To Eleisha's relief, Robert fell into step behind him. Wade followed. Rose's eyes filled with hope as she watched them.

Not too bad, Eleisha flashed into her mind. *It's a start.*

Rose looked at her. *No, not too bad.*

Mary Jordane was beginning to panic. She'd been looking for Eleisha since the night Julian landed in San Francisco . . . and come up with nothing.

It wasn't that she'd lost her ability to track the dead.

The problem was that an overwhelming *sense* of the dead seemed to be everywhere. Since coming back into the world of the living, she'd encountered only a few other ghosts.

But a weird, misty veil of death hung over this entire city—along with too many other ghosts who were all dressed in old-fashioned clothes. In desperation, she'd finally talked to the spirit of a sailor down on the docks to try to find out why.

His answer was not helpful.

Apparently some stupid earthquake happened in the past here . . . like a hundred years ago! Who cared what happened a hundred years ago? You couldn't even buy an iPod back then. But a bunch of people who weren't ready to die and who weren't expecting to die got squished or buried or burned up in fires, and their spirits ended up tied to apartments and houses and restaurants and bars.

A ghost who remained in this world, who was tied to a person, would pass over either into the gray plane or the afterlife once the living person finally died as well. But a ghost tied to a *place* remained on this plane as long as the place still existed in some form.

So Mary was having trouble picking up the slightly different "blank spot," as she called it, among all the life energy that helped her separate the living dead from the ghosts. It was frustrating, and it was pissing her off, and Julian was getting impatient.

He'd called her back last night, and he was really mad when she couldn't tell him anything yet. He scared her worse than he ever had before.

Tonight, she worked harder to separate the blank spaces in the fabric of energy, to shift through and find the *right* kind of undead presence. She couldn't really explain the difference, even to herself, but the first time she'd felt Eleisha, the signature had been more . . . solid than a ghost.

She struggled to find that signature again. It was hard against the sea of death all around her, but she wasn't going back to Julian empty-handed.

About an hour past dusk, she felt something, and she materialized slowly behind a statue in the Golden Gate District. She focused again and instantly felt a much stronger rift.

She blinked out, followed the path, and rematerialized inside some kind of fancy garden with no flowers.

There was Eleisha. Sitting on a bench.

Good! Good! Good!

She wanted to dance. Julian could finally calm himself down.

But then she looked more closely and saw two extra people she'd never seen before, and both of them were undead. She lodged their faces in her mind—because Julian would ask her a billion questions—and she tried to drift a little closer without being seen.

One of them, a man with a nearly shaved head and a broken nose, was talking to Philip.

Philip looked around. "This place is too open, no? Come."

They all started leaving the garden, but Mary didn't worry. She had them now. She could blink out and follow.

As their small group approached the apartment door, Wade had an uncomfortable feeling growing in his stomach that he could not quell and he could not identify.

Rose fished for her new keys. Wade had called a repairman and had the door fixed that morning.

She let everyone inside, and Robert looked about the place, taking in everything as if preparing to offer approval or disapproval. Maybe that was the problem? Robert was perfectly polite, but Wade didn't care for the way he looked at Eleisha, Philip, and Rose, as if they were inferiors to be pitied.

Or as if they were children?

Something didn't feel right.

Even worse, neither Eleisha nor Philip appeared to notice.

Rose closed the door.

"So," Robert said, still looking around. "You all plan to live together in someplace called Oregon? In an old church you call the underground?"

"Yes," Eleisha said, sitting down and taking her boots off. She'd never liked any shoes inside a house. "We'll buy it as soon as we get back."

"And then what will you do?"

"Do?" she repeated. "Look for more of us. If you survived, others could have survived."

That was another thing. Just how had Robert survived when Julian seemed to have beheaded every other telepathic vampire in Europe?

Robert looked back at Eleisha, and for the first time, he seemed to be studying her hair, her face, her small hands. "I don't think you'll find any others like me."

"Maybe not, but there could be others like Rose. We

have to try. We'll bring them back with us to the underground, and they won't have to be alone anymore. Wade can train them."

"Wade?" he asked in surprise. "No, they'll need a proper master to train them."

The anxiety in Wade's stomach began expanding.

"But, Robert, he already understands what to do," Eleisha argued. "He's so good at it that Philip and I were able to figure out—on our own—how the elders must have fed without depopulating entire areas."

Seamus had not yet appeared, and since arriving at the apartment, neither Philip nor Rose had said a word. They were just watching and listening.

But as Eleisha spoke this last sentence, the *feeling* inside the apartment seemed to change, and Wade's thought patterns grew hazy.

"None of you know anything about the laws of your own kind," Robert said. "If we're to live together, the laws must be learned and obeyed. They were created to protect us from ourselves and others."

As he spoke, the words landed smoothly on Wade's ears. Of course Robert was correct. A proper teacher, an elder vampire was the only one who could help the newer ones protect themselves. And he would guard them all in the meantime. They were in danger without him.

Why hadn't Wade seen this before?

Looking around the room, he could see that Rose also agreed. Philip was still simply watching the entire exchange. But then Wade's gaze fell upon Eleisha as her expression grew frightened.

She glanced at Wade and flashed out.

It's protection. He can seduce by making us all feel protected.

The truth of this hit him, breaking the spell. He couldn't believe how strong the feeling had been.

He flashed back. *Can you counter him?*

Robert turned toward him, as if he could hear their exchange, and Eleisha did not answer.

Mary managed to follow them back to an old apartment, and then she was at a loss. She couldn't exactly materialize outside the windows and start peeking in, and she didn't know where they were inside.

Focusing, she tried to pinpoint their undead signatures, and she materialized slowly inside some kind of bedroom, making sure she was alone before fully manifesting. She could hear Eleisha's voice coming from the room outside and knew she was in the right place.

Good.

Not much of what they were saying made sense. Eleisha was talking to some guy she called Robert— must be the one with the shaved head—and he was talking back to her about laws and training and a bunch of other boring stuff.

Mary was trying to remember it all as best she could, when she felt *someone else* in the apartment, someone who was really dead, another ghost. The presence was coming closer, and for some reason, it scared her.

She blinked out.

Since arriving, Julian had not left his hotel suite at the Fairmont.

He couldn't move around freely until he had some

information on Eleisha's location. He'd had a good deal of time to think, and if Eleisha had indeed managed to locate another vampire, this woman called Rose, it was likely that she had been created right around the time he had taken matters into his hands in 1825.

She had not been listed in Angelo's book, and Angelo kept careful records. But why would one of the makers create a new vampire and keep her a secret? That wasn't the way of the elders.

Had she been trained at all? Was she telepathic? Did she know anything of the laws his predecessors had followed?

It also troubled him that he did not know what had caused Rose and Eleisha to seek each other out in the first place. Or how had Eleisha managed to find her?

The air shimmered, and Mary appeared by the fireplace.

"There's another one!" she exclaimed immediately. "And I think I felt a ghost in their apartment!"

Instead of growing more accustomed to her outbursts and lack of manners and her grating voice, he only seemed to hate her more. What was she saying? Another one?

"Slow down. Another what?"

"Another vampire, besides that Rose lady from the letters . . . or at least I think I saw Rose. But there's now a man named Robert, with a shaved head and a broken nose, and I could almost see through his eyes."

Julian froze.

"He kept on talking about laws and training and stuff. I think he wants to go back to Portland with them."

Julian put one hand to his mouth, almost unable to take this in. His hand was shaking. Robert? Impossible. Robert was gone.

But Mary had just described him right down to his clear eyes.

One of the telepathic elders who'd plotted to destroy Julian still existed?

The rules had changed.

The game had changed.

Everything was different now.

chapter 8

Robert didn't stay long, saying he had things to take care of at the warehouse. Eleisha had no idea what these things might be, but she wasn't sorry when he left.

As of yet, he had not stated whether he was going home with them or not—and she didn't know which answer would be better.

Rose closed the door behind him and a tense silence followed. She turned around. "He said he'd be back tomorrow night, but he must be overwhelmed by all this."

"I think we all are," Eleisha answered.

"I have some business to do in my room," Rose said, walking quickly across the floor and disappearing from sight. Wade was sitting on an antique couch, and he didn't look happy. Oddly, Philip seemed fine, but then he'd known a good deal about Robert already.

Eleisha went over and sat down close to Wade. "Don't worry. We won't let him take over," she said. "If he comes with us, he's just another member of the household."

He nodded, his white-blond hair hanging in his eyes. "Okay." He relaxed slightly. "I didn't think you noticed."

"What? That he sees himself as lord of the manor and us as his peasants? Yeah, we noticed."

"I warned you," Philip said absently from across the room.

"When we came here, I just didn't expect . . . anyone like him," Wade said. "You talked about finding vampires like Rose, scared, hiding." He looked over at Philip. "I guess I thought you'd be the badass of the group."

Philip smiled. "I am."

"So you don't mind if he comes back with us?"

Philip shrugged. "I don't care either way. This whole thing is for you and Eleisha, not me. If he does come, he won't stay long. Angelo told me Robert never stays long." He turned to Eleisha. "But he's better than I remember, and he didn't try to hurt you or Wade."

"Did you expect him to?" Eleisha asked.

"I thought he might be trying to draw us all out at once, and I don't think I could fight him by myself. If he went near you, I told Wade to shoot him in the chest or the face, to stun him so I could take his head."

Eleisha sat up straight. Philip said this with all the passion of someone ordering breakfast at Denny's. Wade glanced away, having the good taste to at least appear embarrassed.

"That's what you expected to happen tonight?" Eleisha asked.

Philip shrugged again as if the question wasn't worth an answer. "Wade, I'm bored and there's no DVD player. Do we have cable here?"

Wade stood up and headed for the television, apparently glad for the change of topic. "No pay channels, but I can probably find us a movie if you don't mind commercials."

"I hate commercials."

"That's the best I can do."

Wade started channel surfing until Philip said, "Oh, stop there . . . No, go back. That was *Die Hard*. I'd watch commercials for *Die Hard*."

"Okay." Wade looked around. "Seamus, are you there? This is a pretty good movie." Nothing happened, and Wade frowned. Apparently, Seamus was not interested in watching movies with Philip. "I'm going to order a pizza."

With Philip entertained, and Wade ordering pizza, Eleisha sat quietly, trying not to think about what could have happened tonight had Philip felt threatened. Gunshots and beheadings at the Japanese Tea Garden? But then again, Philip considered scenarios she did not. And vice versa. Maybe they needed each other even more than she'd realized.

She glanced over at Rose's bedroom door. Once they got everyone back to the church, and they could begin setting it up as a proper safe house, all this distrust would be over. The sooner the better.

"I'm going to go check on Rose," she said.

Walking to the bedroom, she decided not to knock

and opened the door to find Rose just sitting on her bed, staring into space.

"Eleisha!" Rose said in surprise.

Eleisha slipped in and closed the door. "I didn't really think you had business to finish. You can't sell the place overnight, and you can do your banking from anywhere."

Rose looked lovely, sitting there in her green dress with her hair down over her shoulders. It suddenly occurred to Eleisha that in the past, back in Scotland, Rose had hardly given a thought to her appearance, sometimes forgetting to even brush her hair. Like Philip, she had changed over the decades.

"You're upset with me for finding Robert," Rose said.

Eleisha hesitated. Was she upset? She walked over and sat on the bed. "No." Then she shook her head for emphasis. "Of course I'm not. This was our plan. You looked for one of us in a clever fashion, and you found someone. I just didn't expect him, and you have to admit that he'll . . . take some getting used to. But we won't leave him behind if he wants to come, and I think he'll want to come. We just need to get started. I'd like to buy plane tickets for tomorrow night."

"Tomorrow night?" Rose's voice wavered. "So soon?"

"It's best. I should make arrangements to buy the church. Then we can set up rooms for you and Robert, and do a bit more work on the place. Then we start looking for anyone else still in hiding." She paused. "That was smart how you found Robert, looking for news reports. How long can Seamus be away from you before he starts to weaken?"

"Not long," Rose whispered, but her eyes looked far away. "Plane tickets?" she repeated. "We'll be trapped high in the air, won't we? What is that like? Will we have our own small room on the plane?"

Eleisha blinked, suddenly realizing Rose had never been on a plane. "Oh, it's like what you see in the movies. Just rows of seats."

"Seats? With everyone sitting all together out in the open? We will be trapped in the air, among all the passengers and all the windows?" She stood up, crossing her arms as if she was cold.

"It's not that bad. Truly. It's the fastest way, and I promise to take care of you. We'll be home in a matter of hours."

"No. . . ." Rose shook her head, her eyes growing glassy and wild at the same time. "I could not do that. We must have a cabin . . . where we can shutter the windows and lock ourselves away."

Eleisha blinked. "A cabin, like on a train?"

"Yes, yes . . . the train."

The air shimmered.

"I think we should do as she says, Rose," Seamus said, appearing next to the bed with a worried expression. "I *felt* something in the guest room tonight. It vanished, and I've been trying to track it down."

Eleisha looked around. "Felt something? What?"

"I don't know. Something dead, but it wasn't one of you . . . more like one of me."

"A ghost?"

"Maybe."

Did Seamus know any other ghosts? Speak to them?

"But I've never felt one inside the apartment before, and with all this going on . . . ," he said, moving closer to Rose, "I think we should leave."

Rose lowered her head and didn't answer him.

Eleisha suffered a few seconds of frustration. A train from San Francisco to Portland could take nearly a full day, but then she took in the sight of Rose's anxious face and her frustration faded.

It didn't matter how they got home.

"Don't worry, Rose," she said. "I'll get us a cabin on the train."

Julian sat in a linen-covered chair in his suite, holding his fist to his mouth. A part of him had always known. In the wee hours of the day between sunset and dusk, he sometimes felt panic rising that perhaps an elder had somehow escaped him, slipped away to hide and wait. Or he even feared that perhaps Angelo had missed one—or two—from the listings in his book. Once fully awake, these fears left him . . . but they always returned.

And Eleisha had found one.

Eleisha had found Robert Brighton.

Julian did not understand how he'd been tricked. He'd cut off Robert's head and watched his body turn to dust. But only an elder would know of the laws, and Mary had described him in detail.

If Robert began teaching the old laws, then everything Julian had accomplished to protect himself would perish. He would be the aberration again.

If Robert had survived, escaped . . . could there be others like him?

Yet one truth was clear.

Eleisha was managing to do something Julian could not: draw these vampires in hiding out into the open.

He realized that he could not kill her yet. He would not kill her yet. He was still the hunter, only this time, she was the hound. In just over a month, she had found two others and drawn them out of hiding. Rose was not important just now. Mary had relayed that Rose still required "training by a proper master." If this was true, then she knew nothing of her own kind or their history.

But Robert had to be destroyed before the week was out. In years past, he would have murdered Julian for merely existing—and Robert was fully telepathic.

To Julian's further discomfort, Mary had relayed word-for-word conversations that seemed to suggest Wade was also telepathic, but the girl must be wrong. He did not see how this was possible. Wade was mortal. But what if . . . ? The implications of the timing and Eleisha's sudden manifestation of psychic abilities left him almost too unsettled to think.

Julian tightened his fist. What to do?

He could not reveal his presence yet or the fact that he was hunting again, not when his prey appeared to be gathering into a group. He'd often taken out two vampires at once by stepping from the darkness, beheading one of them instantly, and then killing the second one as he or she was hit by the first one's psychic explosion. Julian was not as affected and maintained his ability to strike.

But four vampires? No, that was too many.

But if any one of them learned of his presence here

too early, they would band together as never before, and he would lose the element of surprise. How could he manage to pick off one or two before they learned he was hunting again?

Strength in numbers.

They were joining forces, and he had no one. Well, he did have Mary, and in spite of her repellent nature, she had proven herself useful. Did he need more numbers?

He shook his head.

No, he existed alone. He believed in the purity of remaining alone—as all his kind should. Unnatural, undead beings who fed on mortals should function alone, not pretend to be some kind of human *family*. The very thought repelled him. He was convinced that the behavior of the elders, their need for each other's company, and their close physical proximity to each other must have generated the first inklings of their telepathy, of their twisted need for laws, in the first place.

He was sure of it. . . . Centuries and centuries ago, one vampire must have become aware of this power and begun assisting the others. Why else would a new vampire have to be "taught" by his or her maker? Why else would a new vampire need an elder to awaken such abilities?

That thought brought him back to Robert.

He had to do something!

Strength in numbers.

He took his fist away from his mouth. If . . . *if* he created a vampire to assist him, the obvious choice would be to pick someone strong, an intelligent and resilient fighter. But he could not bring himself to do this. No, he would have to pick someone who could be controlled and easily dispatched if necessary, but also someone who yearned for more than what he had, someone who could be used and tempted.

Julian would need to find the right type. But he was not telepathic, and he was not a good judge of mortals by simply studying their faces, especially Americans. They all looked the same to him.

He glanced around the room. "Mary, are you still here?"

She materialized by the fireplace, seeming somewhat put out. "Yeah, I'm here. You give up on staring into space?"

"I need you to find someone."

"What? Again? I told you. I know right where they are."

"No, I need you to find a mortal."

"Someone still alive? How am supposed to do that? Even if I had the right name, I can't exactly turn pages in a phone book. . . . Well, I guess you could turn them for me and—"

"Quiet!" he ordered, wishing he could strike her. "Listen to me. I need you to find a specific type of mortal." He closed his eyes, visualizing. "A man in his late teens or early twenties. He lives in near squalor, not homeless, but in some shabby apartment where he watches TV at night. He has a job but makes just enough to scrape by. He has failed in relationships with women, but he believes success is a matter of luck, and that if only he had wealth and drove a BMW, then all his problems would be solved."

When he opened his eyes, Mary was floating right in front of him. "Geez, Julian."

"Can you find someone like this?"

"Here? Sure, the city's full of guys like that. You probably couldn't swing a Barbie doll by her hair without hitting one. I just can't believe you know that much about people."

"Find one," he said coldly. "Tonight. And come back with his address."

Mary materialized inside a darkened doorway near the mouth of an alley. She'd already been looking around the city for an hour.

In spite of her flippant words to Julian, Mary was having a tough time locating the right man. Although she'd never paid attention at school, she wasn't stupid, and she knew *exactly* what kind of guy Julian was looking for.

She would never admit it, but in the past few nights, she'd felt more satisfaction with herself than she had in all of her previous life. There was something satisfying about tracking Eleisha in secret and always finding her, about traveling wherever she chose with a freedom that no other ghosts seemed to enjoy.

Mary was unique.

She hadn't even thought about her parents in several days. Even though Julian was a cold-blooded bastard, she was starting to kind of . . . well, *like* the tasks he gave her. Weird.

Focusing on the task at hand, she spotted a FOR LEASE sign on an empty shop next to a video store, and she got an idea.

Blinking out, she blinked into the empty shop and moved up alongside the window to peer into the street. She could tell a lot about people by the movies they rented.

She started to study everyone who came out of the video store and walked past her.

The first guy was bald and weighed about three hundred pounds, and he was stuffing movies inside his coat like he was ashamed. The films were probably porn.

Nope. Too perverted, she thought.

Next, a couple came out arguing loudly because she'd wanted to see *Fried Green Tomatoes* again, and he'd wanted to rent *The Fast and the Furious* with Vin Diesel. They weren't carrying any movies, just arguing.

Nope. Too married.

The next guy was tall and good-looking, wearing tight pants and a tank top. His hair was perfectly gelled, and he had a movie in each hand: *The English Patient* and *A Room with a View*.

Nope. Too gay.

Then a slender man of about twenty, with shaggy brown hair, came out of the video store alone. He was wearing jeans, a leather jacket, a backpack, and a pair of ancient Adidas athletic shoes that must have once been white. His shoulders were hunched forward, like he was closed off to everyone else.

Mary looked down at his right hand. He was carrying two movies. The one on top was *Spider-Man* with Tobey Maguire. When the film slipped slightly, she saw the one behind it: *Spider-Man 2*.

This guy had promise. He liked movies where an ordinary boy gets bit by a spider and becomes a super-hero that Kirsten Dunst would consider sleeping with.

She let him get a little ways down the street, and then she blinked out, rematerializing in an alley down the street so she could keep tabs on him. She repeated this process several times until he reached an apartment building in the Mission District and went inside.

The stairwell was empty, so she managed to follow him up to the fourth floor without being seen. Then he went inside.

Apartment 4-E.

She thought she was on the right track with this one, but she still wasn't sure, so she blinked out and tried to gauge the distance to the back of a small apartment, rematerializing again—poised to wish herself into nothingness—and finding herself alone inside a dirty bathroom. The door was open, and she heard the television come on.

Peering around the door, she saw that he didn't even own a couch, just a shabby overstuffed chair and a TV and one end table that looked like it'd come from a garage sale. He had no other furniture in the room. Looking up, she saw a Keira Knightley calendar hanging on the wall. The light on his answering machine was not blinking. He had no messages.

He put the first film into his DVD player, sat in the chair, opened the backpack, and pulled out a bag from McDonald's.

She'd seen enough.

Blinking out, she stopped once downstairs to get a

better look at the building—and then the mailboxes—scanning for the resident of apartment 4-E.

Jasper Nesland.

She blinked out again, focusing on Julian and rushing back to the suite.

"Come on," she said, before she'd even materialized completely. "I think I've got him."

Jasper Nesland ate his Quarter Pounder with Cheese and tried hard to focus on *Spider-Man*.

Watching the story of Peter Parker usually made him feel better, but he'd had a bad day—bad week actually—and he shouldn't have stopped at the video store and spent eight bucks on movies.

He'd been working for a year at the Quickie Mart on 19th Street, always keeping an eye out for something better. Paying the rent on this rat-hole apartment ate up almost everything he earned, but he just never seemed to get a break like everyone else.

When he was seventeen, his mom ran off to Sacramento with her newest boyfriend—and they didn't invite Jasper along. He'd never known his dad, and it sometimes ate away at him that he didn't have parents to help him out. But since Jasper couldn't change this fact, he'd decided to keep himself afloat.

He worked hard to pull his own weight. He didn't smoke. He rarely drank. He knew a bright future was waiting just around the corner, with money and respect and pretty girls. He just had to wait for some kind of break and be ready to pounce.

Then, earlier this week, he found out his landlord was raising the rent by eighty dollars, and yesterday, his boss had cut his hours, due to business slowing down because of a brand-new Circle K down the street.

Today, he'd felt so bad, so down about everything, that he'd spent forty dollars on lottery tickets, just hoping to get lucky, but he'd come up with nothing, and now he was out forty dollars and might have trouble even making this month's rent.

He shouldn't have rented these movies.

But he had, so he tried to forget everything and keep his eyes on the TV and his mind on Kirsten Dunst. He sighed. If only he had a decent car.

Somebody knocked on his door, and he jumped slightly.

Who could that be?

Even desperate salesmen wouldn't come to this part of the city. He didn't move and the knock sounded again, louder this time.

He stood up and walked over. "Who is it?"

"Open the door."

When the words reached his ears, a cold feeling began to crawl over him. He didn't want to open the door, but he was afraid not to. Something in that voice wormed through his body, filling him with terror of what might happen if he didn't unlock the door.

His hand moved as if functioning on its own, flipped the latch, and turned the knob.

A large man stood in the hallway. He had pale skin, dark hair, and expensive-looking clothes . . . black slacks, a dress shirt, and a long coat.

He walked in and Jasper backed up, his fear increasing.

What the hell was going on?

The man closed the door and locked it again. Then he looked about the apartment.

"What do you want?" Jasper managed to ask.

But when he spoke, the man's head swiveled rapidly back, his eyes narrowing as if Jasper shouldn't dare speak.

Fear hit him. He'd never been so afraid in his life. He'd never felt anything like this, and he sank to his knees, too shaken to remain standing.

The man strode over and grabbed the front of his shirt. Jasper wanted to scream, to beg, but he couldn't even speak. He felt himself being slammed against the wall, and then to his shock, the man pressed in closer and bit him on the throat.

No . . . more than bit him. Jasper felt teeth tearing into skin, puncturing deeper, and this time he did try to scream, but nothing came out. He bucked and fought and pushed, but the man was as solid as a moving statue, and he was drinking Jasper's blood.

After a few minutes, Jasper couldn't struggle anymore, and he could hear his heartbeat growing slower and slower, until it barely beat. The man let go of him, letting him fall to the floor. Was it over?

To his horror, the man knelt down, ripped the veins of his own wrist open, and shoved the bleeding wound into Jasper's mouth. He started choking, and the man ordered, "Drink."

Again, the voice filled him with fear, but the blood flowing down his throat tasted good. He obeyed and started drinking.

Then the world went black.

*   *   *

Julian waited in the shabby apartment for several hours. He still had time before dawn and didn't want to be seen carrying an unconscious body.

Finally, Jasper's eyelids fluttered and opened.

"Get up," Julian ordered.

Jasper saw him and cried out, crab-stepping backward to press against the wall.

"Just get up," Julian repeated coldly.

Jasper put his hand to his throat, which was nearly healed. "What did you do?" he whispered.

"I gave you a gift." Julian motioned to the dingy living room. "You're going to leave this place with me and never come back. You will have all the money you could ever want . . . anything wealth can buy. Your body is much stronger now, and you will never grow old. But you can't go into the sunlight, and you'll drink blood to live."

He let the words sink in. Most mortals would be horrified at a statement like this, but not Jasper. His eyes shifted back and forth as he absorbed Julian's words.

"I can hear every car outside," he said softly. "I can hear the people walking in the street." He touched his throat. "Vampire?" He rushed to the bathroom. "No, I can see myself in the mirror!"

Julian wanted to sneer. "Of course you can," he answered.

Had he made a mistake? He would only settle for a servant he could completely control, but this one seemed even more vapid than Mary.

"So, what do I have to do?" Jasper said, turning from

the mirror. "For all that stuff you said ... about money?"

Maybe he wasn't so stupid. But as of yet, he had no true idea what had just happened to him, and he was already trying to hedge an advantage. This creature had desires. He could be worked upon—and controlled.

Julian was pleased. "You just need to pass a test ... when I tell you."

chapter 9

The following night, Eleisha sat at the kitchen table watching Wade as he got the water boiling and then scrambled a few eggs. Philip was in the shower, and Rose was packing—although Eleisha suspected she was so anxious over the impending journey that she just needed some time alone in her room. So far, Seamus had not appeared tonight.

"What time does our train leave?" Wade asked, placing a tea bag into a mug.

"Just past midnight, from Jack London Square."

"Did you tell Philip not to hog all the hot water?" he asked, bringing her some tea.

She looked up at him, and he stopped with the mug in midair.

"What's wrong?" he asked.

"Why do you think Philip is being so cavalier about

Robert now, and he's so hostile about Rose? You'd think it would be the other way around."

Wade dropped into the chair beside her. "Because neither one of us seems to like Robert."

"What?"

"Think about it. You threatened Philip back in Seattle. You told him you wouldn't forgive him if he stopped you from finding Rose. Then you got me interested in helping her, too. You exchanged letters with her, and you want her company. He sees Rose as a threat to your time and affection—maybe even to mine."

Eleisha blinked. "No, even Philip isn't that self-involved."

Wade pursed his mouth at her as if she'd said something stupid, and he stood back up to get his eggs.

Out in the sitting room, she heard a soft knock on the front door, and she tensed. That would be Robert.

"I'll get it," Rose called from her room.

Wade scooped his eggs from the pan onto a paper plate, and he sat down beside Eleisha with his own tea. Voices carried from the sitting room, and then Eleisha looked over to see Robert standing in the archway. He was quite possibly the most physically intimidating person she'd ever met, and she didn't know why. He wasn't even as tall as Philip.

Maybe it was his eyes.

He carried over one shoulder a narrow nylon bag that stretched down to his thigh, and he was looking around the kitchen at the bright pots of herbs and the teakettle and egg pan on the stove. Then his gaze moved to Eleisha and Wade sitting at the table.

"Is there more tea?" he asked.

That was the first moment Eleisha felt any kind of connection to him. She remembered waking up after her first night here and how wonderfully comfortable it had been to just sit in a kitchen and drink tea with other people. How long since he'd enjoyed such a simple pleasure?

"Yes," she said, getting up. "Come and sit. Wade, you finish your eggs."

She made Robert a cup of tea and brought it to him, deciding not to beat about the bush, as they didn't have a great deal of time. "We've decided to leave tonight. I reserved two adjoining cabins on an Amtrak," she said.

"So soon?" he asked.

"There's no reason to stay, and I should start making arrangements to purchase the church. I can give you our address in Portland if you need to think this over and perhaps join us later, or you can come with us tonight."

"Tonight? I don't have a ticket."

"I bought one for you last night when I booked ours."

He stood up, ignoring his tea, seeming uncomfortable. "You bought me a train ticket on one night's notice? How much did that cost?"

"Cost?" She shook her head. "I'm not sure. I won't pay the Visa bill until the end of the month."

"It's all right, Robert," Wade cut in. "Eleisha doesn't . . . she doesn't need to worry about money. It's fine."

Maybe Robert liked to pay his own way?

Philip walked into the kitchen wearing nothing but his Calvin Klein jeans and rubbing his wet hair with a towel. He half turned to grab a mug out of the cupboard, exposing the white cigar burns on his shoulders.

At the sight of him like this, Robert froze, as if recognizing him for the first time, and the tension meter in the room suddenly shot up.

"What?" Wade asked in alarm, looking at Robert.

Philip stopped rubbing his hair and took the towel away, glancing down at himself, and then he locked eyes with Robert, but with some kind of intense realization dawning on his face until Eleisha wondered if the two of them were sharing a memory.

"Eleisha," Philip said slowly, putting the empty mug down. "You'd better take your shower while I get us packed."

She hurried over to him, still not sure what was wrong. "Of course. Can I borrow a sweater? I didn't bring enough clothes."

"Sure."

He backed out of the kitchen and then turned around. Eleisha followed him to the guest room.

"What was that about?" she whispered.

"Nothing." He turned away. "Go take your shower."

She never pushed him when he got like this, so she gathered up some clothes to wear, not paying much attention to what she grabbed.

Considering his mood, this was hardly the most opportune moment, but she wanted to speak to him before they left.

"Philip," she said to his back, "Rose is afraid of traveling, and I want you to look out for her, be kind to her, protect her like you do for me and Wade."

He glanced over his shoulder, and she could see his expression darkening. This would be so much easier if she could just use her gift, but he'd feel it, and afterward, he'd blame her.

"Rose is like Robert," she said quickly, "just someone we're trying to help. She'll never be the kind of friend that Wade is to us, and she will never be what you are to me."

The anger in his profile vanished, but he didn't answer.

"Be kind to her," she repeated, hurrying out toward the bathroom.

But she stopped halfway. Looking back to see Philip packing his bag, she walked to the kitchen, pausing in the arch. She needed a more concrete idea of how this night was going to play out, how their future was going to play out.

"Robert," she said. "Are you coming with us tonight?"

He was sitting at the table beside Wade again, and he studied her for about thirty seconds. "Yes," he said finally. "I'm coming."

Julian brought Jasper back to the Fairmont, allowing him to stay in the suite. He had also introduced him to Mary—so there would not be any drama occurring from her frequent and sudden appearances. If Jasper could so easily accept the reality of vampires, he should have no trouble with ghosts.

And he didn't.

More important, Jasper's awe at his opulent surroundings was most satisfactory. He'd probably never even seen a suite like this outside of a movie. His body was still completing the change, but Julian wanted to send him hunting soon.

Julian had a fairly good idea what Jasper's gift would be once it surfaced. But in all his years, Julian had never trained anyone, never acted as master. He'd turned only two other vampires—his father and Eleisha—and that had been nearly one hundred and seventy years ago.

He hadn't taught Eleisha to hunt. Edward Claymore handled all that for him.

He was pondering exactly how to broach the subject with Jasper. But he cringed inwardly at the thought of another conversation. He didn't like having such human filth anywhere near his suite, much less sleeping in it, and it bothered him that he could not completely rely on his gift to cow his new creation into reluctant obedience . . . as Jasper must *want* to succeed.

Obtaining anyone's willing agreement had never been Julian's strong point, even when he was alive.

"So, where'd you get all your money?" Jasper asked, turning circles inside the suite while reexamining everything. "Do you have some kind of mental power that lets you find lost treasure?"

Good God.

He made Mary look like a Mensa candidate.

"No," Julian answered, using all his restraint to remain civil. "I inherited an estate and made sound investments."

"Inherited? Sure. You're lucky."

"If you are to attain full strength," Julian said, changing the subject, "you'll need to feed, and I would prefer not to travel outdoors myself any more than necessary. I want you to listen to me carefully."

He expected some questions, some argument, some form of reluctance at his mention of feeding, but Jasper just turned and looked at him with glowing eyes. Maybe the change had finished quickly? Jasper appeared to have lost any lingering remnants of mortal ethics.

Julian was about to begin explaining the best methods for drawing someone off alone into the darkness when the air in the room shimmered and Mary appeared, looking even more dramatic than usual.

"They're going to leave!" she shouted. "Tonight!"

Julian didn't even tell her to calm down. "What?"

"Yeah, I couldn't stay long. . . . There's something in that apartment that keeps trying to find me. But I was alone in the sitting room for a few seconds, and I heard Eleisha and Wade talking about a train leaving at midnight from Jack London Square! They're going home to Portland."

Julian put his fist back to his mouth again, but this time he was simply thinking. They were leaving sooner than he expected.

He did not wish to destroy Eleisha yet—and possibly not for some time—if she was going to continue seeking other elders who might be in hiding. He needed her to find them, and he wanted her to view the church in Portland as safe so that she would remain there and he could keep track of her. She was weak of character and did not like being alone. He believed that no matter who he killed, she would keep on looking, keep on trying.

So he had to destroy Robert before they left San Francisco, and he couldn't risk this if Robert was traveling with three other vampires—and a mortal who Mary swore was a telepath.

Julian had to thin the group. But how?

He forced himself to calm, to think.

He couldn't expose himself yet, and his only possible tools were Mary and a newborn vampire.

Jasper could hardly stand up to Robert or Philip.

But would he need to?

From what Angelo had told him long ago, Julian understood that although the newly turned were not immune to each other's gifts, even a young untrained vampire could defend against a straight telepathic attack, to a degree, by putting up a mental block. Julian was the only exception to this, as he had no psychic defense at all.

He turned to Jasper. "Your test has come earlier than expected. I have enemies trying to leave the city . . . as Mary has just told us. I need you to keep them from leaving. Mary will guide and assist you."

"I will?" Mary asked uncertainly. "How can I help him?"

"You can show yourself if need be," he answered. "I want them to feel pressure now, to feel that they are attacked from several sides. I just don't wish them to know I am involved."

"So, I can, like . . . pop out and scare them if I need to?"

"Yes."

She smiled. "Okay."

"How will I know who they are?" Jasper asked, looking more uncertain, even nervous.

Forgetting Mary and turning his attention back to Jasper, Julian described all five members of the group, starting with Eleisha and finishing with Rose. He did not know if Rose and Philip were becoming telepathic, but he was harsh in his warnings about Eleisha and Robert—and he mentioned Mary's questionable assertions about Wade.

"If need be, you can use your own mind to try to push them out," he said. "But your goal is to avoid that need."

"How?"

"By keeping to the shadows, staying out of sight until the last second."

Julian did not bother to add that this strategy had always worked for him in the past because his undead condition combined with his complete lack of telepathic power made him invisible to others of his kind until they actually *saw* him. Otherwise, he was a black, empty hole in the night, and they could not sense his presence at all.

Jasper might not have this advantage.

"Once you find them," Julian went on, "Mary will work to break them up. You must stay near them but out of sight until you have a close proximity to one or two. Don't try to attack more than two, and don't strike until you know you can take one of their heads instantly. This will incapacitate the other one and give you time to take the second one's head."

He also didn't mention that it was possible the psychic release from the first one could incapacitate Jasper as well . . . but he was new and may not be as heavily affected.

"Take their heads?" Jasper asked.

Julian tried not to grimace, having forgotten to whom he was speaking. "Yes." He lifted his sheathed sword from where it lay on the mantel. It troubled him to send Jasper off with a two-hundred-year-old sword, but there wasn't time to get another one.

"Come here and watch me," Julian said, pulling out the blade.

He showed Jasper how to properly grip the hilt and position himself for a hard strike. Then Jasper practiced the act himself. Surprisingly, he took to the sword quickly, swinging it with decent balance and speed.

"Good," Julian said with a nod. "Just aim for the throat. You'll notice your hand-to-eye coordination is much sharper now, and you are stronger." He moved closer to Jasper, reaching out to grip the hilt. "But no matter what you do, do not attack Eleisha."

"That blond girl you talked about first?"

Julian allowed a small wave of fear to seep out, enjoying the satisfaction of watching Jasper's face turn paler.

"Yes. If you kill her, I'll tear your head off myself. Do you understand?"

He let more fear seep out.

Jasper's hands began to shake. "Yeah, I got it."

"Also," Julian added, running possible outcomes through his mind, "you would do best to avoid Robert if possible. He's the strongest, and you should leave him to me. But you can target the others, and I want at least two of them dead." He cut off the flow of fear and tried to make his voice sound comforting—not an easy feat. "If you succeed, and you keep them from leaving, I'll make certain you have everything you could want: clothes, cars, rooms like this one, anything."

Jasper's eyes glowed again. "Where do I start?"

Julian weighed possible options. Jasper would have to try to catch them in the open, so that Mary could help split them up.

"Go to the Amtrak station. Wait for Mary to help you track them, and when they arrive, make sure you cut them off." He paused. "But you'll need to be at full strength, so you should feed first."

"How do I do that? I mean . . . is there anything I need to know?"

Once again, if it were possible, Julian would have smiled. Perhaps he had done well turning Jasper.

"A few things," Julian said, and he began to explain the best tactics for hunting.

Jasper walked out onto Mason Street wearing Julian's long coat with the sword hidden underneath and five hundred dollars in his pocket—just like something out of a movie.

He almost couldn't believe what happened to him. Maybe those years of bad luck had been his just due while his life built up toward this moment, this night. In all his fantasies, he could never have imagined this.

He was immortal. He was unstoppable. He was rich.

And this was so much better than what he'd seen in vampire movies. He felt like something right out of

Highlander, walking down the street with a sword hidden under his coat.

He had a mission.

But Julian had said he'd need to feed. As of yesterday, Jasper had never once broken the law—but only because he didn't like trouble. But now, trouble didn't seem like such a big deal. . . . In fact, it seemed new and shiny.

He turned down Sacramento and headed toward Huntington Park, which was mainly a haven of upscale condos and town houses. Sacramento Street was way too busy, so he slipped in between several apartment buildings and looked around for the darkest section of a parking lot. He just kept walking for a while until he spotted a young woman who came out of a security building and walked beneath some trees toward a silver Lexus. He couldn't see—or hear—anyone else close by.

A beep sounded when she hit the button on her keys to unlock the car, and he came up behind her.

"Can I get a ride?" he asked, wondering what would happen after he spoke. Julian had explained how a gift would surface to help him hunt. Julian's gift was fear, and that would be awesome, but Jasper kind of hoped his would be more like that of the Philip guy Julian told him about. That would be the best.

The girl turned to look at him, and his interest went up several notches. She was pretty, with long blond hair, wearing a tight pink T-shirt and small diamonds in her ears—the kind of girl who normally wouldn't bother to spit on him.

She didn't seem startled and glanced at his coat. "You borrow that from your big brother?"

He went cold. She was making fun of him?

"No, it's mine," he lied defensively.

But his words sounded different this time, and her expression changed. He felt something flowing out from his body as he recounted all the times people had ignored him or discounted him or rushed to be away from his company.

The girl suddenly looked like she felt . . . sorry for him.

"I didn't mean to say that," she said. "It's been a long day."

The feeling inside him increased until she was looking at him like he was some sort of lost puppy. Her eyes filled with sympathy.

"Poor thing," she said. "You said you need a ride?"

Pity? His gift was pity?

No!

He wanted to wipe that look off her face as fast as he could. He should be feared, desired. There was nothing about him to be pitied! Not now.

As these thoughts passed through him, her expression wavered, and he remembered that Julian said his gift would help him to hunt more quickly and quietly, but he had to keep it focused. He didn't want to mess this up, and he rushed to her before the sympathy in her eyes completely faded. He grabbed her, clamping one hand over her mouth before she could scream, and he jerked the back door open with his free hand, pushing her halfway inside the car and then shoving her down beneath him. The sword hampered him, but he couldn't believe the strength in his arms and hands, and he pinned her down easily, driving his teeth into her neck, still keeping his hand over her mouth.

She struggled and tried to scream but kept getting weaker. The blood tasted so good, he was gulping it down, feeling the strength in his body growing stronger, and then he saw pictures passing through his mind . . . her father playing golf, her mother drinking from a martini glass, her sixteenth birthday party with a bunch of adults she barely knew, a string of boyfriends in polo shirts. . . .

The images faded. Her heart stopped.

He wanted it to go on, but she was dead.

"Hurry up," someone said from behind him.

He jumped back out of the car and whirled around, his right hand going for the sword. Then he saw Mary's transparent form standing a few feet away from the car. He hadn't actually talked to her yet, but in truth, she looked more like the girls he'd known in high school, and even as a ghost . . . she seemed more familiar to him than the girl he'd just fed on.

"You better get moving," she said. "They're not at the apartment, and I can't find them. That means they're on their way. Julian told you to feed fast and get started."

"Don't tell me what to do."

"Yeah? Well, you don't know Julian yet. You screw this up, and he'll make you sorry."

That scared him and he looked around, debating on the fastest way to get to the train station.

"Just take the car!" Mary said. "Her keys are right there on the ground."

She was making him feel stupid, and at the same time, he didn't want to do all this alone.

"You'll meet me there?" he asked.

She tilted her head to one side, looking at him. "Yeah," she said, sounding nicer now. "I'll meet you."

He grabbed the keys. Then he slid the dead girl's body farther into the backseat and slammed the door. Attempting to climb into the driver's seat, he found he couldn't sit while wearing the sword, so he took it off his belt and leaned it on the floor of the passenger side. Then he was somewhat unsettled by the alien-looking dashboard. He'd learned to drive in an old Dodge Dart.

"But you'd better hurry," Mary said, and she blinked out.

He started the Lexus.

He still couldn't believe his gift was pity.

As Eleisha walked through the large doors of the Jack London Square station, she was beginning to worry about Rose—who was growing more and more anxious with each passing moment. Her eyes were turning glassy. Her face was beginning to look pasty rather than pale, and her hands were shaking.

From their very first meeting, Rose had never tried to hide her fear of traveling, of leaving the safety of her home. But throughout the course of her undead existence she'd managed two successful—and long—journeys on her own. Then again . . . in fairness, the last one had been well over a hundred years ago. She had been holed up in her apartment for a long time now, leaving it only when the need to hunt grew desperate.

Although she was the one who expressed a desire to

join Eleisha and to begin a new purpose, perhaps she had underestimated her own terror of truly leaving the safety of her home?

Eleisha didn't know how to help her.

After walking a few steps into the brightly lit train station, Rose faltered and then stopped, blinking in open fear at the sights all around her. A modern-day Amtrak building must look quite different to her than a station had in 1870.

Philip walked up behind Eleisha and leaned close to her ear.

"What's wrong with her?" he whispered.

"Shhhhh," Eleisha said. "You know she's afraid of traveling. I just didn't think it would be this . . ." She trailed off.

Robert and Wade both seemed equally concerned, but when Wade took a step back, Eleisha stopped him and dropped her bag. "Let me."

She walked toward the doors, reaching out to stroke Rose's arm. "We'll be hidden away in our cabin soon."

She could feel Rose's arm shaking and suddenly felt at a loss for words. Was this more than simply a fear of traveling? Eleisha had never dealt with a full-blown phobia before. Maybe she should have let Wade handle this?

"Isn't this too soon?" Rose whispered. "Should we not take more time to . . . get used to each other, to steel ourselves for this journey? Doesn't that seem wise?" Her eyes shifted back and forth. "Let us go back to my home. We can leave for Portland in a few nights. . . . Yes, a few more nights."

Eleisha's heart began to sink. Rose would say anything to put the impending journey off. Of course she would feel better once they'd reached their cabin, but here, in the bright lights of the station, Eleisha could think of no way to comfort her.

And therefore she decided not to try.

"No, Rose," she said firmly. "We're going tonight. Just take my hand."

Suddenly Rose's expression turned completely calm, almost blank. She looked right at Eleisha and said, "Before we board and begin searching for our cabins, could we find a ladies' room? I need to splash some water on my face first."

The request brought some relief. At least Rose sounded rational.

"Of course." Eleisha called out to Philip, "Wait here. We'll be right back."

He frowned. "Why?"

She held up her palm. "Be right back."

Taking Rose's hand, she made her way down the vast cavernous station, passing people and check-in counters without really noticing them. Rose's hand had stopped shaking, which was a good sign. They turned a corner around the Departures board, and she looked at Eleisha.

"What are you wearing?"

Eleisha glanced down at herself. She had dressed in a bit of a hurry, in white sneakers, faded jeans, and Philip's Ralph Lauren V-neck sweater—with the sleeves rolled up and the bottom hanging halfway to her knees.

Rose wore sandals and a loose black dress that flowed when she walked.

"I've no idea, really," Eleisha answered, smiling, feeling better now that Rose was acting more like herself. "I just grabbed something out of the suitcases."

She was still smiling when she spotted the ladies' room sign near an exit to the parking lot. "Oh, right there."

Just then, Rose stopped walking and gripped down hard on Eleisha's hand, causing her to stumble. When she looked up, Rose's eyes were glassy again—lost and wild at the same time, as if the last few moments and her request for a splash of cold water had never happened.

"Eleisha," she said slowly, "you and I should go back to the apartment. We'll have tea in the kitchen and talk all night."

Her voice was smooth, and it tingled in Eleisha's ears. The station grew hazy. Rose's idea did sound lovely—so inviting.

But they were already here. They had tickets.

"No, we need to board soon, and Wade is—"

"The men will be fine," Rose said, her voice sounding smoother, softer. "You and I will go home, and they can leave tonight. Don't you think we need some time to ourselves?"

Eleisha's mind filled with images of sitting huddled at the kitchen table with Rose, sipping tea, talking together of things that mattered, just the two of them. Why hadn't she thought of this before? Rose always knew what to do.

"Wade can take Philip and Robert, and we'll all meet in a few nights at the church." Rose's voice went on. "Can you see our homecoming? They'll be so glad to see us when we arrive."

The lights of the station seemed too bright. Images of arriving at the church and meeting Wade and Philip passed through her mind. Of course this was best.

"Come home with me," Rose whispered.

Eleisha followed Rose out the exit and into the ground floor parking lot. The air was colder, and she looked out into the numerous lines of empty cars.

Something was itching, scratching at the back of her brain.

"This way," Rose said.

The scratching grew uncomfortable as Eleisha looked around. What were they doing in the parking lot?

"Rose, why are we . . . ?"

Her companion looked back in alarm, and Eleisha's stomach lurched. Rose was inside her head! She pushed back hard, fighting to gain control of her own senses, and Rose's expression shifted to panic.

She turned and ran, moving so fast that she vanished between the cars.

Eleisha stood stunned. Then she reached out wildly with her thoughts, trying to clear her mind and connect with Wade.

Rose is running! She's in the ground floor parking lot. Hurry!

Nothing came back, and she had no idea if he'd heard her. She bolted after Rose.

chapter 10

Jasper made a hard turn with the Lexus and squealed through an entrance to the station's parking lot. He slammed on the brakes, skidded to a stop, grabbed the sword, and jumped out of the car, dropping to a low crouched position.

"Now what?" he said aloud. "Are they here? Where do I go?"

If Julian's enemies were inside the building, he knew he'd already lost without a fight. He and Mary were supposed to cut them off.

Please, don't let them be here yet, he thought.

Mary appeared suddenly, swiveling her transparent head as if she was listening. "Yeah, they're here but . . . wait. That way!" She pointed across the lot to the right. "Somebody's still outside. One of them is running, over there."

Closing his eyes, he could hear the sound of running feet, but he didn't see anyone.

Relief flooded him. He must be more afraid of Julian than he'd realized.

"Remember to stay hidden!" Mary said.

Gripping the sheathed sword, Jasper slipped alongside the countless parked cars, moving quickly toward the sound.

Wade waited, somewhat impatiently, with Philip and Robert. He tapped his foot and glanced at his watch. It was already eleven forty.

What in the world was Eleisha doing?

It wasn't that he didn't trust her judgment, and it was clear she was trying to help Rose through this . . . but they really needed to board.

At least his other two companions seemed okay with each other. The tense moment from the kitchen had passed as soon as Philip dried his hair and donned his usual designer clothes. Wade had no idea what transpired between them in the kitchen, but he certainly didn't have time to worry about it now.

Robert was still carrying the narrow canvas bag over his shoulder, and Wade had packed his gun and Philip's machete into the same brown suitcase.

"Can you see Eleisha coming back yet?" Philip said. "I can't see her anywhere."

Robert swiveled his head to look around, and just then, Wade was hit hard by what felt like a telepathic shout.

Rose is running! She's in the ground floor parking lot. Hurry!

The shock made him buckle forward, tripping over two bags and falling to the floor. He caught himself on his hands.

"Wade!" Philip shouted, reaching to help, and people around them began to stare.

Wade grabbed Philip's arm. "Go," he managed to say. "Rose is running, and I think Eleisha's chasing her. They're in the ground floor parking lot."

Robert was rushing toward the far exit doors before Wade completed his last sentence.

"Don't leave that brown bag, Wade!" Philip called, running after Robert. "Don't lose it."

Only then did Wade think to reach out and try to contact Eleisha. But he couldn't feel her anywhere. She just seemed to be gone—or maybe out of reach. He struggled to his feet, grabbed the brown suitcase with their weapons, and started running, leaving the other bags behind.

Eleisha ran after Rose, dodging between cars and debating on whether to call out or not. The parking lot was nearly empty of people, but she could see a family half hidden by a column about seven rows down, all climbing into an SUV.

Eleisha ran on, catching a glimpse of Rose's black dress vanishing behind a white van up ahead, and she ran faster.

"Rose!" she called, throwing caution away. "Please stop. We'll go back to the apartment!"

She would have promised anything in that moment.

The air in front of her shimmered, and a brightly

colored form appeared from nowhere . . . a transparent girl with magenta hair, waving her arms and baring her teeth. Eleisha swerved and smashed into the side of a car.

She bounced off and hit the concrete ground, rolling quickly to try to get up. The girl ghost was coming toward her, making snarling sounds. Eleisha crawled backward in confusion and a surprised fear that made thinking difficult.

What was going on?

"Seamus!" she called.

He flashed into view beside her.

"Go!" he barked at her in his hollow voice. "Get to Rose!" Then he focused on the girl ghost, his angry eyes narrowing. They were both transparent, but here in this modern parking lot, Seamus looked even more like something from a bygone era with his draped plaid, hand-sewn breeches, long shaggy hair, and the sheath on his belt.

The girl ghost drew back at the sight of him. She stopped snarling and waving her hands. Her eyes widened.

"Oh, geez . . . ," she said. "No way."

She vanished from sight. So did Seamus.

Rose screamed, and the sound echoed off the concrete columns stretching down the lot. Then Eleisha heard a loud clanking sound. She dashed forward, skidding around the back of the van, and she could not believe the sight before her.

Rose was crawling backward, trying to use one of the garage columns to protect herself . . . and a slender man in a long coat was chasing her with a sword. He swung hard but missed her by inches, smashing the blade against the column. Eleisha sensed no life coming from him at all.

He was one of them.

"Get away from her!" she yelled.

He stopped, letting the tip of the sword drop when he saw her. Rose looked lost and frightened, still crawling backward up against the column. Eleisha didn't hesitate.

She let her gift flow and tried to permeate his mind. She didn't know him. But if he was telepathic, he'd be able to resist the kind of attack she'd used on Julian, and he was standing so close to Rose that Eleisha didn't want to take any risks.

She let her gift flow, and she worked to soak it inside of him. He shouldn't hurt her . . . he should come to her . . . walk over to her . . . protect her.

His face went blank, and he took a few steps, dragging the sword. She had him.

"Eleisha?" he said.

He knew her name?

Suddenly, she felt something coming from him . . . a feeling of how tragic his life had been, and she could not help a wave of pity rising inside her. She wavered, and her connection broke.

He blinked, straightening and staring at her in shock. Then he saw Rose right beside him and he roared, raising the blade and swinging hard.

"No!" Eleisha screamed.

The tip of the sword sliced through Rose's throat, not severing her head, but black blood sprayed out onto the concrete.

The strange vampire backed up at the sight, as if he couldn't believe what he'd just done. But then he drew his sword arm back again. Eleisha had no weapons and her gift had failed, but without thinking, she ran forward, getting between him and Rose, shouting, "Don't!"

He halted in midswing.

Philip's voice rang out from somewhere behind them. "Eleisha!"

"Here! We're here!" she called.

Rose was toppled to the side, bleeding from her throat. But at the sound of Philip's voice, her attacker swiveled his head around desperately, as if he didn't know what to do—or maybe he was expecting help. With one last wild look at Rose, he turned and fled around the column, vanishing from sight. Eleisha dropped to her knees beside Rose.

"Philip!" she cried out.

He came running around the van with Robert on his heels. They both skidded to a stop, taking in the sight of Rose on the floor with her throat half-severed.

"It was one of us," Eleisha began babbling. "With a sword. He cut her and ran. Oh, God, Philip, he tried to take her head off!"

"Where?" he asked.

"There," she said, and pointed behind the column.

Philip held out one hand. "Robert!"

Robert threw him the long nylon bag he'd been carrying. Philip caught it and took off running again. But then Robert came over and dropped beside Rose—whose eyes were closed, the dark pool around her growing.

"What do we do?" Eleisha asked him. "I don't know what to do."

*   *   *

Wade hadn't been far behind at first, but he couldn't keep up while carrying the suitcase. He'd seen where Philip and Robert had run, so he came huffing upon the scene behind the van, unprepared for what awaited him.

The reality registered in stages.

It took him a second to realize the darkness spreading around Rose was her blood. He didn't think he'd ever seen Eleisha hysterical before.

Robert was kneeling on Rose's other side, his face emotionless.

"She needs blood right now," he said.

"Blood," Eleisha repeated in a whisper. "Would it heal a wound that bad?"

She put her wrist into her mouth as if to bite it, but Robert reached out and stopped her. "No, it won't be strong enough from one of us. Her cut is too deep, and she needs pure life force from a mortal." He didn't even glance over but said, "Wade, hurry."

Eleisha's forehead wrinkled. Then she saw Wade standing there with the suitcase. "Wade? No . . . that will hurt him, drain him."

"Get back," Robert ordered her.

Wade rushed over, kneeling by Rose's head. The sight of her up close left him shaken. Her throat was severed more than halfway through. "What do I do?"

"No—" Eleisha tried to say, but Robert cut her off as if she hadn't spoken.

"Give me your wrist."

"It's okay, Eleisha," Wade said, reaching out. She was beyond upset, and Robert could certainly be handling this differently—but he was right.

Maybe Eleisha realized that, because although the shock on her face melted into misery, she didn't try to stop either of them. Robert took Wade's wrist and punctured his teeth into a vein.

It hurt.

Wade didn't wince, and he let Robert guide his wrist into Rose's mouth, squeezing blood past her lips.

"What if she's too far gone to drink?" Wade asked.

But then Rose opened her mouth and clamped down on his wrist. The pain of Robert's teeth was nothing in comparison, and he couldn't help crying out. His hand . . . his entire arm was burning as she drained life force away from him, sucking in savage gulps. He gasped a few times, leaning over her, and he could hear Eleisha making small strange sounds beside him. Then he felt Robert's fingers on his throat.

"I'm sorry I cannot put you to sleep," Robert said to him. "Eleisha, get ready to pull him back when I tell you."

Wade's head grew light, but he could actually see Rose stop bleeding, and although her wound didn't close, the internal section appeared to be knitting together. He wondered if he was hallucinating.

He could feel his heart slowing down.

"Now," Robert barked, pulling Wade's wrist out of Rose's mouth.

Rose snarled and snapped after it, but Robert held her down, and Wade felt Eleisha jerk him backward. Then he was lying on the concrete floor, and she was holding his head in her lap, rocking him back and forth. He was dizzy and weak, and his mind wandered. Rose had stopped fighting Robert and lay quietly now.

"God, I hope no one walks by and sees this," Wade murmured.

For the most part, they were hidden between the column and the van.

"It doesn't matter," Eleisha said, and she laid him down on the floor. She untucked his shirt and ripped a strip off the bottom, tying it tightly around his wrist.

"What the hell is going on?" a low voice with a French accent demanded, and Wade looked up to see Philip standing over them.

Eleisha didn't answer and pulled Wade's head back into her lap.

"There was no other way," Robert answered, still sounding emotionless. "Where's the vampire?"

Still angry, Philip shook his head once. "Gone. I lost him."

Robert stood up. "We can't stay here. Philip, find something in that bag to hide Rose's throat and cover her dress. Anything will do," he ordered. "Then get her on her feet. Wade, you'll have to walk, too, but we need to board that train. Right now."

When Eleisha looked at him, her expression was flat—almost bitter.

She had no reason to be angry. Robert was *doing* all the right things, and yet . . . even drained and weak and dizzy, Wade understood exactly how she felt.

Jasper was bleeding and groveling on the floor of the suite, but the sight of this didn't make Julian feel any better.

He kicked Jasper's side again, watching him roll hard against the fireplace.

"What do you mean, you *think* you took her head?" Julian demanded.

Jasper was gagging, black blood dripping down his chin, and he tried moving up to all fours. "I cut through most of her neck! I swear, Julian, her head was hanging by a thread!"

He crawled backward, and Julian was suddenly too disgusted to kick him again. Unless Rose's head was severed, she would heal after feeding.

"You said Mary would help me!" Jasper shouted. "And you didn't tell me Eleisha could make me see things . . . feel things!"

Julian put his fist to his mouth. Where exactly was Mary? This situation was bad, and he was completely in the dark. Jasper, the fool, had run from the station parking lot after botching up any attempt to decrease the numbers in Eleisha's group. Then he'd left! Just left them there.

Julian ground his teeth.

"Mary Jordane!" he called.

Her transparent form stumbled as she appeared near the terrace.

"Hey!" she exclaimed. "I'd just gotten back to the station to look for Eleisha. Why'd you pull me away?"

"Where have you been?" Julian demanded. "Did you leave Jasper to fight alone?"

She crossed her arms. "They've got their own ghost. A big guy who looks like something right out of *Braveheart*. I had to take off."

Julian lowered his fist. "What?" Another ghost? "Can he injure you? Do anything to harm you?"

"I don't know! I wasn't waiting around to find out.

He can't travel as easily as me, so he must be tied to one of their new vamps."

Eleisha's group had a ghost? This unsettled him. It leveled the field too much. "What do you mean, 'right out of *Braveheart*'?"

"You know: his clothes, his hair. He looks about eighteen, but he's old. A lot older than the earthquake ghosts here in the city." As she said this, she noticed Jasper bleeding onto the carpet. She frowned. "Geez, Julian, you didn't have to do that."

He focused his cold anger upon her.

"You left Jasper," he said.

"I had to, but I went back as soon as I could. Did he nail one of them? I found a big pool of blood on the parking lot floor."

Julian turned away, fighting to keep himself from slicing off Jasper's head and banishing Mary tonight. "Where are they?" he asked softly.

She shrugged. "I don't know. They probably just got on the train."

"No, they couldn't have made their train," Jasper choked, trying to stand up. "I had 'em scattered for too long, and that Rose woman was a mess."

Julian looked at him.

Although Jasper's words made sense, he did not yet know enough about his own kind. Julian tried to *think* like Eleisha—what she would do. She was a survivor by nature . . . but she was also flawed by her obsession over taking care of others. He believed her capable of finding a way to board that train in time, whether Rose's throat was half-severed or not.

Yes. He almost nodded to himself. She—and her

companions—were most likely on the train to Portland.

Unfortunate, but not a complete loss yet.

"Mary, check the apartment, just to be sure they haven't gone back." He walked toward the telephone on the end table. "Jasper, go clean yourself up," he said, picking up the phone and hitting zero.

"Front desk," a professional-sounding woman answered.

"Yes, I need an Amtrak schedule sent to my suite. Then arrange for a rental car. I'll want it within the hour."

chapter 11

R ight as the train began to move, Wade dropped to sit on a small bench-style couch against one wall of their cabin. His head was still light, and his wrist hurt, but otherwise, he was starting to feel better.

Once everyone was inside, Robert locked the door.

Rose eased down beside Wade, wearing his jacket, but when she moved, the collar slipped down past her shoulder.

To his amazement, her injured throat was almost healed, the wound appearing only as an angry red line. She was clearly shaken but conscious and fairly calm.

"Do you want me to close that shutter over the window?" he asked.

"I'll do it," Philip offered, slipping past them.

Eleisha kneeled down on the floor beside the couch.

Rose's face twisted in a pained expression. "I'm so

sorry," she said with a harsh rasp. "I don't remember very much after we walked into the station . . . until . . . I saw the sword coming at me and then I woke with Wade's wrist in . . . You know how badly I want us all to reach Portland. I'm so sorry."

"It's all right," Eleisha soothed her, touching her forehead. "I didn't realize how hard that would be for you. It's not your fault. Do you feel better in here?"

Rose looked around the small cabin, at the closed window and locked door. She nodded.

"Just exactly what happened out there?" Robert demanded, stepping past Eleisha and opening the adjoining door to their other cabin. He stood in the doorway to give everyone else more room.

Even so, the quarters were tight.

Still kneeling, Eleisha began to talk in short bursts, telling them about a ghost who'd flashed in front of her suddenly and how Seamus had then appeared, and they'd both vanished.

Then she described the vampire who'd attacked Rose.

"He seemed new," Eleisha whispered. "Like he didn't understand my gift or his own or how they work."

"Julian's behind it," Robert said. "He must be."

"We don't know that," Philip said, surprising Wade—as Philip always tended to suspect Julian. "He works alone. He doesn't make servants to help him."

"He made Eleisha," Wade said.

No one spoke for a few moments, and then Robert asked, "Was the ghost working with this vampire?"

Eleisha's forehead wrinkled. "I don't know. But it

seemed like she was trying to scare me off, to keep me away from Rose. I do think the sight of Seamus frightened her."

The implications of this left Wade shaken. He had no idea why a ghost and a vampire they'd never met would go to such lengths to attack them.

Rose lifted her head weakly off the back of the couch. "Seamus," she rasped. "Are you there?"

A slight blur marred the view of the shuttered window close to where Philip was standing, and then Seamus materialized. His expression was troubled.

"Well?" Robert said, as if it was the only necessary word.

Seamus looked over at the couch. "Rose! What happened to you?"

She leaned her head back again. "I'll be fine."

"What happened?" he repeated.

"Did you find that . . . girl who jumped out at me?" Eleisha asked.

His transparent eyes narrowed. "No, I tried, but she moves so quickly, blinking from place to place like nothing I've ever seen."

"Do you . . . have you ever spoken with other ghosts?" she asked quietly.

He hesitated. "Yes, but they were like me, tied to a place or to someone in this world. This girl is different."

"Why would a ghost work for Julian?" Robert asked, not really speaking to anyone.

"We still don't know it's Julian," Philip answered. "We don't know if the ghost and that vampire are even connected. We don't know anything."

"Except that we need to get home!" Eleisha cut in, and the strain in her voice caught Wade's full attention. "Once we're back at the church, we'll be safe . . . and we can figure some of this out." She closed her eyes and whispered, "Let's just get home."

Rose reached out to stroke her hair. When Wade looked back toward the window, Seamus was no longer visible. Wade was beginning to suspect that he found engaging in conversation among their group to be unpleasant—or maybe it was still too new for him.

But Eleisha was right. They were now inside a cabin, with their weapons, heading for Portland. At the moment, they should keep their focus on getting home to the church.

Although weakened, at least Rose was behaving more like her calm self again, though she looked less elegant wearing Wade's jacket over her blood-crusted dress. He'd have to go through his suitcase and find something else for her to wear soon.

She looked around the clinical cabin. "This is so different from . . . You should have seen our cabin when we traveled here from the east."

Eleisha opened her eyes again, seeming relieved at the change of topic. "What was it like?"

"I had a bed and a porcelain basin for water. Embroidered curtains on the window . . . a satin comforter. It was like a little hotel room. Robert, did you ever travel by train in those days?"

"No."

"Times have changed," Wade said, also glad to be speaking of more mundane things. "But at least between both cabins we have four bunks."

He realized he was thirsty, probably feeling dehydration from losing so much blood, and he looked over at Philip. "Would you mind going to the food car and picking up a few bottles of water? And maybe Rose could use a cup of tea?"

"I don't mind," Philip answered.

"No," Robert ordered. "She's fine for now, and we should stay in these two cabins, keep together with our weapons. Wade, there's a sink right there if you need water, and a porter will come by in a few hours to take food orders. You can get anything you want then."

The cabin fell into a tense silence again. Philip pressed his lips together tightly, but he looked uncertain at the same time, as if unsure what he should do.

"Robert," Wade finally said, and he could not keep the edge from his voice. "I agree we should be cautious, but you don't make the decisions for any of us. Philip is going to walk out the door and go buy some bottled water and get Rose a cup of tea. He might even get me a ham sandwich. Do you understand?"

Robert's face betrayed nothing. No hint of emotion crossed his eyes. Then he stepped backward into their second cabin and closed the inner door.

Wade sighed, thinking he might have handled that differently. Philip looked surprised. Eleisha and Rose both looked uncomfortable. But something had to be done.

"You still don't mind going for the water and tea?" Wade asked Philip.

"No, I don't mind. I'm bored in here, and this trip will take forever. What will we do when I get back?"

"I'll think of something."

The moment Philip slipped out, Eleisha turned toward Wade. "You're starting to handle him pretty well."

"I watch you do it enough," he said.

"What's wrong? You sent him off over more than just a bottle of water."

"I think somebody needs to talk to Robert . . . before we get home," he answered, "I don't think he'll listen to me, and Philip would just make things worse."

Eleisha glanced away. "I know. I've been thinking the same thing. I'll do it."

Wade was almost embarrassed by the relief he felt. She'd already had a long night, but they had a long way to go, and something had to be done right now. She had a way of making people see reason. It was a gift she never quite recognized.

"Keep Philip out if you can," she said, standing up.

Rose reached out to touch her arm. "Robert is just following his nature, Eleisha. Remember that."

"I will, but if we're all going to live together and look for others to bring in, he's going to have to understand . . ." Eleisha trailed off. "I'll go talk to him."

She knocked softly on the connecting inner door, opened it, and slipped through.

Wade closed it securely behind her and looked around the small cabin that he and Rose now occupied alone. Then he went back to sit with her.

She seemed all right as long as they were locked away by themselves with the window covered. "You should get some rest," she said.

She sounded sad and a bit lost again, and he remembered that no matter how badly she wanted to begin a new existence with a new purpose, she was still leaving her home of a hundred years. Perhaps he should distract her.

"Rest?" he answered. "I don't think so. We need to think of some way to entertain Philip. Have you ever seen him when he's bored? It's not pretty." He pulled a deck of cards from his bag. "Do you know how to play poker?"

Julian gripped the steering wheel harder.

He'd rented a new Ford Mustang and pushed the needle past seventy, racing up Interstate 5. The Amtrak schedule lay on the seat between himself and Jasper, who was staring out the window. It had been a quiet trip so far—thankfully.

Before leaving San Francisco, they had taken the time to break into an antique store and steal Jasper a trench coat and his own sword. It was not exactly a quality blade, but it would work.

Once on the road, Jasper had fallen silent. His face was still cut, but he'd stopped bleeding.

Finally, he asked, "What makes you so sure they're on that train anyway?"

Julian looked into the rearview mirror and into the backseat as he saw the air blur, and Mary appeared.

"You were right," she said. "I hid behind some shelves near the dining car and Philip walked right past me. They're on the train."

Jasper turned from the window and looked at Julian in astonishment—almost respect. "So how far are we going tonight?"

"As far north as we can get before dawn," Julian answered, glancing down at the Amtrak schedule. "We'll take cover and sleep out the day. Then we start again. But between all their stops and one layover, they're on a twenty-two-hour route, and they'll have to change trains in Eugene tomorrow night. We'll be waiting." He paused. "But we need to find some way to keep Robert from getting off inside the station. We need to get him outside. A train yard is a good place, an excellent place, for our needs. It's full of nooks and shadows."

"And then what? You just step out and cut his head off?"

Jasper still didn't understand the difficulty of this or the need to strike from the darkness at the perfect second. But Julian had no doubts now. He had been an unstoppable hunter once, and the memories were all coming back.

Eleisha slipped into the second cabin to find Robert standing by the window and gazing at the landscape as it raced by. Everything about him looked so hardened, from his lean face to his worn boots. He struck her as lonely yet inaccessible at the same time.

"I'm sorry about that . . . that moment with Wade," she said. "But we all managed to survive for a long time before meeting you."

"You're too young to know anything."

"Philip and Rose are over two hundred, and I'm not far behind."

He moved toward her, and the tense expression on his face eased a bit. "Rose told me that until just recently you've spent your entire existence taking care of Julian's father."

She nodded. "Yes, but I didn't mind. I loved William."

"That's why you're so different, not like one of us at all."

In spite of everything they'd been through tonight, she couldn't help smiling. "Maggie used to say that all the time."

"Maggie?"

"Philip's lover when he was first turned. Then he turned her, too."

His jaw tightened, and his eyes clouded with anger again. "Oh, her." He walked back to the window.

Eleisha worried that she might never understand him, but she had come in here for a reason. "We're glad to have you with us, but you need to stop behaving as if you make our decisions. Can you do that?"

He nodded once without looking at her and then said, "I know you can't help what you are, but you don't understand anything. There are laws we have to exist by . . . that we did exist by. Julian's maker, Angelo Travare, broke two of those laws, and a nightmare started that hasn't stopped."

"What are you saying?"

He dipped his head, looking so unhappy that she felt sorry for him.

"I don't know how to tell you," he whispered. "I don't think I could make you understand."

Words were certainly not Robert's strength, but he seemed desperate to convey the meanings of these "laws." She was drained and tired, and dawn was still hours away. The last thing she wanted to do was share consciousness with Robert. But once home, she wanted them all to be able to start moving forward—and that would take mutual understanding.

Reluctantly, she sat down on the floor. "Close the window shutter. You don't have to tell me anything. Just show me. Take me back."

He frowned. "Take you back?"

"Don't you know how to share memories?" she asked, puzzled. "You must. We've all shared our memories, even Rose. Come sit here. You just think back, and I'll follow inside your head."

Still uncertain, he sat on the floor in front of her. "I just focus on a memory and you can see it?"

How could he not know this? He was five hundred years old.

"Yes, go back as far as you need to go."

"I only need to show you one."

"All right," she answered. To the best of her experience, none of them had ever shown each other a single memory—as the flow always started in one point and just continued until it finished or somebody managed to pull away.

"Just relax and think back," she said, closing her eyes.

She reached out for his thoughts, stretching her consciousness into his.

Think back, she projected. *As far back as you need*.

She felt a moment of panic inside him as her consciousness meshed with his, and then his memories began to surface, and then she lost awareness of herself, falling into his past.

chapter 12

Robert

Robert Brighton cared nothing for titles or power—or even for family. His grandfather had been a soldier, his father had been a soldier, and he never considered any other life than following the same path.

He didn't mind the simple designation "man-at-arms," and he was loyal to the lord he served.

In the year 1514, his lord, Thomas Howard, was named Earl of Surrey. And Robert, at the age of twenty-three, had already been in his service for five years. He rejoiced in his lord's success.

By this point he had followed Thomas Howard into wars with Spain and Scotland, and he liked traveling from one battle to the next.

The course of his life simply followed that of his lord's, and this was comfortable, with a natural kind of flow that Robert desired. His left arm was broken once and his nose twice, but he always healed enough to fight again. He did not think into the future. He preferred living day to day, and the earl made certain the needs of his closest men were always met. Robert had little to consider besides loyalty, courage, and following orders—and he excelled at all three.

The earl's first wife died of consumption, but Robert had barely been aware of her existence. He was almost equally unaware when his lord had remarried in 1513 to Elizabeth Stafford, daughter to the third Duke of Buckingham.

A man-at-arms like Robert would hardly be included in the wedding party, and he and his lord were rarely at home. He'd seen Elizabeth a few times, but she was barely sixteen at the time of the marriage. Later, he wished he had taken more note of the event, as it came to shatter the course of his life.

After the Battle of Flodden Field in Scotland, to Robert's disappointment, his lord began growing interested in the political arena, and they spent more and more time at court in Eltham or Lambeth Palace—wherever the king was residing. Robert hated inactivity, and there was little for him to do. But he enjoyed those weeks when the court made preparations to "move," and then the hordes of Henry VIII's household took to the roads for a short journey.

Always acting as guard to his own lord, Robert liked the traveling and the break in monotony.

There were brief stints when the earl took time to rejoin his new wife, either at court or their seat at Arundel Castle in Sussex or their family home at Kenninghall, Norfolk. As a result they had a son named Henry and a daughter named Mary, but again, Robert barely noticed these domestic happenings.

Then, in 1520, his lord was given the thankless task of "putting Ireland in order," and Robert rejoiced once more. The following year they fought in France. They were merciless, burning all of Morlaix. After this, Robert hoped the earl would not be recalled home, and he got his wish. They were sent back to Scotland, killing men and ravaging lands, and Robert felt nothing but respect for his lord.

Then . . . in 1524, Thomas Howard's father died, and so he became the third Duke of Norfolk. As a reward, he was allowed to go and live in his own house in Kenninghall. At first, Robert thought little of this. By this point, he was thirty-three years old and quite resigned to going wherever his lord went.

Upon arriving at Kenninghall, Robert found out that he was to live inside the manor, as head of the household guard. This appointment honored him. He was placed in charge of the watch, arranging schedules and making certain his instructions were maintained.

He sometimes worried about missing the traveling and the fighting, but perhaps it would not be so bad to oversee the Kenninghall watch. His lord had a young son who would soon need training, and there seemed to be plenty to keep a man like Robert occupied.

There was only one problem.

His lord and lady hated each other.

Whereas Robert had barely noticed his lady before, he was now faced with her on a daily basis. Nearing her late twenties, Elizabeth was tall, slender to the point of being spindly, with dark hair and a widow's peak. She dressed carefully, paying attention to each detail down to her earrings matching her gown, but Lord Thomas somehow always managed to find fault, criticizing her in front of the servants, humiliating her whenever he could.

Robert found his lord's actions base. . . . Worse, he found them common.

Thomas was fifty-one, with a narrow face and a nose so long it seemed to stretch from above his eyes to the top lip of his mouth. His brown hair was thinning, but he, too, dressed carefully, often wearing his robes of state at home.

He had never spent much time around his wife, Elizabeth, and now one of his main pleasures seemed to be verbally torturing her.

One night, she walked into the dining hall wearing a forest green gown with a matching headpiece, Spanish in design, as was the current fashion. They had six guests for dinner that evening.

"Good God," Thomas said. "You look like a brown scarecrow. If you're going to wear that color, the least you could do is cover your face in powder."

Elizabeth froze in her tracks. Several guests tittered. Several glanced away in embarrassment.

Robert tried not to wince as he stood near the door. He was ashamed of his lord. A man of honor did not humiliate his wife.

Yet as uncomfortable as he found the situation, Robert never imagined it could get worse.

He was wrong.

Although Thomas Howard did not particularly *like*

women, he found many of them enticing, and as far as he was concerned, the lower the class the better for his appetites. In addition, he was hardly discreet, and Robert began growing more unsettled by his lord's behavior.

One of the household women was of particular concern. Her name was Bess Holland, and she was Lady Elizabeth's washing woman. She was small and buxom with a mass of reddish curls and green eyes. She had a way of walking, while carrying a basket on her hip, that could cause an uproar among Robert's own men, and she was well aware of it. Had he been the steward in charge of the household servants, he would have dismissed her.

Unfortunately, he was not the steward.

Soon, it was clear that his lord was sporting with Bess behind closed doors as often as possible. They didn't even try to be quiet.

Again, Robert winced, but he said nothing. It was not his concern.

On the battlefield, his lord was magnificent. As a husband and father, he was lacking.

Robert chastised himself for such thoughts and vowed to remain loyal.

But when an old friend who served Thomas Boleyn stopped by on an errand one day, Robert almost asked him about possible openings among their house guard.

This got him thinking on travel and battles again, wondering if he should offer his services elsewhere. He was beginning to despise his lord and pity his lady.

The problem with Elizabeth was that she allowed

Thomas to hurt her. Robert could see this in her eyes. If only she had ignored his barbs, let them vanish in the air, and pretended he had never spoken, he might have eventually relented. But she kept on trying to improve herself to keep him quiet. She flinched visibly at his cutting words, and yet she kept on trying to please him. That was her mistake. She had no other way to fight back, as he held all the power. Robert longed to tell her that the secret to fighting him was through complete and absolute disregard.

But of course he said nothing.

Then, one night, he was making his house rounds, and he heard screaming upstairs. He flew forward, drawing his sword, taking the steps two at a time. He ran for the nursery.

His lady was still screaming, but he checked himself in the doorway upon hearing his lord's voice inside.

"Stop squalling, you hag!" Thomas shouted.

"A house?" Elizabeth screamed at him. "You bought her a house, for everyone to see?"

In horror, Robert realized his lord and lady were having a loud argument that many of the servants could probably hear. He stepped up closer to peer inside, and he saw little Henry and Mary up against the wall with their nurse, staring wide-eyed at their parents. Robert felt sick. He wanted to get them out of there.

"At least she does not lie beneath me like a motionless bag of sticks!" Thomas roared back.

"She is a churl's daughter who was nothing but my washerwoman!"

Robert started slightly as the truth sank in. Lord

Thomas had purchased Bess Holland a house of her own and had set her up as a mistress—and he had done so publicly.

"How could you? How could you stain our family name like this?" Elizabeth was sobbing now. "You will give her up. I demand you to give her up!"

"You demand—?"

His sentence was cut off by a loud crashing sound, and Robert stepped up to the door, not caring if he was seen. Lady Elizabeth was on the floor with her mouth bleeding. Thomas reached down, jerked her back up to her feet, and struck her again. She fell back against a small table, and he kicked her.

The nurse pulled both of the children closer and covered their eyes.

Thomas hit his wife over and over again until she was unconscious and lying in a bleeding heap on the floor.

Robert just stood there in the doorway. He could not interfere. But something inside of him snapped, and he knew he could not stay in this house.

Though Thomas was panting, his rage finally seemed spent. He glanced at the nurse and his children and then strode out the door, stopping in brief surprise at the sight of Robert just outside in the hallway.

"I heard shouting, my lord," Robert said instantly. "I feared for your safety."

Thomas said nothing. He didn't even order Robert to fetch help for Lady Elizabeth. He just brushed past and headed for the stairs.

Robert ran into the room, kneeling by Elizabeth and calling to the nurse. "Go get help! Run and find young

Francis on watch out front. Tell him to break off one of the house doors and bring it up. Then send for a physician." He paused. "And get the children out of here!"

Relieved at the sight of him taking charge, she shooed the children out, and he knelt there, alone, with Lady Elizabeth. She was still breathing, but she looked so broken that he feared even touching her without some assistance, and he did not want to try carrying her in his arms. After battles, he'd seen wounded men hurt worse if their backs or necks were already injured when someone tried to pick them up.

A commotion sounded downstairs as people burst into action, and all he could do was wait for his guardsman, Francis, to hurry upstairs with the doctor.

Lady Elizabeth recovered slowly, but word of Lord Thomas' brutal actions—and the reason for the dispute—spread quickly. Striking one's wife, even beating her, was not uncommon for men of his station. But beating her with his fists and feet into an unconscious state was . . . unseemly at best.

The third Duke of Norfolk decided to go back to court and continue his fight in the political arena. Robert requested to stay behind—and his request was granted. Thomas could barely look at him after the scene in the nursery.

Robert was determined to change his service and yet the prospect filled him with sorrow. He had served this house since he was eighteen. He was trusted here. The thought of starting over with a new lord seemed overwhelming. And as of yet, he could not leave Lady Elizabeth in her current state.

So he stayed.

With the duke gone and Bess Holland gone, the mood of the household improved somewhat. But as Elizabeth recovered physically, she appeared to deteriorate mentally, and she was sometimes seen whispering to herself.

Robert saw this himself one day, when she was out in the gardens with her mouth moving rapidly, but no one stood nearby. Her ribs had healed and she no longer bent over when she walked, but he believed she would keep the small scar on her upper lip.

Against all his training and belief in propriety, he walked up to her. "Are you well, my lady?"

She jumped at his voice and squinted as if not recognizing him for a moment. "Oh, Robert . . . yes, I am well. Even better soon. All will be well soon."

She walked down the path, her lips quiet and still now.

Better soon? What had she meant?

The trio arrived several nights later—hours after darkness had fallen and long past when respectable guests might come calling.

Robert was in the kitchen, drinking a mug of ale before starting his final rounds, when young Francis stuck his head in the door.

"Sir?" he said.

"What is it?" Robert stood up.

"You'd better come."

Robert followed to the great dining hall, where he found three figures illuminated by a burning candle: two men and a woman. The men were dressed like ruffians in baggy trousers and loose soiled shirts, their hair lank and greasy. They wore cutlass-styled blades on their belts. But he glanced at the men only briefly before his gaze fell upon the woman . . . perhaps only a girl? And he stopped walking.

The moment he entered, she turned and stared at him with large black eyes—true black like her wild hair. She looked maybe nineteen years old, with the pale, glowing skin of someone who seldom went outdoors. Her nose was small, and her mouth was heart-shaped. She wore a burgundy skirt and white blouse with a thin vestment over the top, laced up tightly. She was slender and her hips were narrow, yet the tops of her breasts swelled above the laced vest. Gold rings dangled from her ears, and bracelets clinked on her wrists.

Robert had seen gypsies before, but not one like her. When she turned to look at him, the top of her blouse slipped slightly, exposing her fine-boned shoulder, and he was hit by a rush of physical desire stronger than anything he'd ever felt before. His mind filled with images of her lying beneath him, clawing at his back.

He drew in a breath, cursing himself, and straightened, pushing the images away.

"What are you doing in here?" he demanded.

"We have business with your lady," the young woman answered.

"I don't think so," he answered.

Such rabble had no business with Lady Elizabeth. How had they gotten this far into the house? He'd have Francis on night watch for a month.

"Are they here?" a breathy voice called from the entryway outside, near the bottom of the stairs.

To his surprise, Lady Elizabeth nearly ran into the dining hall. She wore no headpiece, and strands of her hair fell about her face, sticking to her chin. She was holding her skirt off the floor. Robert had never seen her in such an undignified state.

"Oh . . ." she breathed at the sight of the strangers. Motioning toward a back room where the duke sometimes held intimate conferences with other lords, she said, "Quickly, in there."

"My lady?" Robert asked in confusion. Had Elizabeth indeed called for these . . . people?

She ignored him and hurried past, moving toward the strangers.

The girl was still staring at Robert, almost as if she knew him. Though shaken by his own reaction to her, he had no intention of allowing Elizabeth to take these three into a back room alone. The men looked like thieves or lowborn assassins—or both.

He walked after his lady, gripping the hilt of his sword.

She held up one hand. "Wait out here," she ordered.

He couldn't believe what was happening. Elizabeth had never deigned to look at such people, much less speak to them.

"My lady?" he repeated, uncertain what to do.

But she ushered all three strangers into the back room, and he was powerless to do anything but obey her orders. The gypsy girl continued to stare at him until the door was closed.

He walked over in near panic and stood directly outside, ready to break through the moment he was called.

Then he noticed Francis was still standing across the hall in the archway, equally disturbed.

"You're dismissed," Robert said. "I'll speak with you later."

Francis went pale, turned, and left.

Robert didn't want anyone else here. His fears did not surround only his lady's safety. What was she doing? His mind raced for any reason she would call upon armed vagabonds in the middle of the night, and the only possible answer left him cold.

She was arranging to have someone murdered.

Only two choices were possible: either the duke or Bess Holland.

He paced before the door, searching for some way out of this. Though troubled by her actions, he could not blame Elizabeth. How might anyone react to the treatment she'd received? But he had to stop this. If the target was Bess, his lady would only bring further shame and scandal upon the house. And if it was his lord . . .

He listened to the low voices beyond the door, hearing mainly Elizabeth's and the smooth tones of the young woman. Elizabeth's voice rose several times, and at one point, he thought she sounded horrified, but he couldn't make out the words.

Thinking more clearly, he rationalized that his lady would never arrange to have her husband murdered. Even if she managed to keep her life afterward, she had too much to lose by way of title and wealth and position were she to be found out—and he did not believe she would risk the future of her children. No, she was going to punish Bess.

Beyond the door, Elizabeth's voice rose again, and the door was jerked open. She stood on the other side, looking out at him. Her features were drawn tightly, her eyes full of pain. But she appeared more composed now.

She stepped out of the room. "Robert, please have them escorted out." Her voice was ragged. As the strangers seemed to slide into the dining hall, he noticed the young woman carried a velvet pouch. Elizabeth had paid them already? What was going on?

"Francis!" he barked, hoping the guardsman was within earshot.

"Sir?" Francis appeared the archway.

"See these people all the way out of the gates."

Robert wasn't leaving the hall—not yet. The gypsy was staring at him again. He tried not to look at her as Francis led the strangers out. They went quietly. As of yet, he hadn't heard either of the men even speak.

Then he was alone with Lady Elizabeth.

"Robert," she whispered. "I almost made a mistake tonight. But I changed my mind. I could not . . . could not . . ."

The relief flooding him was so intense his legs felt weak. She had changed her mind.

"You paid them?" he asked.

"For their time. For their trouble. For their silence."

In the moment, it did not shock him that she was speaking to him of such things, as if he were her brother or cousin or her equal.

"What will you do now?" he asked.

She lifted her head to look at him. "Think of my children. I must work for their futures. I have no way to fight my lord."

"Then don't," he said coldly.

Her brow wrinkled.

He hesitated only a few seconds before the words came pouring out. "Do you not see why he chose Bess Holland? Your washing woman? Who would cut you more? Ignore the fact that Bess exists. She is not worth your notice. When the duke speaks to you cruelly in front of others, regard him with disdain or pretend he has not spoken. Show him that he is not worth your notice."

Her eyes shifted back and forth as she listened, absorbing Robert's counsel, appearing as if such a tactic had never occurred to her.

"Yes," she whispered.

Then she looked him in the face again, and they suddenly both realized the inappropriate nature of this discussion considering their ranks. And they were both acutely aware of everything that had taken place in the last hour.

Robert stepped away. "I should make my rounds outside," he said.

She did not bother responding to him but walked to the other end of the hall, out the arch, and toward the stairs.

He sucked in a deep breath and steadied himself on the edge of the table for a moment, and then he, too, fled the hall, going outside into the cool night air as fast as he could.

He did not want to be in the house.

The thread that had held him here protecting Lady Elizabeth was broken. This had become a madhouse of dark secrets and hatred, and he wanted no part of it.

He kept walking, not even checking in with the guards outside, just walking, until he reached the outside of the stables. He could hear the horses moving about inside, and the sound was slightly calming—or at least grounding.

"Do you like being out at night?" a smooth voice asked from his left.

He whirled and felt his heart stop briefly as the gypsy stepped from behind a tree. The sight of her made him tense up again. His experiences with women were limited to the occasional girl along the road, and only in his much younger life.

"I had you escorted out," he said.

"You did," she answered lightly. "I came back."

He moved closer, intending to grab her arm. "I won't have assassins near this house."

"I'm not an assassin," she said. "My companions are, but I met them only a few nights ago, and I bet them five sovereigns your lady would change her mind once she heard the details."

He stopped. "What?"

She shrugged. "I saw her face when we first made arrangements, at a tavern in the village. To dream of murdering a rival is one thing; to hear the effects of poisons or drowning or strangulation is another. I knew she would change her mind."

"A tavern?"

Then he remembered that Elizabeth had gone into the village for a while a few evenings ago. He'd stayed behind and sent a small contingent along as escort.

The gypsy girl was so close that even in the darkness he could see every detail of the lashes around her black eyes. Her close proximity made his chest ache, and he fought to keep his hands at his sides. Did she not fear being alone with him in the night?

"Why did you come back?" he whispered.

"For you."

He didn't move, and the sound—or perhaps the quality—of her voice changed.

"You long to leave this place," she murmured. "To run and seek adventure, to travel, to see other sights and hear other sounds."

As she spoke, the pain in his chest faded, replaced by excitement. Her words began to create pictures in his mind of the wonder of constant travel, living on the road with her, and she . . . she would never be at a loss for something new to explore. She was a fountain of ideas and adventure, always delighted by the joys of the journey.

She embodied everything he had ever wanted.

"Come with me," she whispered, moving close enough to speak in his ear. "Come with me now. I've waited for you for a hundred years."

A hundred years.

"Get us two horses," she whispered. "The front gates are open. Your men are asleep. No one will see us."

He didn't even stop to think.

Less than half an hour later, they were riding out the open front gates.

Deep inside the forest, he watched her building a fire, and the reality of what he'd done began to sink in.

Had she put some kind of spell on him?

He'd abandoned his lord's house with the front gates wide-open and left all his men asleep!

His hands were shaking by the time she finished the fire, and the small twigs crackled and burned.

"What did you do to me?" he demanded, wondering how fast he could get back and yet hating the thought at the same time.

"Nothing you didn't want," she answered. "My gift only works to that degree on a certain few . . . those who love the journey more than anything."

Her voice had changed again, falling like music on his ears, and he began to forget the open gates. He forgot his men. He forgot his lady.

"Your gift?" he asked.

"Where do you wish to go first?" she asked. "Germany? The south of France? Italy?"

"Italy," he repeated in wonder. He had always longed to see Italy. But her words offered more than travel. He could see pictures of her laughing on a foreign beach in the night air. He could see her offering idea after idea for the next place to explore, the next delight to uncover. For the first time in his life, he did not feel alone.

She held both hands out to him, and he walked over to grasp them. Her black hair smelled earthy and musty. Her face was lovely, exotic and delicate at the same time.

"I've looked for so long," she said. "You are protection itself."

He didn't know what that meant. He didn't care.

"But you have to agree," she said.

"Agree?"

"If you come with me, we'll live only by night, but we'll live forever. You have to learn the laws and obey them. You won't age and you won't die, but not everyone wants this. You have to tell me that you agree, or I cannot go further."

Live only by night? Forever?

He had no idea what she was saying, but again, he didn't care. He only knew he could not live now without the perfect vision of traveling the continent with her at his side.

"I'll agree to anything you want," he whispered.

She smiled, exposing white even teeth. "I knew you would. I knew I had finally found you."

She kissed him.

He grabbed the back of her head and pressed his tongue into her mouth. She drew him to the ground by the fire, and he ran his hand down to her waist, pinning her with the weight of his chest.

"No, roll over," she murmured.

He obeyed her, and then she was sitting on top of him. She was so light he could barely feel her weight.

"My name is Jessenia," she said, "and you are my other half."

She leaned down, and he expected her to kiss him again. But she moved her mouth to his neck, and before he realized what was happening, she drove her teeth into his throat. The pain was blinding, and he bucked hard to throw her off. But she held on, gripping him and draining his blood.

His mind went blank.

Then he was lost again in the glorious images of rocky beaches with saltwater spray, new cities to explore, ancient churches, lush forests, mountains . . . and Jessenia always beside him, always smiling and laughing or lost in wonder or offering ideas for the next place to go. The pain in his throat vanished. The beating of his heart slowed and slowed. So lost in the lovely visions, he was only dimly aware of his heart. He saw himself sitting with Jessenia at a fine inn, and she offered him a goblet of red wine. He drank deeply. It was delicious.

Then he opened his eyes and found himself lying on his back with her on top, leaning over him . . . and her torn wrist was in his mouth. He was drinking her blood. He was gulping in mouthfuls.

Shock hit him like cold water.

"Don't stop," she whispered. "Not yet."

And he couldn't stop. She caressed his face and murmured in his ear. A few moments later, everything went black.

When he next woke, he could hear all the insects of the forest.

He turned his head and saw Jessenia sitting near him. She crawled closer and smiled.

"You're awake. I did not know how long you would sleep."

He felt different. The fire was long out, but he was not cold. Memories came rushing back, and he knew he should be horrified, enraged. He should want to kill her.

But he didn't.

With her face leaning close to his, he only wanted her to wash those perfect images of their journeys through his mind again.

"Can you walk?" she asked. "We should go and stay

at an inn until you've completely finished the change and you're ready to feed. But you cannot feed without me along at first, not until you've learned how."

"Feed?"

"Just come."

She drew him up to his feet, and they untied their horses, leaving the dead fire behind and the small patch of ground where Robert lost one life . . . and began another.

The first weeks of his undead existence passed quickly, but he never forgot them.

He was not a fanciful man, and he took no stock in myths and superstitions.

So this new reality—clearly no myth—was something he accepted as an event he could not change.

He might have questioned more, even regretted more, had Jessenia not been at his side, helping him every step of the way, or as much as he allowed her to help. He never realized how alone he had been before her.

She was just a slip of a girl. A gypsy sprite.

Yet she bubbled over with life to a degree that left him in awe. He would have died for her.

Not long after the night by their campfire, he began growing uncomfortable, hollow and agitated.

"We need to go out," Jessenia said.

They left their inn and walked among the people of the village. He wasn't even sure which village.

"Where are we?"

"It doesn't matter yet," she answered, looking around. She spotted a smithy with a red glow coming from somewhere inside. "This way."

When they reached the front doors, she stopped him. "Just try to watch me, but don't come all the way in until I call for you."

He frowned in confusion, but the hollow feeling inside him was growing worse, and she had always known what to do before. So from the side of the doorway, he watched her go in. She approached a young man standing by the brazier with a steel mallet in his hand.

The young man looked up in surprise, but Jessenia smiled.

"Sorry to bother you so late, but my horse has gone lame, just down the street. He's bad enough that I didn't want to try to make him walk. Could you come take a look? I can pay you."

The man laid down the mallet and took off his apron. His face was sweating. "I don't mind. I could use a rest from this anyway."

But Jessenia did not move to leave. Instead she looked around the smithy. "Are you here all day?" she asked. "Do you ever wish to go someplace else, someplace far and strange?"

Robert heard the change in her voice, and he was beginning to recognize the difference between her voice for dreams and her voice for communicating. The blacksmith's eyes glazed over almost instantly, and he sank to his knees as Jessenia continued talking, lowering her voice to a soft pitch.

"To walk along the shores of Italy, with the blue sky and blue sea . . ."

Robert was hit by a stab of jealousy so strong he almost walked in and grabbed her by the throat. What was she doing? Sporting with another man right in front of him?

"You see a ledge jutting from the rocks. You walk over and lie down beneath it, breathing the warm air. You fall asleep."

The blacksmith lay down in the straw on the floor.

Jessenia looked up. "Robert," she said softly. "Come now."

Confused, he walked in, still angry at her, but uncertain what she was doing. She knelt down on the floor.

"Like this," she said, picking up the blacksmith's wrist. Carefully, she sank her teeth into his veins. Something on the edge of Robert's awareness told him he should be shocked, but he wasn't.

Jessenia pulled her teeth out. "Come and feed. I'll keep him asleep."

He walked over and knelt on the other side of the sleeping man. Then he took the blacksmith's wrist and bit down, drinking blood as he'd once swallowed ale from a wooden mug.

"Be careful," Jessenia said. "Listen for his heart. You can't take too much."

The blood tasted sweet and salty at the same time. He could feel the life and strength growing in him. Images of the man's life passed through his mind, of work and family and spending holidays in the north. The hollow ache vanished. He gulped in more mouthfuls.

"No!" Jessenia pushed him away. "You never kill to feed. You can kill to protect us. You can even kill for money, but not to feed. Else you'll endanger all of us. Do you understand?"

He did not understand.

She placed one hand on the blacksmith's head and closed her eyes. Then she opened her eyes again, took a small knife from her boot, and turned the bite marks on the man's wrist into a straighter line.

"I've altered his memory," she said. "He won't remember me at all. When he wakes, he will remember cutting himself on that sword lying halfway off the table. Then he will remember fainting."

The sense of this was beginning to dawn on Robert, but he still didn't grasp what she meant by "altered his memories." How?

"Don't worry," she said. "You'll be doing this on your own soon. We should go." She smiled. "Tonight we set out. Where shall we go first?"

Feeling strong and filled with anticipation, he followed her.

Robert decided upon France, so he and Jessenia made their way to the coast and found passage on a ship to cross the Channel.

The ship sailed about an hour before dawn.

"Tonight, we'll go up and watch the water racing past the bow," she said.

Huddled in their cramped quarters belowdecks, Robert thrilled at even the prospect of this crossing. Jessenia made every moment enticing.

The air was still dark outside, and he felt wide awake. Somehow, she'd seemed different to him tonight. She kept studying his face almost as if she was hungry.

She came to him, sitting beside him on his bunk. "I can feel your gift," she said. "It's getting stronger."

So much she said was still a mystery.

"I love your gift," she whispered. "As you love mine."

For the first time since that night by the campfire, she reached up and kissed him. He pushed her back to lie on the bunk, and he pressed his mouth down hard over hers, running his hands down her slender waist as she moved her hands up to grip the nape of his neck.

In spite of his desire, his body did not respond in its usual way, and he ran his hand over the tops of her breasts. His need for her, his urgency grew, but his body still betrayed him.

Then . . . he felt Jessenia inside his mind, her thoughts reaching for his, entwining with his, and her sense of adventure, her joy in journeys, was suddenly part of him, drawing upon him, and as he thought of them together in strange places, a feeling of fierce protection began to build inside him. No matter where they went, no matter what they saw or what they did, he would protect her from people, from the sun, from poverty, from everything.

Her passion for adventure began to combine with his desire to protect inside of him . . . inside of her until he could no longer tell the difference. The joining and meshing of half-mad drives went on and on in waves through his body until he felt it build to an almost intolerable bubble, and then it burst and his body shuddered in a shock of intense pleasure. Jessenia was still gripping the nape of his neck, and she gasped aloud— as if she still needed to breathe.

"Robert," she was saying over and over in his ear. "I knew, I knew."

He pressed his nose against hers. He was still shaking.

He had never imagined emotions like this, drives and needs like this. She had been inside of him, and he inside of her.

What had she done to him?

Her body began to relax beneath his, and she turned her head to one side.

"I knew as soon as I saw you," she said.

Years passed.

Jessenia taught Robert to develop and focus his telepathy. He learned to seduce with his gift. He learned how to hunt safely, and he learned why this was so essential: to protect the secrecy of his own kind.

He learned the laws as Jessenia taught him.

The first law was the most important. Never kill to feed. So she'd taught him this one immediately.

The second law prohibited any of their kind from making more than one other vampire in the span of one hundred years. Apparently, the physical and mental energy it required was so great that making another one before one hundred years passed could produce weak or flawed results.

The third law prohibited any of their kind from making a vampire without the express consent of the mortal. Turning a mortal against his or her will was a sin.

Fourth, the maker was required to teach the new vampire all methods of proper survival—again to protect the secrecy of the others.

"What happens if someone breaks one of the laws?" he asked one night.

She looked surprised. "None of us would break them." She paused. "The maker takes immense responsibility in turning a mortal, so we consider our choices carefully, as they will be long-term companions. I know vampires who are natural teachers who have turned mortals out of a need for a student. I have seen some who sought a mother or a father figure."

"What did you seek?"

"I sought you." She grabbed his hand. "I looked so long for you."

It troubled him at first that she would never answer certain questions. Where had she come from? Who was her maker? He did learn that she was right around one hundred years old, but where had she been for the past hundred years, and who had she been before that?

She told him not to ask.

Over the years, he did come to understand that her love of traveling was an overwhelming drive, and yet she had learned to fear doing so alone. She told him she'd been searching for a companion who was a soldier, but not a common soldier. She sought one who saw the importance of rules and laws and order and yet at the same time was capable of feeling pity, of feeling love. Most of all, one whose gift would be seduction through the promise of protection . . . and one who would protect her.

"Connections like ours are rare," she said. "Your gift and mine create fire when we join them."

And they joined frequently. He could never get enough of the feel of her body in his hands or of tangling his gift with hers until they both shuddered with waves of pleasure and exhaustion.

"But you have no obligation to me," she said. "After training is complete, there are no laws to tie the new ones to their makers."

He grasped the back of her hair. "Why would I ever leave you?"

She smiled.

Each night was as full and interesting as the last. He found out quickly that Jessenia enjoyed the company of most mortals, and she was often involved in intrigues similar to that of the night he'd met her. He shook his head in wonder when she told him more details of how she'd seen the two assassins in a tavern, and she'd seen Lady Elizabeth's face. Afterward, she made friends with the men easily, and then bet them five sovereigns that the lady would back down.

Jessenia was a good judge of character.

She and Robert traveled through France and Italy, meeting new people and sometimes staying in villages or towns for months at a time if the place pleased them. Once, Robert even helped a local constable solve a series of murders—involving young girls. Robert followed the smell of blood to a chapel and found the body of a girl in a secret space beneath the altar. He read the mind of the priest and found a mad predator hiding behind a serene face.

The constable paid Robert well for his help. Jessenia and Robert earned some money in these intrigues, but normally they simply took it from their feeding victims— and then would leave behind memories of a robbery.

As time passed, Robert took over this element of their existence, and he always managed to keep them adequately stocked with money.

Jessenia spoke a number of languages fluently. In the early days, Robert knew only French and a bit of Spanish, but as his telepathy increased, he learned how to draw meaning from words by reading minds. Soon he spoke fluent Italian.

He did think back now and then upon Thomas Howard and Lady Elizabeth and how he had abandoned his position—abandoned the house with the gates wide open after Jessenia had put his guards to sleep.

But that seemed a different life.

"It was different," she told him. "But you are still yourself. Your years as a soldier, of serving the duke, of pitying his wife . . . these made you into who you are."

"And what made you into who you are?" he asked.

She turned away from him, something she rarely did. "I invented myself."

He did not press further.

After twenty years together, she began introducing him to other vampires, and this offered him more new experiences. He found out that she set up several message posts in every country, and she would stop occasionally to pick up letters.

As with people, he enjoyed the company of some vampires more than others. His least favorite was an elderly German scholar—turned late in life—named Adalrik. Robert found Adalrik to be decent and kind, with a solid old house outside of Hamburg. But he and Jessenia spent several months at the house one summer, and Robert had almost nothing to do for the entire visit. Jessenia could read and write several languages, including Latin, and she tended to get lost for hours in Adalrik's library. Robert could barely read English and had no interest in learning anything else. But her concern for Robert's pleasure always took precedent, and she soon assured him they would move on.

In Italy, however, over the years they stayed numerous times at a villa near Florence with a lovely woman named Cristina and her maker, Demetrio, and Robert did not grow so restless there. Demetrio was an artist from the Renaissance. He was full of good conversation, yet he always treated Robert like a social equal. Cristina was a kind hostess, and they were both clearly fond of Jessenia.

Unfortunately, after being turned, Demetrio had developed a discomfort with unfamiliar places, and he rarely left the villa except to hunt.

"It happens sometimes," Jessenia told Robert quietly. "Demetrio's maker was gentle, but he had a difficult time adjusting to the change. I've heard if the experience is traumatic, and the new vampire recovers for months in one familiar place, he or she may come to fear open spaces or places unknown."

Robert felt pity for Demetrio.

Still, the four of them drank red wine on the terrace and played at dice games and told stories to each other. Their times together were always pleasant.

But Robert's favorite visits always took place in a manor outside of Harfleur in France that belonged to a near-ancient crusader, Angelo Travare. He and Robert had a good deal in common and enjoyed each other's company. Although he, too, could be prone toward scholarly nonsense, his penchants tended to change upon whom he was with, and he played the old soldier in Robert's presence. Once Angelo decided to travel with them, and the three of them spent the better part of a year touring Spain. But Angelo was sometimes given to deep melancholy, and Robert often sensed the man was lonely—very lonely. Traveling with Robert and Jessenia did not alleviate this but rather made it worse.

"You two are good to me," he said one night. "But you only see each other. You only need each other."

Robert could not deny this, and the next night, Angelo left them to head back for France.

Three hundred years slipped by, and Robert found some pleasure, some wonder, in every single night. He and Jessenia traveled through Portugal and then Greece. They spent years in Austria and then Poland, and later found delight in Prague. They explored forests and beaches and mountains. Sometimes they found inns—or even rented rooms—for a longer stay. Sometimes they slept in abandoned hovels. Sometimes Robert camouflaged a black canvas tent in the forest, and he made them their own shelter for the day. Jessenia never questioned his decisions or his abilities, and he never once failed her.

The best thing about traveling in this slow, exploratory fashion was that after a hundred years, they simply went back to England and started all over again . . . and everything was different.

At the turn of the nineteenth century, they heard that Angelo had finally created a surrogate son for himself, a Scot named John McCrugger. Robert was glad to hear the news. Now Angelo would not be so lonely.

But he did not think long on this, as he was too lost in the bliss of his own constant companion, his lively sprite, Jessenia.

He believed their love and their journeys would go on forever.

Then, in 1820, everything began to change.

They had just crossed the border from Switzerland into northern Italy, and Jessenia stopped at one of her message outposts to see if she had any letters waiting. She did.

"Oh, look," Jessenia said with a smile. "It's from Demetrio. Let's find an inn, and I'll read you the news."

A half hour later, they were sitting at a table, making plans whether to take rooms or travel on the next night, when Jessenia opened the letter, and her expression changed. Her smile faded and her mouth began to tremble.

"What is it?" Robert asked in alarm. He had never seen her like this.

Her hand was shaking as she held on to the letter.

"Jessenia! What's wrong?"

"Angelo . . ." She was trying to speak and kept failing. Robert could not read Italian, so he waited.

"Angelo has broken the laws . . . several of them," she managed to say. "He made a second son, a Welsh noble, two years ago, and then a third one, French, only a year after. Demetrio says the Welsh one has no telepathic ability at all, and the French one is feral and cannot be trained."

Robert fell back in his chair. "That cannot be right. Is this something Demetrio heard or saw? I cannot think . . . Angelo would never . . ."

Three new vampires in the span of eighteen years?

"We have to go to Harfleur," Jessenia said. "We should leave tonight."

This was a journey without joy. Robert kept turning the possibilities over and over in his mind, but he could not think of how these last two vampires could feed without killing. Why would Angelo, the oldest among them, break laws set up for the protection of them all?

No, it had to be a mistake. Something had been mistranslated.

They arrived in Harfleur.

It was no mistake, and the scene Robert found was worse than he imagined.

He walked inside the stone manor and saw something moving stealthily up ahead. A figure emerged into the entryway, and Robert actually took a step back, holding his arm out to guard Jessenia.

The creature moving toward him barely seemed human. It was a man with long red-brown hair who might have once been handsome but who now wore the expression of a mindless animal. His feet were bare and he wore no shirt, with blood smeared across his face and chest. He snarled savagely.

"Philip! Get back!"

Angelo strode quickly up behind this creature and took his arm. The creature calmed somewhat, but Angelo did not look happy at the sight of guests.

"Robert, I was not expecting you."

Robert just stood there with no idea what to say. He couldn't believe the sight before them, and he continued holding Jessenia back.

"Forgive me," Angelo said. "This is Philip Branté.

Excuse his state of undress. He just came in and I must have his shirt laundered."

Judging by the blood smeared all over the creature's face, Robert could only imagine what his shirt must look like. And this pretense at a polite introduction was insulting.

"Send him away," Robert choked. "We would speak to you alone."

Angelo looked at him through cold eyes for a long moment and then turned to the creature. "Philip, my boy, you stay here. I need to speak with our guests."

The creature snarled again but moved to the side, half turning to expose what looked like a mass of round white burn scars across his shoulders. Robert cautiously drew Jessenia past him. They followed Angelo to the library, where Robert slammed the door.

"How could you?" Jessenia whispered. "Angelo, how could you? Demetrio says there is another one . . . who has no telepathic ability at all."

Angelo sat in a large wooden chair by a table. An open book lay upon the table near a bottle of ink and a wet quill.

"Yes," he said, "that is Julian, but I am working to help him develop his abilities. I believe it is only a matter of time. Philip improves each week. At first he could not even speak, and he now understands language quite well."

"Why?" Robert exploded, sick of this calm response from Angelo. "Why would you do this?" He paced along the length of the study. "They have to be destroyed. Both of them!"

"I will decide what is best," Angelo said slowly. "And I will take responsibility for my own actions."

Jessenia was watching him with sad eyes, and her countenance seemed to affect him much more than Robert's anger. Tonight, she wore a rich green skirt with a white blouse and silver hoops in her ears. Her beautiful face was a picture of sorrow. Robert felt sick.

Angelo walked over to her. "I wanted the company of men, as in days long past. One was not enough. I wanted sons again."

"It doesn't work that way," she whispered. "You know it doesn't. Why couldn't you have been happy with your young Scot?"

"I am happy with him. But he wasn't enough." He paused, touching her face with his slender fingers. "I will no longer follow laws I don't believe in, and I swear I will make this right. I just need time."

"How are they feeding?" Robert demanded.

Angelo did not answer.

"What are their names again?" Robert asked, "Julian and Philip? Have either of them shown any tendencies for mental power?"

"Not Julian. Not yet, but in all other respects, he is whole, and his gift is strong. I believe Philip's telepathy will surface quickly once I begin his training. But he has no memories of his previous life, and it is too soon to press him."

"Then keep him on a leash!"

"He is my son!" Angelo roared back.

"Angelo," Jessenia said, looking more composed. "If you won't train Philip now, right now, then he must be destroyed, and so must Julian if he does not develop telepathy. You know this."

"Leave me," Angelo answered. "Go back to your travels. I will deal with my own family."

There was nothing they could do. Vampires did not fight among each other.

Jessenia started for the door. "I cannot believe that you, you of all among us, chose to break the law. You endanger us all."

With nothing left to say, Robert followed her out.

Although deeply shaken, they could only hope that Angelo would adhere to his word. It was Angelo's place to destroy his sons if need be—which was already the case in Robert's opinion—so they had to believe he would do the right thing.

Needing some sort of comfort, some sense of familiarity, they decided to go back to England for a few years, and they crossed the Channel again, later taking rooms in London. Jessenia wrote to let Cristina and Adalrik know where they were staying, and yet she remained sad, a shadow of herself, for several months. Robert worried about her.

But London proved a lively place in 1821, with many sights and distractions, and soon she joined with him again in their bed, running her hands up his chest, filling his mind with the promise of tomorrow.

They heard nothing worrisome from their friends. Perhaps Angelo had lived up to his word?

Then, in 1824, Jessenia received a letter from Adalrik with news he'd only recently learned. Apparently as far back as 1816, Angelo's first son, John McCrugger, had turned his own serving man, Edward Claymore, into a vampire, and later, Philip, the feral one, had turned his mortal lover, Margaritte Latour, as well . . . long before the hundred-year mark. Law upon law was being broken due to Angelo's breach.

Robert was uncertain what to do, and Jessenia was frightened.

About a year after this, strange psychic onslaughts began to hit them without warning. Most were weak, as if coming from a great distance, but some were strong and painful. In the same moment, they would both see images and memories of other vampires, sometimes hundreds of years played out in moments. Neither of them knew what this meant.

In 1826, the last letter arrived . . . and it was from Cristina. Jessenia read it aloud, almost as if she were sleepwalking.

> Oh, Jessenia, my dear one, I think we are lost.
> Angelo is dead. His son John McCrugger is dead.
> Our sweet Adalrik is dead.
> Several others, whom you have never met, are now dead.
> I have hidden some events from you, but in recent years, many of us began to counsel Angelo to destroy Julian and Philip . . . most pointedly Julian, who shows no sign of developing his telepathy and will never be able to follow the first law. Our gentle counsel soon turned into demands and, to my shame, . . . threats of taking this matter upon ourselves. We fear Julian learned of our urgings. He must have believed Angelo would eventually relent to us.
> Julian's presence cannot be felt and he is coming from

*the darkness to take our heads. I do not know how he is
finding us with such ease and haste, nor how none of us
has managed to hold him with a telepathic defense.*

*You and Robert must find someplace to hide, some-
place you've told no one about—not too far. I will send
another letter soon. You know Demetrio will not leave
the villa, but I expect more news within a few nights.
Knowledge is safety.*

With my love, Cristina

Jessenia dropped the letter onto the floor.

"We're leaving here tonight," Robert said. "We'll
hide up north."

"No," she whispered. "I want to wait for her next
letter."

The letter never came.

A few nights later, they were hit with waves of memories from Demetrio first . . . followed shortly after by
Cristina's.

Once she had recovered from the onslaught, Jessenia
began to pack her few things. "We're going to Italy, to
the villa, to make sure they are safe."

"Italy?" Robert repeated. "No."

"You are a soldier!" she shouted. "Demetrio is an
artist! Would you not protect them?"

He grasped her hand. "I would protect you first."

"Please," she whispered. "Please, Robert. None of us
will survive by hiding. We have to fight. This Julian is
still a newborn. His luck will not hold."

They began the long journey back to Italy, to the
villa, where they found two piles of dust, just inside the
terrace.

Jessenia fell to her knees. "It is them," she said. "My maker told me that we turn to dust. They are gone."

This was the first time Jessenia had ever mentioned her maker.

"We have to go," Robert said. "We need to leave this place now." An unfamiliar and unpleasant feeling had begun crawling around inside him. He couldn't quite place it, but he believed it was fear. "Jessenia, come. There is nothing you can do."

She let him lead her through the front doors, into the dense gardens. Cristina had always liked thick, wild gardens. Jessenia stumbled out ahead of him, and he longed to comfort her, but what could he say?

His mind was churning with decisions over the best possible place to take her and hide, when she walked past a mulberry tree, and the darkness beside her seemed to move on its own. A glint arced through the air, and her head flew off her body before his eyes could absorb what was happening. Her body fell forward with a slight thud.

Before he could even scream her name, a wave of memories hit him.

It was nothing like what he had experienced back in England. He was only a few feet away from her, and he buckled from the impact, rolling on the ground. And what he saw . . . He saw her dressed as an English lady in the fifteenth century in a velvet gown and headpiece with her hair pinned beneath. He saw a vampire with a wizened face lecturing over a small pile of books, hitting her hand with a wooden pointer, and going on with the lecture. But her name was not Jessenia back then. It was Jane.

The memories went on as if Jessenia was speaking to him.

The wizened vampire had wanted a daughter with imagination, and he'd chosen her. He seduced her agreement through promises of travel and learning. But he was coldhearted and cared nothing for her well-being.

Yet only when he allowed her to begin meeting other vampires, such as Cristina and Demetrio, did she understand the loneliness of her existence. She wanted a different life.

She ran away.

She was alone and lost and frightened—even of some mortals, once she learned her gift did not work well on those with little imagination.

While traveling with a group of gypsies, she changed her way of dress, her hair, her name. She learned the power of her gift. She began looking for a companion, and she could see him in her mind. She would never break the laws or make someone too soon, but still . . . she searched.

And then she found Robert.

He saw image after image of himself, the way she saw him. She thought him handsome, with his lean face and broken nose. She loved the way his presence changed the way brutal mortals treated her. Harsh men would only need glance at Robert and then look away. None of them came near her. Robert was the real thing. A hardened soldier. He protected her, saw to her needs, loved her, and he asked almost nothing in return. All he wanted was for her to plan their next journey, their next delight, their next exploration, and to share in her enjoyment. He washed away the pain of the past and took everything upon himself. Every night, she looked at him and wondered if he was real. . . .

Robert was choking from unbearable physical and emotional pain when his vision cleared enough to see the blade arcing down at him, and on instinct he rolled to one side.

The sword sliced through the front half of his throat, sending a spray of black blood into the air. He finished his roll, bleeding onto the ground, and looked up to see a dark-haired man standing over him, raising the sword again.

Julian.

It had to be.

Robert flashed out telepathically, rage and hatred giving him strength. The sword stopped in midair as Robert held him there. He wanted this creature to suffer for hours! But the blood kept flowing into the dirt beneath him, and he was growing weaker by the second. The world grew hazy before his eyes. He couldn't get up. He couldn't fight. Soon, he was going to lose the mental connection.

Then he would die.

Had he allowed himself to think, he would have chosen death, but the survivor embedded so deeply inside him took over, and he used a simple telepathic glamour, the same kind he might use on a feeding victim, to alter what Julian saw.

Still standing above him, Julian stepped back, looking down.

Robert managed to stay inside his mind, and Julian

saw a headless body on the ground, slowly turning to dust. He looked around, seeing Jessenia's body turning to dust as well.

His work was complete.

After a few moments, he turned and walked away.

Robert lay there, bleeding into the dirt, unable to move, realizing that when the sun rose, he would burn anyway.

He didn't care.

Jessenia was dead.

Her memories tortured him. Why had she never told him of her past? He would have comforted her. He writhed in pain just thinking about the way she saw *him*. She saw herself as the taker and him as the giver, when he saw it the other way around. Why had they never spoken of such things?

He wanted the sun to rise.

Just before dawn, a gardener came up the path and gasped loudly, running to Robert's side.

"Oh," he cried, kneeling down and leaning over. "Can you move?"

Robert couldn't get up, but he could move his arms. Again, the survivor, the soldier of Norfolk, took over, pushing everything else away. Robert grabbed the gardener and jerked him down, driving his teeth into the man's throat and draining him. He drank until the man's heart stopped.

It was the only time he ever killed to feed.

The wound in his throat closed slightly, and he dragged himself into the house.

*   *   *

In the early years after Jessenia's death, Robert sometimes burned with enough hatred to attempt tracking Julian, to take revenge.

But that fire faded after a while. He was sometimes hit by the distant, much weaker onslaught of the memories of dying vampires—he now knew what they were—and in the dullness of his nightly existence, he lost interest in revenge.

It wouldn't change anything.

It wouldn't bring Jessenia back.

As a mortal, he had often been told that time heals all wounds, but this proved untrue. Each night, he woke up reaching for Jessenia, and each night, the absence of her body, her laugh, the way she always turned to lie facing him in the bed, came crashing down as he saw the empty space and felt the same agony.

It never went away. . . .

chapter 13

"No!" Robert gasped, summoning all his strength to wrench himself away.

He grabbed Eleisha's shoulder and pushed her. She struck the bathroom door and fell. Her expression was wild and confused.

He wanted to kill her.

She had invaded him and seen everything, all his private thoughts and his past. He had relived it all. He could still taste Jessenia in his mouth.

"I'm so sorry . . . ," Eleisha choked out. "Robert, I'm so sorry."

He crawled toward her, wanting to get his sword and take her head.

"If you were sorry, you wouldn't have done it!" he spat.

"Jessenia," she whispered, her eyes still lost. "I'm so sorry."

He stopped.

She covered her face with her hands. "Why did you show me all that? You said *one* memory."

"Show you? You took it!"

Then he wondered how. How could she make his life pass by to the degree of reliving it?

"No, you went all the way back. . . . Robert, you loved her so much. I wish you hadn't shown me. . . ." She faltered and lowered her hands. "Angelo caused all this. Philip doesn't even know."

Robert's rage began to fade. She was as distraught as him. Her blond hair covered part of her face, but he could still see her pained expression.

"Oh, God . . . and Philip," she went on. "That's why you didn't know him at first."

Crawling closer, Robert felt a strange release in talking of these things. He had never spoken about the past, but she knew it all anyway. Nothing would change that now.

"At first, I didn't even recognize him in the park," he whispered.

"But he looked more familiar when he walked into the kitchen with his hair a mess and his shirt off?"

"Yes, and then I saw *him* again, and it all came back. I think he remembered, too."

Her face was only a few inches from his, and he could see how rapidly her mind was working.

"The laws," she said softly. Then she pushed herself to sit up. "None of us know anything. None of us were taught anything."

"It's not your fault."

Her voice was beginning to calm, and he still

couldn't comprehend what she'd just done to him, but if she hadn't forced those memories, if she hadn't *tried* to invade his past, then she was taking in a great deal of unwanted information about a past that had spawned her existence.

"Only the first one applies," she whispered.

"What do you mean?"

"That we don't kill to feed." She huddled against the bathroom door with her arms crossed. "I can see now . . . understand everything you've been saying since you found us. I swear, Robert, that I would help you teach those laws and live by them. But I won't ever make another vampire. Neither would Philip now, and Rose wouldn't even think it. Only the first law applies, and I've taught Philip how to hunt without killing." She paused. "I haven't talked to Rose about that, taught her anything. Have you?"

"Yes, the first night I arrived."

"Then we'll be okay, Robert. . . . We will." Her face twisted in sorrow again. "I'm so sorry about Jessenia."

Her sympathy was so raw. It didn't help. Nothing would help, but she mourned for his loss as if it happened yesterday.

And yet she knew far too much about him. She even knew he'd killed the gardener to survive. He was not certain how he could come to terms with how much she knew.

"That book on Angelo's table," she said. "Philip told me that Angelo taught him about you from a book, one that Angelo had written himself, called *The Makers and Their Children*."

Robert tensed. "What?"

"Yes, he told me that Angelo believed he and Julian should know about other vampires sharing their existence."

A knock sounded on the other side of the inner door.

"Eleisha," Philip called. "The sun will be coming up. Let me in."

Philip had done exactly as Wade asked, and he left Eleisha to talk to Robert, but they'd been in the other cabin for a long time, and he didn't like it. He understood that Eleisha should be the one to tell Robert to stop ordering everyone around.

He knew the others sometimes thought he was simple, but he understood.

It's just that he'd expected a short conversation, and they'd been in there for hours. What could they possibly be saying all this time?

Finally he knocked on the door.

"Eleisha, the sun will be coming up. Let me in."

Wade had already prepared the lower bunk for Rose, and he was in the process of pulling out the top bunk for himself.

Eleisha slid the door open.

She looked different. Paler than usual. Shaken.

He didn't like this.

He stepped forward into the cabin so she'd have to move back. "The sun is coming up," he repeated.

"Okay," she answered. "We should get these bunks down." She sounded tired.

"Philip," Robert said, "Eleisha told me Angelo was

teaching you about the elders from a book he'd written."

Philip glared at him. Is that what they'd been talking of? Hadn't Eleisha already been through enough tonight seeing Rose's throat cut and Wade having to feed her? Now Robert was bringing up ugly dust from a distant past that didn't matter anymore?

"Why?" he asked, not bothering to keep the anger from his voice.

"What was in it?" Robert asked. "Were there details?"

Eleisha was looking at him, too, so Philip finally nodded. "Yes, places they lived, their makers, children, loves, hates, anything Angelo knew. But I didn't pay attention then. I was different."

"Could Julian have taken that book?" Robert asked.

"He could have taken anything. He cut off Angelo's head and told me to run. The house was empty."

Eleisha looked down at the floor, and Philip had had enough of this.

"None of that matters anymore," he said, folding the couch into a bunk. "We need to sleep."

Whatever Robert was fishing for, he must have gotten it because he stopped asking questions. But something was still different—something between him and Eleisha. Philip could feel it.

"Eleisha, I'll sleep on the floor," Robert said.

There. It was in his voice. He spoke like he knew her. He'd never done that before.

"No need," Philip answered shortly. He took his boots off and climbed into the lower bed, lying down, waiting to see what would happen. Eleisha knelt beside the bunk, looking so small and sad that he wanted to grab her, or maybe kick Robert in the face, or both.

"Can I sleep with my back to your chest today?" she asked.

And then everything was all right.

He rolled and moved over so she could press her back up against him and he could hold her with his right arm.

Robert watched this without a word. Then he pulled out the top bunk.

Normally dormant the instant the sun came up, Robert lay awake longer than usual. Maybe Philip was right.

Even if Angelo had a kept a book with details of places and habits and histories of all the vampires in existence nearly two hundred years ago, and Julian had used that book to find and destroy the ones like Demetrio and Cristina . . . did it matter anymore?

Julian might even have used such a book to lie in wait at the villa for Jessenia, believing she would come to check on her friends. This thought made his chest hurt.

But did it really matter now?

Jessenia was gone, and decade upon decade had crawled past him.

He was traveling in the company of vampires with either no training or a bizarre training from Wade that had given Eleisha abilities he'd never even heard of— and that she couldn't control. They were foreign to him, these vampires. A new breed.

But Eleisha had given him a gift he'd never expected . . . a second life with Jessenia. He could still smell Jessenia's hair, feel her soft skin on the tips of his fingers, hear her laughter. His eyes drooped from exhaustion, but he feared going to sleep in case he could not still feel her when he woke up.

With effort, he looked over the side of the bunk down at Eleisha, sleeping with her head pressed into the curve of Philip's throat below his chin.

What am I doing here?

But this small alien group stirred something inside him that he hadn't felt in a long time. He wanted to get them home safely.

That meant some part of him must still be alive.

Shortly after Eleisha woke up that night, everything seemed a little better.

They'd left the door between the cabins open, and she looked inside the second cabin to find Rose and Wade already up. Rose's throat looked about the same, but Wade was moving around more easily and seemed to have some of his strength back.

Eleisha moved in to join them while Robert and Philip were busy turning the lower bed in their cabin back into a couch and then securing the upper bunk into the wall.

"Morning," Wade joked, and she smiled at him. He was still getting used to their upside-down world. But he hadn't seen her since sending her off to speak with Robert the night before. "Everything okay?" he asked.

Everything was far from okay, but she knew what he meant. "I think so."

Rose settled onto the couch again. She somehow

looked smaller, and Eleisha realized she was wearing some of Wade's clothes, and her lovely streaked hair was tangled.

"How long now?" Rose asked.

Eleisha walked over and glanced down at Wade's watch. "In about an hour, we'll have to change trains in Eugene. But we'll make it home tonight." She crouched down. "I know it will feel strange at first, but you'll like Portland. You can even grow herbs outside in our garden."

Rose didn't respond for a few seconds. The thought of a new home must be daunting. But the church was safe and solid, and she would see that soon.

"And we'll start helping the others soon after?" she asked.

"Yes. As soon as we're settled, we can start out the same way you found Robert, researching newspapers for similar stories."

"We should just set up computer and Internet access," Wade put in. "I could research newspapers from all over the world."

"Good." Eleisha nodded. "We'll use one of the ground floor offices behind the sanctuary."

Rose was looking at them both oddly, as if they were missing something.

"What?" Wade asked.

"Well . . . we've already found one, or he found us," she said. "That vampire who attacked me was probably made in some random moment like I was. Eleisha, you said yourself he didn't seem to even know how to use his gift properly. But he could be as old as any of us, and he's struggled on his own for years without discovering enough of himself. He may need our help more than anyone."

Eleisha was struck silent. Rose wanted to help the savage vampire who'd tried to take her head off?

"What about the ghost?" Robert asked from the inner doorway.

How long had he been standing there?

"I have a ghost with me," Rose answered calmly. "And those two could have nothing at all to do with Julian. Philip once thought Seamus and I must be working for Julian, and neither of us has ever seen him."

"You didn't attack anyone," Robert said.

Eleisha was not at all sure about trying to help the vampire from the parking garage—as he seemed beyond help.

"I'm just saying that if we encounter him again," Rose said to Robert, "you and Philip should think twice before pulling your swords."

Robert raised his eyebrow.

Eleisha wasn't sure what to believe. If Rose was correct, and this stranger had just been some randomly created vampire who'd been set adrift and ended up in San Francisco and attacked them out of fear, then they were hiding and taking great precautions for no reason. That thought was comforting in a way, and if true, it meant they would arrive home tonight with no further trouble.

But Eleisha could not accept this explanation. He was at the station the same night they were trying to leave the city, and he appeared to be attempting to stop them, and the girl ghost's actions had been aimed at keeping Eleisha away from Rose. It just all seemed too . . . planned.

However, Robert's insistence that Julian was behind it all seemed equally hard to accept. She had been inside of Julian and felt his fear. She believed he would keep the oceans between them.

"Well, taking guesses isn't going to help," Wade said. "All we can do for now is get home and then make a pact that no one goes out at night for a while."

"Except for me," Philip said, looking in from the other cabin over Robert's shoulder. "I can take care of myself." He glanced at Eleisha. "But no hunting alone for you."

Eleisha ground her teeth. How had this conversation suddenly turned to her?

He seemed about to say more and then stopped when he saw her face. To his credit, he glanced away as if realizing how condescending he sounded, and her anger at him faded. He was just being overprotective, and he had a tendency to say whatever came into his head.

To make matters worse, she realized that she *didn't* want to go hunting for a while without him, and considering his more limited telepathic abilities, she didn't want him going hunting without her. She feared either one of them being without the other's protection. Did that make her a coward?

She felt him inside her mind.

Sorry.

Her eyes flew to him in surprise. Was he apologizing?

It's all right, she flashed back.

Then he pretended that nothing had happened.

"Wade, you should eat food," he said, "and we should play at cards again. You still owe me money from last night."

"That's because you cheated and tried reading my mind on the last hand. I don't owe you anything. And I think you still owe Rose forty dollars."

Had they been playing cards? That seemed a good way to pass the time. Robert stepped aside to let Philip pass into the cabin.

A few moments later, Rose, Wade, and Philip were engaged in a game of poker.

"Full house, aces high," Rose said at the end of the third hand. "You're right, Wade. This was an easy game to learn."

Philip dropped his cards in a huff, and Robert actually laughed. Eleisha had never heard him laugh before.

"I didn't know you liked games," Eleisha told Philip. "Do you know how to play chess?"

"Chess? Ugh," he answered. "Angelo tried to teach me. Boring."

"Do you own a set?" Robert asked her.

"Not anymore, but we could get one in Portland."

"I'll play it with you."

As Eleisha settled back on the couch, she almost forgot why they had run for this train in the first place. They almost seemed like friends on a holiday. Robert's promise to play chess with her brought up more unbidden fantasies of their future at the church, living together, drinking tea in the kitchen, playing board games in the sitting room . . . just like everyone else.

"Philip! Stay out of my head," Wade snapped, holding his cards closer. "You know I can feel it when you try that."

And the hour rolled by.

Wade had a decent dinner—chicken breast, rice, and salad—which an attendant brought to their cabin, and after eating, he acted as dealer for a round of blackjack. Before Eleisha knew it, they were pulling into Eugene.

"Everybody, get ready to move," Robert ordered, and for once, nobody seemed to notice or mind.

A knock sounded on the outer door.

"Porter," a man called through.

Robert slid open the door. "Yes?"

"I'm sorry, sir, but we've had an overbooking on the Express to Portland. All the cabins are filled except for one small half cabin, and I'm not certain it would accommodate your needs."

Rose looked up in alarm, and Eleisha moved quickly to the door. "I paid for two adjoining cabins on that train," she said around Robert's shoulder. "We have a traveler in our party with . . . special needs. You'll have to bump somebody else."

The porter looked at Rose settled on the couch with a blanket across her lap. He ignored Eleisha and spoke to Robert. "We still have ten minutes to departure. Would you like to come and examine the half room? Perhaps it might be suitable?"

"It's only a three-hour trip," Wade said. "But I don't want to make Rose move until we know where we're taking her. Just go and make sure we'll all fit." He looked at the porter. "If not, you'll have to make other arrangements for us."

Robert picked up his long nylon bag and slung it over his shoulder, following the porter out into the hall.

"I'm coming, too," Eleisha said. She had made certain Rose would have comfortable accommodations in a setting where everyone could stay with her. This was unacceptable.

She glanced over to Philip. "We'll be right back."

He nodded, and she knew he'd keep watch over Rose and Wade.

After sliding the door closed, she followed Robert and the porter only a few cars down, and then the porter led them down a set of metal stairs outside.

That was the first action she found out-of-place. She'd expected him to lead them into the station where they could board the Express from a well-lit, cavernous area and take a quick look at the cabin.

But they were outside in the night, gazing across multiple sets of tracks.

"That one," the porter said, pointing to the left up ahead.

He led them along their own train, and Eleisha suddenly didn't care for all the shadows and black spaces in between the cars. Was it common for Amtrak personnel to escort passengers right along the tracks like this? The situation felt wrong. She took her first close look at the porter. He was thirty years old, average in weight and height, wearing a wedding ring and no coat. The night air was cool . . . and he was sweating.

They were almost to the front of the train they'd come in on. The Express to Portland was one track over, just up ahead.

She reached out and tried to pick up any surface thoughts coming off the porter, and she almost tripped upon feeling the waves of fear inside him.

At least I can make the house payment. Laura won't even know I lost the money. I couldn't just pass up two grand.

Someone had paid him two thousand dollars? For what?

They were passing the front of their own train.

The night air by the first car seemed to move, and she saw the glint.

"Robert!" she called in warning.

He was directly ahead of her, and she shoved him. The blade slashed down, catching the back of her hand and the top of Robert's shoulder in the same swing. He cried out as he fell sideways. Eleisha fell to the ground on the momentum of her push.

She rolled, looking up in disbelief and shock to see Julian standing over her in a long black coat with a sword in his hand.

A wall of fear hit her with full force.

Wade looked down at his watch and shifted uncomfortably.

"They've been gone almost ten minutes" he said. "We're going to miss the Express." Where were they?

Philip lifted the sliding shutter over the window and peered out. "Something's wrong."

"Maybe she's still arguing with the porter," Rose said. "She looked so angry about that mix-up."

Philip looked back at Wade. "Maybe we should just go?"

"No," Wade said, opening his bag, strapping on his

gun, and pulling on his jacket. "You stay with Rose. I'll just take a look. They must be on their way back. It's better if we can make the switch all together."

He slipped out into the hallway, closed the door, and made his way down the train. A few cars down, he came to an empty car with an open doorway.

Moving to the steps, he peered outside. Looking to the right, toward the end of the train, he was surprised to see how far the cars reached behind him, all the way into the large train station, which appeared to be a good four-minute walk away. He couldn't even see the end cars. Would Eleisha have gone that far? He didn't think so. Tracks stretched in both directions. He wasn't sure where to look.

His growing discomfort turned to anxiety.

Where had the porter taken Eleisha and Robert?

Jasper walked into a bathroom stall of the men's room inside the train station. He wasn't crazy about the trench coat, but he liked the new sword hidden beneath. It was a lot lighter than Julian's.

He only waited a few seconds, and then Mary appeared.

He was relieved to see her.

"Julian says only two of them came out," she said, tilting her magenta-tinted head, "but one is that Robert guy he's after, and the other one's Eleisha, so it's okay. He's waiting up ahead now—found a good hiding spot. The other three are still on the train from San Francisco, and it's about to pull out, so they're going to get stuck if they're too scared to get off by themselves. He says you should get on and look for a chance to kill one or two of them alone if you can break 'em up. He said that train is heading east toward someplace called Bend. They'll panic when they figure out Eleisha and Robert aren't coming back to get them . . . and that they're going the wrong way."

Jasper blinked a few times.

Julian wanted him to get on the train and start hunting on his own?

He thought about this. He knew he'd screwed up badly back at the station, and he was still pretty shaken by Julian's reaction, but the payoff was worth it. He just had to prove himself.

"Which train?"

They all looked the same, and the station reader board was confusing.

"When you go out of the men's room, just turn left. You'll step right on."

"I don't have a ticket."

"It's all right. You just have to hide someplace and avoid the ticket collectors."

The thought was kind of exciting. "Okay."

"I'm going to check in with Julian, and then I'll come find you again."

He nodded, slipped out of the men's room, turned left, and got on the train. Once again, he was starting to feel like someone right out of a movie. It was his first time on a train.

Pretty cool.

Eleisha fought the overwhelming fear, knowing she could resist it as she had once before.

She had to press her thoughts into his, get control of

him, but the waves kept coming until she felt sick, and she couldn't focus.

Almost the instant Julian completed his first swing, he swung upward again and took off the porter's head. The sight of the body falling and blood spurting from the stump shocked her. Too many events were occurring at once. Robert was trying to crawl up and unzip his bag, but his shoulder was bleeding and his expression was locked in fear—and he'd never felt Julian's gift like this before.

Julian raised the sword and was about to rush toward Robert again, when Eleisha gathered any scraps of control she had and used her mind to push into his thoughts with a single word.

Stop!

He sidestepped in shock, and his dark eyes widened. Instead of swinging the sword, he kicked her, and she rolled. Dust flooded her mouth and she tried to push up to all fours. The pain in her side made her cry out at once.

Then Julian was gone, and Robert was on his feet with a long polished sword in his right hand.

He didn't even look back at Eleisha before he bolted forward. Was he trying to run down Julian?

"Robert!"

She struggled up to her feet and stumbled after him, but he didn't go far.

"Which way?" he shouted. "Which way did he run?"

She hadn't seen Julian vanish, and she reached out with her thoughts, trying to pick up anything. "I don't know!"

"Get over here! Stay away from the front of that train."

Confused for a second, she saw all the nooks and shadows around the front cars—with no overhead lighting.

She ran to him, half limping, worried Julian might have broken her ribs. Robert's head was moving back and forth. They were now closer to the passenger cars near the end of the Portland Express. He looked at one open door with a floodlight above. The train was about to pull out.

"There," he barked.

"What? No, the others are still on the first train! We can't just leave them."

"Eleisha, I can't sense him. I don't know where he is. We have to stay in the light!" He glanced back once more down into the shadows where Julian had been hiding. Then, without warning, he bent down rapidly, reached around the back of her thighs, picked her up, and ran for the open door of the Portland Express.

"No!"

She fought him but couldn't even make him slow down. In desperation, she reached out with her thoughts, trying to make a connection to Wade.

Stay where you are! Julian is outside! We're on the other train. Wade! There's nothing I can do. Stay out of the shadows. Find a way to meet us back at the church.

Robert jumped through the open door a half second before it slammed shut behind them, and the Portland Express began moving north.

*   *   *

Wade stepped outside for a better look to the left, up toward the front of the train, and thought he saw something. . . . A glint reflected by an overhead light? Then he heard shouting, and his heart skipped a beat.

He pulled his gun immediately, but he wasn't sure whether to run toward the shouting or not.

Then his knees nearly buckled when a telepathic shout hit him, exploding in his mind.

Stay where you are! Julian is outside! We're on the other train. Wade! There's nothing I can do. Stay out of the shadows. Find a way to meet us back at the church.

"Eleisha!" he yelled, watching the Portland Express begin to move.

He tried for a mental connection, but he couldn't reach her.

Turning, he quickly climbed back aboard the train from San Francisco. He had to get to Philip and Rose, to tell them, to warn them.

Julian was outside.

He could say this to them without flinching . . . but how, how was he ever going to tell Philip that they had just lost Eleisha?

chapter 14

Eleisha heard the door *whoosh* shut.

Robert put his back to the wall inside the stairwell of the train and slowly let her slip down until her feet touched the floor, but he still kept his arm tightly around her. She could feel his body shaking. The reality of what had just happened was sinking in.

Julian hadn't stayed away. He had come from the darkness swinging a sword.

She'd been wrong all along.

And now her friends would suffer.

She choked at the thought of Wade and Rose being left behind, but one face surfaced in her mind, causing more pain than she could believe.

Philip would be blind with panic.

Robert's left shoulder was bleeding and so was her right hand, but she made a fist and pounded it against him several times.

He held onto her and let her hit him.

"Philip is so afraid of being alone!" She wanted to sob. "Do you know what this is going to do to him?"

"I did it for him!" he hissed in her ear. "How do you think he'd feel tomorrow if I let Julian take your head? How do you think he'd feel the night after? And the night after that? We have to survive by moving between one moment and the next. Do you understand?"

She stopped hitting him and just stood there, letting him grip her too hard.

"They're all alone now," she whispered. "They can't fight Julian. I don't think Wade would know what to do."

"He won't follow them. He'll come after me first."

He released his arm slightly, and she moved back to look up at him. He wouldn't look down at her, and his face was taut.

"You don't know that!" she hissed quietly. "If he thinks Rose or Philip have turned telepathic, he could just as easily go after them."

"It isn't just telepathy," he whispered back. "That's what Philip thinks because it's all Julian told him . . . all Angelo told him."

Eleisha tensed and let his words sink in. No, it wasn't just telepathy. She had seen that in Robert's memories. Julian feared a resurgence of the laws. He feared vampires making connections with each other again, teaching the laws, practicing telepathy, and learning to feed without killing.

He would come after Robert.

"Where do we go now?" she asked.

When he didn't answer, she fished their tickets from the pocket of her jeans, looking at the cabin numbers she had reserved.

"That porter was bribed to lie to us," she said. "I think if we go to these cabins, we'll find them empty."

He nodded once, but he still didn't look at her.

Julian pushed the Mustang's speed past eighty. Glancing at the wheel, he saw his left hand trembling and he fought to control it.

He had *missed* his swing.

The setup was flawless, Robert had walked right past him, and he'd missed.

In all his years hunting, he'd never missed his first swing, not once. What was wrong with him? What happened?

Was Eleisha able to sense him? Feel him as the others couldn't? No, if that was true, she could have zeroed in on him afterward.

But she'd been inside his head during the fight! Just for a split second before he kicked her. He could not risk that again, and he could not—would not—kill her yet.

What was he going to do?

Robert knew he was there, knew he was hunting again.

Julian forced himself to calm, thinking back over the few seconds just before chaos erupted in the train yard. He'd timed it perfectly, and the porter was bringing Robert directly past him. Robert was out in front of Eleisha. . . . Julian had waited, as always, until the right second . . . and then Eleisha called a warning and pushed Robert.

Had she seen a light reflect off the sword?

In the past, rumors of the way he hunted eventually spread to a point, but the vampires of the distant past were fairly scattered, mainly communicating through letters to anyone besides a direct child—or the child to the maker. Most had no idea how he was locating them or taking their heads.

Robert knew.

This thought made him wonder how Robert had escaped him back in the past, as he clearly remembered cutting off Robert's head . . . but then he remembered that he'd killed Jessenia first. Afterward, he'd taken his swing at Robert, seen the dark blood spraying out, and the world had grown slightly hazy. Had Robert made him see something which wasn't there?

If so, that would not happen again. He had to kill Robert on a first swing.

Only now Robert and Eleisha would be looking into the shadows.

Julian glanced down at the Amtrak schedule on the seat beside him, trying to decide what they would try next. They were on an express train with only one brief stop in Salem—but the end stop was Portland, so Robert would reason that Julian believed they were running to Portland, and his built-in protective instincts would never allow him to lead an enemy from the final train station straight to the church.

They didn't even realize Julian knew about the church.

No, Robert would want to get off in Salem and rent or steal a car for that last hour home, trying to throw Julian off the trail.

Or at least Julian fervently hoped he would.

But no matter what happened, Julian had to finish this before they got home. He had to make Eleisha believe the church was safe. He could not attack anywhere near that place or she might not continue trying to seek out the others in hiding and bring them in.

With the remnants of a plan forming, he felt slightly better—nearly certain that Robert would take Eleisha off the train in Salem.

He just had to get there first, and he had to know the layout before he arrived.

"Mary Jordane," he called.

She materialized on the passenger seat beside him, looking around in some confusion at the inside of the car.

"Where have you . . . ?" she asked. "Did you mess up?"

He bit down on the inside of his cheek to keep from snarling at her.

"I think Jasper's all set," she said. "He's on the train with the other three."

"What?"

He'd forgotten about Jasper. At this point, Philip, Wade, and Rose were not his main concern—as Rose appeared to be nearly helpless, Philip didn't know anything of the laws, and Wade was a mortal.

But Robert was dangerous. He had to die.

"Look down at this map," Julian said, ignoring the fact that she'd spoken. "Go ahead to the Salem train station and find the nearest car rental lot. Then examine all possible routes to the lot from the station's main or back doors and return to me."

"What, you're going to try the same thing again? They don't exactly strike me as stupid."

He didn't answer her, but he did agree. If Eleisha and Robert were looking for him in the shadows of doorways or alleys, he'd have to try something else.

Wade could see Philip hanging halfway out the cabin door up ahead, and his stomach lurched.

Their train was slowly starting to move.

"Where is she?" Philip demanded. "We have to go now! Where do we go?"

Wade struggled for what to say and then just blurted out, "She's already on the other train, and it pulled out a few minutes ago. I think Julian attacked them in the yard and they had to run."

He waited for the words to sink in, and then Philip did exactly as he expected—pushed him aside and ran down the hall.

Wade could not stop him physically, but he fired out telepathically.

Stop! Eleisha's gone, and you can't leave Rose.

Philip stumbled and halted, turning around, his face a mask of hate. Wade knew it wasn't aimed at him, but he didn't move any closer.

"How?" Philip spat. "How do you know any of this? Did you see it? If you did, why didn't you bring her back?"

"I didn't see anything!" The accusation made him angry. Could Philip ever give one thought to what somebody else might be feeling? "She shot me a few warnings . . . like she was screaming in my head. She told us to stay here, that Julian was in the yard, that she was on the other train, and we should all meet at the church. That's all I know, Philip, and you have to keep it together!"

The rage on Philip's face only increased. He strode back, shoved Wade inside the cabin, and started giving orders.

"Get up, Rose," he barked, which sounded strange in his French accent. He fastened the machete's sheath onto his belt and put on his coat, buttoning it. "Wade, is your gun loaded?"

"What are you doing?" Wade asked in alarm, standing in front of the door. Rose looked frightened already, but she was on her feet.

"We're going to jump," Philip answered flatly. "We'll steal the first car we find, and I'll get us to the Portland train station."

"Jump? What if he's still in the yard?"

"He's after Robert!" Philip shouted. "He wants Robert's head, and Eleisha will try to stop him! We have to get to the Portland station before the train arrives. Julian will find a way to get there, and we have to be there first." His voice was calmer now, and he looked at Rose. "Can you jump?"

The train was just beginning to pick up speed.

Rose wavered, but then said, "Yes, I can jump. It's my fault we took this train in the first place, and I don't want Eleisha and Robert left alone either."

Philip's anger melted into relief; he held out one hand. "Good. Come."

She came to him.

He led her forward, but then he stopped before the doorway, looking Wade in the face. "I am going to drive very fast," he said in short, clipped words. "If a police-man tries to stop us, we cannot be caught up in a chase, so I will pull over and kill him as he reaches our window. I am telling you this so that you know."

Wade swallowed and didn't know how to answer. Philip certainly wasn't asking permission.

"There's a door to the outside just down here," Wade said, stepping back out of their way and pointing, a little concerned about jumping off a moving train.

Philip and Rose walked out past him, and he followed them down the hallway.

Jasper made his way through the train, trying to think of what he should do. He couldn't exactly knock on the door. He wasn't even sure which cabins they were in.

Where was Mary?

If she was here, she might have been able to tell him. She might also be able to scare one of them into the hallway, but she'd vanished in the men's room of the station and he hadn't seen her since.

He thought hard. Could he pull the fire alarm?

Did trains have fire alarms?

No, that wouldn't work. If he did that, everyone else would come rushing out, too, and then he wouldn't be able to do anything.

How had Julian done this without being seen until the last second?

Well, first things first. Mary *had* told him earlier they were in adjoining cabins toward the front of the train. He'd just have to pick a good spot in the area and wait. Moving quickly, he passed people sitting in basic seats for about six cars.

He opened a door and stepped into an empty car with a door to the outside. Just as he stepped in, the inner door opposite from him opened, and to his shock, Philip walked through . . . wearing a long black coat.

Wade and Rose were right behind.

They all stared at each other.

"That's him," Rose said.

Philip's lips curled back over his teeth, and he charged.

Without even thinking, Jasper turned and ran.

Eleisha was sitting on the floor in their adjoining cabins with her arms wrapped around her knees. She couldn't stop thinking about Philip.

Robert was pacing, but since the cabin was seven feet across, he could take only a few steps before turning around.

"You promised you'd stop making decisions for us," she said.

"I never promised you anything."

When she half turned to look at him, a stab of pain flashed through her side, and she winced. He came over and crouched down beside her.

"Did he break you?"

"I don't know," she answered.

"Let me see it."

He reached out to pull up the side of her sweater—Philip's sweater—and she didn't try to stop him.

A purple-black bruise covered her ribs, and he touched them cautiously. "I don't think they're broken, but you'll need to feed soon."

Suddenly, she wasn't angry at him anymore.

"I really thought he would leave us alone," she whispered. "What are we going to do now?"

His face was so close she could see the shadow of light brown stubble on his jaw. She'd never noticed it before.

"We have to kill him," he said.

She sat up straighter. "What?"

"He won't stop, Eleisha. Now that you've been with me, he'll see you as contaminated." He hesitated and asked, "How did you run him off . . . before?"

She'd never talked about this, not really, but the words started flowing. "I got inside his head, and he couldn't push me out. I took control of his body. I showed him ugly images, anything I could think of: the vampires he'd murdered hunting him down, nailing him to a cross, Angelo lighting it on fire . . . anything. He was writhing, and he couldn't keep me out, and I told him if he ever came near me again, I'd lock him in a nightmare forever. He was so scared. Then Philip grabbed him and kicked him out a window. That was the last time we saw him . . . until tonight."

She'd never seen open shock on Robert's face before.

"*You* came up with all that? You? How could you have known what Angelo even looked like?"

"Philip showed me in a memory, like what I did with you. I saw Angelo die. It was awful."

Robert looked away. Was all this too much for him? He liked his battle tactics cut and dried. Maybe he'd never used his telepathy as a weapon.

She didn't have much else to use.

"All right," he said after a while. "He'll expect us to get off in Salem."

"Why would he expect that?"

"Because he knows I'd never lead him from an end point—and the train ends in Portland." Still crouched, he rocked on the balls of his feet. "We'll head for a rental car lot outside in the dark, taking the shortest route. He'll step out of nowhere and swing at some point. If I can make sure he misses, can you get inside his head before he turns on the fear?"

She couldn't believe what he was suggesting. "Bait? You're going to use yourself as bait? What if he doesn't miss, Robert? You'll be dead, and I'll be rolling around on the ground when your energy breaks, and then I'll be dead a second later!"

"What do you want to do? Go back to the church and lead him right to Wade and Rose?"

She stared at him.

"I won't let my guard down, and I'll make sure he misses," Robert said softly. "You get a hold of him, hit him with anything you can until he freezes, and I'll take his head. We won't be free until he's gone."

"What if he's not waiting for us?" she asked. "What if he doesn't attack yet?"

"I don't know. But I do know we can't lead him to your church, and I can't do this by myself."

She ran his scenario over and over in her mind, seeing various outcomes, and she was frightened. What if she failed? What if she couldn't make Julian freeze again? She didn't want to get Robert killed, and what would Philip do if she didn't come home?

But in the end, what choice did they have?

"We'll get off in Salem," she said. "But if he's there waiting, you better make sure he misses."

"Good." He leaned back against the couch, and he seemed to relax now that they'd come to a decision. His shoulder had stopped bleeding, but his coat was torn and stained.

"Let me try to wash that out," she said, climbing to her feet, "or people will look at you when we get off."

He nodded, slipped out of his coat, and handed it to her. Beneath, his shirt looked worse, but they could cover it once the coat was clean.

"We'll get you some new clothes in Portland," she said, determined to speak of the future as if it would happen.

He opened his mouth and closed it again. She wondered what he was worried about now.

"What?" she asked, turning on the faucet.

"You've said a few times that you're going to buy this church. How are you going to pay for it?"

"With money."

He frowned at her. "You know what I mean. Where are you getting the money? You and Philip both seem to have an endless supply. That coat he's wearing must have cost two thousand dollars."

"At least." Embarrassed, she focused on washing out the bloodstains. "I don't know where Philip gets his money."

Come to think of it, that was a good question. He must have inherited his family's wealth, but he had always made fun of her stockbroker, and she'd never seen him contact a bank.

The irony of her own wealth brought more discomfort, considering what she and Robert were about to do. "Julian always . . . He sent money so I could take care of William . . . a lot of money. We lived with Edward Claymore in New York for years, and back then he handled everything for me. But I wanted control of my own affairs, so I took William, and we moved to Portland. I started investing around 1954, and later, I just learned what to look for, and I made some lucky choices at a ground floor buy-in . . . Coca-Cola, Apple, Microsoft, Starbucks, Exxon."

She paused her scrubbing and glanced at him. He still looked troubled, but he also seemed interested in what she was saying.

"I don't have any money," he said. "I've been living night to night for a long time, just taking a few dollars from people I fed on, and I used almost everything I had left to buy my plane ticket from Russia."

"Why were you living in Russia?"

He shrugged. "It was just a place. I didn't care where I lived . . . but Jessenia and I never traveled there, and I couldn't stay anyplace where we'd been." He paused. "But I always pay my own way, so I'll start contributing as soon as I can pick up a few jobs. I just haven't cared enough to work for a while."

"Jobs?"

He'd been working? Doing what?

"I ran a small business in Moscow for a while where I found lost objects, stolen objects, for people," he explained. "More than half the time, one of their friends or relatives took it, and I just had to read the right mind."

He'd used his telepathy to earn a living? That was clever. She'd never thought of doing anything like that—but then she'd never had to.

His coat looked better. She wrung it out and laid it over a chair. "I've never used my telepathy for much of anything besides feeding or defending myself or reading memories."

At her last two words, he tensed up and then pointed at the floor right in front of where he was sitting.

She joined him, cross-legged, puzzled again. He was changing topics too fast tonight.

"How did you do that?" he asked. "Make me see and feel everything like it was happening?"

"I don't know. Wade taught me to guide the stream, but I can't control where someone chooses to start— like with you. I didn't mean to make you go through all that. I'm sorry."

"Don't be. That isn't what I meant."

He stopped talking, and she had no idea what he wanted, but she could see by the desperate look on his face that he wanted something, and he wanted it so badly he feared asking her.

"What is it?" she asked.

"We still have enough time before Salem," he said quietly. "Can you do it again?"

He wanted to be with Jessenia. He was addicted to someone long gone. If Eleisha did this for him once, would he ask her again . . . and again?

And could she ever say no?

She reached out and grasped his pointer finger to help make the connection stronger.

"Close your eyes and go back. Start wherever you want."

He turned his hand over and gripped down hard on her fingers. It hurt a little, but not much.

"Just think back," she whispered.

chapter 15

As Philip bolted across the empty car after the strange vampire, Wade was once again hit by a sudden telepathic shout.

Stay with Rose!

Philip's voice inside his head felt sharper than Eleisha's, but he was standing in the doorway, so he didn't buckle or stumble.

"Don't kill him!" Rose called after Philip. She looked outside as the train picked up more speed. "Those cars behind us are filled with people," she said more quietly.

Wade stood frozen, trying to take everything in. Philip's brilliant plan to jump off the train—which Wade had never been too sure about in the first place—was rapidly becoming impossible, and just like Philip, he was frightened at the thought of Eleisha getting between Robert and Julian.

Now Philip had gone running off after a vampire in a trench coat, and he was left here with no idea what to do. "Maybe we should go back to our cabin. At least we'll be hidden there."

Rose looked around the empty car with the short stairwell and the door leading outside. Her voice was calm. "No, Philip will come back here no matter what happens. You open the outer door, and we'll wait."

"You're not still planning on jumping?" he asked incredulously. "I think that ship has sailed, Rose. We're going too fast."

"Not quite yet."

For somebody pathologically afraid of sitting in an airplane with a hundred people around, she showed no fear of hitting the ground at forty miles an hour. But her words about Philip coming back to this car made sense. Just what did he plan to do anyway? Pull a machete and take that vampire's head off right in front of the passengers? Why did Philip always have to act first and think later?

"He had to go," Rose said, as if reading his mind—but he didn't feel her. Maybe she was reading his face. "He'd never jump with that vampire right behind us, so he had to at least chase him off. I'm just afraid Philip will catch him . . . and I hope he tries talking first."

"Talking?" Wade asked. "That *thing* tried to cut your head off, and now he's hunting us on a train!"

"We don't know what he's after."

Wade sighed and looked around. Pulling his gun, he motioned to the back of the empty car. "Okay, I'll get the door open, and you wait over there. But if Philip's not back in the next thirty seconds, we're going to need a new plan."

Although he didn't want to shatter Rose's hopes, he somehow doubted Philip would try talking first—and for once, he completely agreed with Philip.

But whatever Philip was going to do . . . he'd better do it fast.

Nothing that had occurred in the last few moments changed the fact that Robert and Eleisha were still alone with Julian coming after them.

Jasper jogged as quickly as he could down the aisles without breaking into a full run, just trying to look like a guy in a hurry. There were too many passengers sitting around.

But he was scared.

It never occurred to him that he might just *walk* into his targets like that—and now Philip was coming after him. He tried to remember everything Julian had told him about Philip.

Savage but not intelligent. He may have developed telepathy by now, but even so, I don't think he'd know how to sense for another of our kind in that way.

Could that be true? Jasper hoped so. Glancing back, he saw Philip closing on him, and he broke into a run without caring what the passengers thought.

Where was Mary? Couldn't she try to blink in and scare Philip for a moment? Just to clear a few seconds of time?

Jasper remembered he'd passed the dining car on the way in, and he ran toward it, passing though doorways and trying to get out of Philip's sight line for just an instant. He could run pretty fast as a mortal, and now his speed made the aisle seats blur past.

As he neared the kitchens, he dashed into a large storage area, hoping Philip hadn't seen him, and ran for an industrial walk-in refrigerator. Once inside, he pulled the door closed and then crouched, using the newfound strength in his legs to jump to the highest shelf, where he crawled behind several large boxes of unsalted butter.

He waited, forcing his mind to be still, not allowing any of his gift to seep out, just playing dead behind the butter.

Nothing happened for a few moments, and he started to think maybe Philip had kept running all the way to the dining car—bypassing the storage room.

Then he heard the sound of the fridge door being jerked open, and he lay completely still. Hidden like this, he couldn't see anything, but Philip wouldn't see him either.

He heard footsteps and a crashing sound as something was knocked over.

"Where are you?" a low voice with a French accent called out.

Jasper fought down the panic, and he lay completely still.

The footsteps echoed away from the fridge and back into the storage room, moving farther away. He only waited a little while and then jumped down quietly, seeing the fridge door open. Philip was gone, and Jasper slipped over to the door, peering out.

He could see Philip down the hall, heading toward the back of the train, into the dining car.

And then Jasper realized he'd done exactly what he was supposed to. Philip was off in one direction, and Wade—a mortal—and Rose—who seemed incapable of defending herself—were alone in a car with a doorway to the outside of the train.

Well . . . awesome.

If he could take out at least two of them, he'd have a success here, and he saw all the things awaiting him: cars, clothes, hotel suites, feeding on girls who'd never have looked twice at him before.

He wasn't going to fail Julian again, and he headed back toward Rose and Wade.

Wade got the outer door open, and he stood on the steel steps, watching the world blur past for a few moments.

"This isn't going to work, Rose," he said. "Even if I could survive the jump, we're too far from Eugene, and all I can see is a line of trees. I don't think Philip's going to find a car out here. We'll have to wait for the next stop and see where we are."

"Do you know the next stop?" she asked.

"No, I'm not even sure where this train is headed now. I think Eleisha said it would turn east."

Rose was standing near the back of the car, and he was just starting to climb up the metal stairs when her expression shifted to fear as she looked to the right, toward the door Philip had run through. Wade couldn't see it from his position, but he raised the gun.

"Wade!" she called out.

He heard the upper door being opened, and he tried to jump up the last three steps, holding out his Beretta.

Something arced down out of the air, and the tip of a blade sliced the back of his hand. He cried out and dropped the gun.

The trench-coated vampire kicked it away, and Wade dodged to one side as the sword came back, crashing into the stairwell's corner.

"Stop it," Rose called out. Her voice was smooth and clear. "That will not serve you, and you can come with us. You'll have a home with us."

Even Wade saw the wisdom of what she suggested. To stop fighting. To go home.

The vampire held his sword in midair. He looked younger than Wade first realized. His blade was slender, more a saber than a sword—but the edge was sharp.

"It's all right," Rose said, taking a step toward him. "Put down the sword and come with us."

The vampire's face wavered, and then somehow he seemed to throw off Rose's aura of wisdom, and in one split second, he snarled, pulling his blade back, about to rush her.

The air shimmered, and Seamus appeared directly in front of Rose. He swung with his fist as if aiming a hard blow.

The transparent fist passed through the vampire, but he still flinched and ducked, as anyone would, and Wade used the only weapon he had left.... Forming an image of Philip running toward them down the aisles, he drove this picture directly into the vampire's mind.

He's coming now, Wade projected. *It's safe outside in the dark. Jump. Jump out the door and you'll be safe. Or he'll take your head and turn you to dust.*

The vampire's eyes widened in terror, and he looked down the stairwell to the open door and the world rushing past.

Hurry! He's coming. He's almost here! He'll take your head. You have to jump.

The vampire moved past Wade, to the top of the stairs, lost in the vision Wade kept pressing on him.

And then to Wade's despair, he felt something pushing back, and he heard hazy thoughts.

No . . . no, he can't be there yet.

This creature was pushing him out, fighting his suggestions.

Yes! Wade projected. *He's almost to the door.*

The vampire's expression altered, and fear turned to rage. He half turned, raising the sword, snarling and aiming at Wade.

An explosion sounded, echoing off the metal walls.

Black blood sprayed from the vampire's chest, and he stumbled down three steps, choking in shock. Another explosion rocked the car, and blood sprayed from his forehead as he fell back through the outer door and vanished from sight.

Wade rushed down the steps and hung out the doorway. He could still see the body lying on the ground, growing smaller and smaller until the train passed him.

The vampire never even moved.

Panting from what felt like emotional exhaustion, Wade looked up into the car. Rose was standing in the middle, holding his gun with both hands. Seamus was still beside her.

"Philip should be back soon," she said calmly. "We'll get off at the next stop."

Still looking at his gun, Wade had no response.

Maybe Rose's wisdom could adapt to any situation.

Julian walked the dark street outside the Salem Amtrak station. The express train was due any moment. He was worried Eleisha might talk Robert into waiting inside the station and calling for a taxi.

But he was also counting on Robert's instinct for complete independence in a dangerous situation. Angelo had known Robert very well—and now so did Julian.

He was walking the shortest route to a Hertz rental car office, and down a side street, he spotted a deep black doorway with a balcony up above it, creating darker shadows.

"How do you know they'll get off?" Mary asked, floating beside him. She was fidgeting, as if anxious about something.

He was too distracted to even find her annoying. "He is a soldier, from a long line of soldiers. He'll get off."

She shrugged, looking down the street. "Shouldn't I get back to Jasper? He's all alone, and that Philip guy seems pretty mean."

"Hmm?" Julian turned from the doorway. "No, leave him. I need you here." He paused, running possibilities through his mind. "All right, this is what we're going to do."

Mary tilted her head, but thankfully, she just listened.

Coming out of Robert's memories for a second time was even harder, and Eleisha had more trouble separating her emotions from his.

She could still taste Jessenia in her mouth.

Somehow, she managed to pull out right after Jessenia's death—before Robert drained the gardener. She would have stopped sooner, but he had such a tight hold.

Once she was able to separate her thoughts and drives from his, she found him leaning forward on the floor, holding himself up by his forearms.

Maybe she should have refused to do this for him? He'd just wanted it so much.

He touched his head to the floor.

"Rob . . . ert," she tried to say, her own voice sounding foreign. "Get up."

He raised his head.

"The train is pulling into Salem," she told him. "We have to get ready."

Without a word, he climbed to his feet. They didn't speak for a little while. What else could they possibly say after reliving all that again?

Eleisha got his coat and buttoned it over his bloody shirt. The coat's shoulder was still ripped, but it looked better.

The cut on her hand had almost closed, and she washed off the dried blood. Her side still hurt.

The tense, angry look he so often wore began returning to his face, and he picked up the long shoulder bag with his sword. Good. Maybe watching Jessenia die again might actually help. As long as he didn't get careless.

"You make sure he misses," she said. The train slowed to a stop. As they moved out into the hall, she said, "What makes you so certain he'll be here?"

"He'll be here. This is how he hunts."

They moved down the hall and through the long aisles to an exit, stepping off into the loud train station. People hurried all around them, and no one even glanced their way.

"Excuse me," Robert said to a young baggage attendant pulling a cart. "Where is the nearest rental car office?"

"There's a Hertz about three blocks away," the attendant answered. "I think it's open until one a.m. Just go out the main doors, turn left, walk two streets down, and then take another left on Baker."

"Thank you."

They walked away, looking around.

"Over there," Robert said, pointing to large glass doors across the station floor.

She followed him outside into the darkness, and he turned left. But now anxiety was beginning to build inside her. If Robert was correct—and he probably was—Julian could be anywhere. The thought made her sick, and she hadn't expected that, or at least not to this degree.

"Wait," she said.

He turned around.

"Give me a second."

His brow wrinkled when he saw her face. "Can you do this?"

She looked down the dark street, and all she could see were shadowy awnings and blackened doorways and the entrances to alleys. But she'd seen the sword coming back in the train yard, and she hadn't been expecting it. Now both she and Robert would be watching.

"Yes," she answered. "Just don't walk so fast."

"Stay right behind me. You know what to do." But he didn't move away yet, hesitating, and then he said, "No matter what happens, I'm glad you and Rose started all this. I'm glad she found me. I'm glad I came." His voice held no inflexion or emotion, but she believed him.

"Let's get this done," she said. "We'll be home tonight."

They were far enough from the station crowds now that he unzipped his bag and took out his sword, gripping the hilt.

The sight of it gave her a jolt. Although she never would have admitted it to anyone, even Wade, she was experiencing an unfamiliar scratching at the back of her mind every time she pictured herself helping Robert to kill Julian—as if some part of her rebelled against destroying her own maker.

But she wouldn't let this stop her.

Julian had killed his maker. So could she.

They walked two blocks down, keeping an eye on all the doorways, and turned on Baker Street, which was dark and empty at this hour.

Robert paused only briefly before beginning this final stretch.

Up ahead, she saw a deep blackened doorway with a balcony above it, and Robert's voice flashed into her mind.

There. Get ready.

He didn't break stride or show any sign of having noticed a thing.

She tensed, ready for Julian's swing . . . when Robert

would swerve and she would need to get hold of Julian's mind in the same instant.

Shaking inside, she cursed herself. She had not expected to be this frightened.

She focused her thoughts, gathering a command to make Julian freeze, and Robert walked past the black doorway.

Eleisha looked for the glint.

And then someone screamed from the doorway. A brightly colored form blurred out from the darkness, screaming, and Robert stumbled back in shock.

At the same time, something large dropped down from the balcony, landing behind him, and a glint flashed with a whooshing sound.

Before Eleisha could even follow what was happening, Robert's head came off his shoulders, and his body fell forward. Julian was standing behind him, and the magenta-haired girl ghost was still screaming.

She fell silent as Robert's body landed on the sidewalk.

His psychic energy burst out and hit Eleisha. She didn't even remember falling beside him.

Wave after wave of memory kept hitting her, and she'd seen so many of them before. Thomas Howard. Battles in Scotland. Lady Elizabeth. Angelo. Countless feeding victims left asleep. Memory after memory of Jessenia and their journeys and the feel of her mouth on his.

Then she saw Rose and Seamus and Wade . . . and she saw herself. Only in almost every memory of herself, she was with Philip, talking to him, borrowing his clothes, sleeping with her head in the crook of his neck on the train.

The memories began fading. The agony of the onslaught was easing, and she was dimly aware of Julian standing over her with a sword in his hand. She couldn't move or muster any power. Robert's memories were weaker but still rushing through her.

I'm going to die.

She wanted to die. Robert was glorious, and she'd gotten him killed. She closed her eyes.

The blow never landed.

When she opened her eyes, Julian was gone. The ghost was gone.

They had just left her lying beside Robert's headless body. She couldn't think or feel and got up on her knees. His head had rolled a few feet away, but the blood had already stopped pumping from the stump of his throat.

She looked around in lost confusion.

Why would Julian just walk away?

The numb sensation was passing, and grief was flooding in to take its place.

Robert was dead.

She reached out to touch the back of his hand, and it was already beginning to crack. Leaning forward, she pressed her nose down on his chest, and she just stayed like that.

If Julian came back to take her head, she'd let him.

Arriving in Portland at one a.m., Philip knew he'd missed the train's arrival, and he drove their stolen car straight to the church. Wade was carsick, and Rose was gripping the handles of the back door, but Philip couldn't slow down.

They'd lost too much time already.

He had the car door half open by the time he squealed to a stop in front of the iron gates, and he jumped out, shoving the gates open and running for the front doors.

"Eleisha!" he yelled, rushing through the sanctuary for the stairs to their apartment below, but he already knew she wasn't here. The place felt empty.

"Eleisha!" he still called out once he reached the sitting room, and he turned a full circle in despair.

She wasn't here.

The next twenty hours were the longest of Wade's life.

In an ugly scene, he'd managed to convince a hysterical Philip they had to remain at the church.

They had no idea where to look at this point, and Eleisha had clearly told him they would all meet back at the church.

Rose sent Seamus out, but he needed some general area to search, and after searching all around the train station, he had come back with nothing. Then she'd sent him to Salem, but again, he did not find Eleisha, and after that, Rose did not know where else to send him.

Thankfully, Philip collapsed into dormancy shortly after sunrise, and Wade waited out the day, sitting on the floor of the sanctuary. But he had too much to think about.

He couldn't stand the thought of Julian getting anywhere near Eleisha.

And what if she didn't come back?

What if . . . what if something happened to her?

This church, their plan for the underground, the life they had been building together would be gone. Rose had the wisdom and the vision. Philip had the strength. Wade had the knowledge and ability to train telepaths.

But Eleisha was the heart.

This would not work without her.

Selfish thought. Wade had never considered what he might do without her, and now all he could think of was himself?

Bastard.

He tried to focus on something constructive. What could he do to find her? He couldn't come up with a single thing. He didn't eat all day. He didn't sleep.

At sunset, Philip came upstairs looking haggard. Rose came up a few moments later—she had slept in Eleisha's room. They still had no idea what to do. Philip opened the front doors and stood on the porch.

Just past eleven o'clock, a taxi pulled up outside the gates, and Philip bounded off the steps.

Then he stopped, frozen in place.

Eleisha met him halfway, and Wade watched from the open doorway, trying not to gasp in relief. She did not run to Philip or grasp his hands or say anything. She was carrying Robert's sword case slung over her shoulder.

Wade walked out to join them, and as he got closer, he saw Eleisha's face.

It was pale beyond her usual ivory and completely empty—as if she had no emotions left. Philip was watching her in hurt confusion.

"Where's Robert?" Wade asked, not certain he wanted to hear the answer.

"Gone," she said with no feeling at all. "Dead. Julian jumped down behind him this time. He left me there on the sidewalk." She touched the case on her shoulder. "I brought back Robert's sword and some of his ashes."

Finally, she looked at Philip. "I'm tired. I'm going to my room."

She moved past them into the church, not even looking at Rose on her way through, and vanished through the door behind the altar.

Philip stared after her, and Wade actually hurt for him.

chapter 16

Julian went back to his suite at the Fairmont and waited.

Jasper crawled in the following night with a hole in his forehead that looked about halfway healed.

Julian wasn't angry. He'd finished what he'd set out to do. He'd taken Robert's head.

And Jasper had managed to keep Philip away long enough.

For now, Eleisha would hide out in the church, but in time—hopefully not too much time—she would begin to seek out others still in hiding.

Julian could wait.

He did not need to fear Eleisha's small group to the same degree he'd feared Robert: an elder who practiced the laws.

In truth, Julian was satisfied enough with how things had turned out that he felt generous.

"I'm leaving you here for now," he told Jasper. "You can keep the suite, and I'll set you up an account with Wells Fargo."

Jasper was easy to control and he wasn't afraid to throw himself into a fight—and both qualities made him useful.

Jasper's mouth fell open, but he didn't say a word.

Mary was floating by the fireplace, looking equally puzzled.

Julian's work here was done. He was determined to wait and discover who else Eleisha might find. . . . Perhaps an unlisted elder or the trained child of an elder who knew the laws and yet never gained Angelo's attention. Who else might have hidden themselves away all these years? Robert had most certainly told Eleisha of the laws, but simply *knowing* about them was a world apart from the vampires who'd practiced such an existence for decades or centuries.

Julian had to be sure Eleisha exhausted all paths, overturned all stones in her search, before she lost her usefulness. Then he would reevaluate what danger she and her companions might pose to him.

Until then . . . he would let her feel that the church was safe.

He picked up his coat and the long cardboard box.

"Mary, I'm returning to Wales tonight. I'll call you from there if I need you. Otherwise, just keep me informed on their movements."

He didn't wait for an answer and walked out the door.

It felt odd that he didn't want to go to his town house

in Yorkshire. But no, he would wait this out at home . . . at Cliffbracken.

He'd be hunting again soon enough.

Philip was at a loss.

Eleisha was not inside her body, but the shell was still walking around with her face. Even worse, Wade and Rose didn't seem to realize she was gone. They both kept saying pointless things like "give her time."

How was he supposed to give her time when she wasn't even there?

The shell began doing some of the normal things he might expect from Eleisha. She had her broker arrange to purchase the church. She helped Wade to sand and resurface the hardwood floor in the sanctuary. She helped Rose set up a bedroom in the second ground floor office. She murmured some approval when Wade set up the first office with a desk and a computer—although she never used it. She even walked at night in the garden with Rose.

But she did not make a move toward searching for other vampires in hiding. She barely spoke.

Because Eleisha wasn't inside this shell anymore.

Philip paced a good deal. He was sick with fear that she might not come back. He tried talking to Wade several times.

But Wade was useless. "She watched Robert die. Just give her some time."

Eleisha's shell slept alone in her own room with the door closed. She would sometimes smile absently at Philip and even let him take her hunting once. But she did not speak much, and he couldn't see anyone behind her eyes.

In agitation, he went out by himself one night and drained the life from a woman behind the Portland Art Museum—and then he dumped her body into a sewer grate.

It didn't make him feel any better.

After two weeks of this, he waited until shortly before dawn, and he went to Eleisha's room. Walking in without knocking, he found her sitting on her bed, gazing at nothing. Her hair hung loose, and she wore a white lace nightgown, as if she just waited for the sun to rise so she could slip into the oblivion of sleep.

The shell smiled at him absently, and his fear only increased.

He closed the door and locked it.

Walking to the bed, he dropped down to kneel in front of her. He remembered the first time he'd met her, in a hotel room in Seattle, where she was protecting Wade. She'd used her gift that night to try to seduce him, to get him on his knees, and he'd found the action amusing.

He wasn't amused anymore, and now he *was* on his knees.

"Eleisha," he said, "we are undead, but we live. Robert didn't really live for the last two hundred years. . . . He just got through his nights. You gave him something he could not give himself, no? A few nights of life."

The shell's face twisted into pained surprise, and she tried to stand up. He took hold of her arms.

"Listen to me!" he said. "I know this because I wasn't

alive either. I wouldn't trade the past few months for five hundred years of just getting through the nights. If we called Robert's spirit up right now, he would tell you the same thing. He would thank you—and Rose—for those nights when he came to life again, and he'd let nothing wash them away."

Something, just a flicker, passed across her eyes.

"I killed him," she whispered. "He's gone because of me." This was the most she'd said to him in two weeks.

"No! He's dead because Julian is mad," Philip answered. "You gave Robert a gift and that's all." Her jaw was trembling slightly, but he couldn't stop himself. "And there are others out there alone, who would risk anything not to be alone anymore . . . if they just knew where to go."

He took his hands from her arms, and she didn't try to stand up again.

"I'll help you find them," he said more gently. "We lost Robert, but Rose is here with us. And now that we know Julian is hunting again, I'll know what to do. It will be different next time. I promise. Whoever we find, I'll get them home."

Another flicker passed across her eyes. "You want to? You want to help us start looking?" she asked. "You'd protect whoever we found?"

"Yes."

He would have promised her anything.

"Wade . . . he bought a computer," she said. "Maybe we could search for news stories when we wake up tonight. Like Rose did, only faster."

It took every ounce of strength for him to keep his

face still. He simply nodded. "We could start tonight." But his voice sounded weak and ragged to his own ears. He was so close, so close to reaching her that he didn't want to press this further—for fear she'd slip completely away again.

He stood up.

She touched his leg. "Don't leave. Would you sleep in here today? Like we did at Rose's and on the train?"

He looked down into her face.

Just like that, Eleisha was back inside her body.

He didn't trust himself to speak and pulled his T-shirt over his head, dropping it on a chair and moving around to the other side of the bed. He lay back onto her pillows, and she crawled over to curl up against him with her head on his shoulder.

"Tonight?" she asked again.

He had failed her in some things, and he kept dark secrets she would never understand. But he'd brought her back, and that was all that mattered. If finding lost members of their kind would keep her with him, he'd go wherever she asked.

"Yes," he said. "We'll start searching for the others tonight."

BLOOD MEMORIES

by Barb Hendee

Eleisha Clevon has the face of a teen angel, but she is no angel. Unlike most vampires, she doesn't like to kill, but self-preservation comes first.

When an old friend destroys himself by walking into sunlight right in front of her, Eleisha is shocked. And what she finds afterwards points to how very sick of his existence her friend had become—piling drained corpses in the basement and keeping records of other vampires' real names and addresses. That's a problem.

Because now, there are policemen on the case: two very special humans with some gifts of their own. They know who Eleisha is—and, even more dangerous, what she is.

National Bestselling Authors
Barb & J.C. Hendee
The Noble Dead Saga

DHAMPIR
A con artist who poses as a vampire slayer learns that she is, in fact, a true slayer—and half-vampire herself—whose actions have attracted the unwanted attention of a trio of powerful vampires seeking her blood.

THIEF OF LIVES
Magiere and Leesil are called out of their self-imposed retirement when vampires besiege the capital city of Bela.

SISTER OF THE DEAD
Magiere the dhampir and her partner, the half-elf Leesil, are on a journey to uncover the secrets of their mysterious pasts. But first their expertise as vampire hunters is required on behalf of a small village being tormented by a creature of unlimited and unimaginable power.

TRAITOR TO THE BLOOD
The saga continues as Magiere and Leesil embark on a quest to uncover the secrets of their mysterious origins—and for those responsible for orchestrating the events that brought them together.

Available wherever books are sold or at
penguin.com

R0054

Also Available from
National Bestselling Authors
Barb & J.C. Hendee
The Noble Dead Saga

REBEL FAY
Magiere and Leesil were brought together by the Fay to forge an alliance that might have the power to stand against the forces of dark magics. But as they uncover the truth, they discover just how close the enemy has always been...

CHILD OF A DEAD GOD
For years, Magiere and Leesil have sought a mysterious artifact that they must keep from falling into the hands of a murdering Noble Dead, Magiere's half-brother Welstiel. And now, dreams of a castle locked in ice lead her south, on a journey that has become nothing less than an obsession.

IN SHADE AND SHADOW
Wynn Hygeorht arrives at the Guild of Sagecraft, bearing texts supposedly penned by vampires. When several pages disappear and two sages are found murdered, Wynn embarks on a quest to uncover the secrets of the texts.

THROUGH STONE AND SEA
Wynn journeys to the mountain stronghold of the dwarves in search of an unknown sect allegedly in possession of important ancient texts. But in her obsession to understand these writings, she will find more puzzles and questions buried in secrets old and new—along with an enemy she thought destroyed...

Available wherever books are sold or at
penguin.com

THE ULTIMATE IN
SCIENCE FICTION AND FANTASY!

From magical tales of distant worlds to stories of
technological advances beyond the grasp of man, Penguin has
everything you need to stretch your imagination to its limits.

penguin.com

ACE
Get the latest information on favorites like
William Gibson, T.A. Barron, Brian Jacques,
Ursula K. Le Guin, Sharon Shinn, Charlaine Harris,
Patricia Briggs, and Marjorie M. Liu,
as well as updates on the best new authors.

ROC
Escape with Jim Butcher, Harry Turtledove, Anne Bishop,
S.M. Stirling, Simon R. Green, E.E. Knight, Kat Richardson,
Rachel Caine, and many others—plus news on the
latest and hottest in science fiction and fantasy.

DAW
Patrick Rothfuss, Mercedes Lackey, Kristen Britain,
Tanya Huff, Tad Williams, C.J. Cherryh, and many more—
DAW has something to satisfy the cravings of any
science fiction and fantasy lover.
Also visit dawbooks.com.

*Get the best of science fiction and fantasy
at your fingertips!*